I0757435

Star People

Mystery of the Hologram

Book One of the Star People Trilogy

By

James Schwartz

Sword and Dragon Press

Sword and Dragon Press

© James Schwartz 2025. Second Edition.

www.starpeopletrilogy.com

ISBN: 979-8-9904877-0-3

This book is entirely a work of fiction. The names, characters, places, and incidents are a product of the author's imagination. Any resemblance to actual persons, living or dead, events or localities is entirely coincidental.

All rights reserved. No part of this publication may be reproduced, stored in a retrieval system, or transmitted, in any form or by any means, electronic, mechanical, photocopying, recording or otherwise, without the prior permission of the author.

Not a single word of this book was written by artificial intelligence.

NO AI TRAINING: Without in any way limiting the author's and publisher's exclusive rights under copyright, any use of this publication to "train" generative artificial intelligence (AI) technologies to generate text is expressly prohibited. The author reserves all rights to license uses of this work for generative AI training and development of machine learning language models.

Acknowledgments

This book is dedicated to the three original flyers who dreamed of building their own air car, Jim, Carl and Fred. And while we were in England, the first alternate, Dave.

I would like to express my gratitude to the following people: Julie, a fabulous wife and editor; fellow author and friend, Jeff Danelek: artist and astronomer, Susan Decker; and Leslie Manville for her help, long ago, with editing the original first draft.

I also want to acknowledge Mary Norton, the author of the *Bednob and Broomstick* series. Her writing ignited my imagination back in those early days.

Chapter 1
Faces in the Window

A flash of light outside the window woke Scott from a dead sleep the way it had numerous times in the past few weeks. It wasn't lightning. It wasn't a storm. They were back. He could tell they had returned by the fearful shivers moving through his body. He just *knew* they were there. He could feel it. And if he listened closely, he could hear the sound of a spaceship hovering just above his house. The sound was a low rumble, much like the sound of the engine of an idling truck off in the distance.

Since it was after midnight on a moonless night, it should have been coal black outside, but it wasn't dark at all. As he lay in bed, from the corner of his eye, Scott could see a very intense white light outside his bedroom window. A bright light, like a spotlight, was shining down from the skies above.

He wanted to turn onto his side and look towards the window to see what was there, but at the same time he was too frightened to move. He was noticing an unusual sensation in his body. He was feeling incredibly tired, but not the same kind of tiredness he felt when he had been running around all day. It was as if he had been drugged and could barely keep his eyes open. But Scott was determined to stay awake. His intuition told him that something wasn't right, and he needed to stay alert, aware and focused.

Then a creepy feeling swept through his body. *It feels like someone is watching me,* he thought. Scott finally got up the nerve to turn over and face the windows to see what was happening outside. When he rolled over, he saw several grey alien figures peering in from the outside. They had cold dark eyes and sad, expressionless faces. It appeared that they were floating, ghost-like, hovering in the air.

It seemed like they didn't have the dexterity to get the window to open, but that wasn't stopping them from trying. Their fingers moved slowly like the tentacles of an octopus, but with a single claw at the end of each digit. There was a scratching sound, coming from the outside, like fingernails scraping against the glass, as they were trying to pry open the bedroom window with those long, skinny fingers.

As he witnessed this, Scott felt trapped, paralyzed, and frozen. It was like one of those dreams where he was too scared to move. Thoughts started to run through his head. *Should I call the police? Should I wake someone up and tell them?* But who would believe him? No one ever believed his stories. He had tried to tell people in the past about the strange things that had occurred. They just made fun of him.

This was the most frightening moment he'd ever experienced. Here he was, being pursued by someone or something that could end his life, but no one ever seemed to care, or take him seriously. He never felt more alone.

At that moment, Scott just wanted to be a normal 15-year-old. He didn't want to worry about aliens that, for some reason, were interested in him. But they wouldn't go away. In fact, things seemed to be getting worse.

Slowly, the latch to the window started to turn, but he couldn't see a hand turning it. *How are they doing that? Are those grey creatures able to open the window latch with their minds?* He knew he had to do something. He jumped out of bed and quickly opened the center drawer of his desk. Buried under a stack of papers was his Swiss Army knife. He frantically pulled open the longest blade and then rushed into the closet to get his baseball bat, closing the door behind him. *If they're going to get me, I'm not going down without a fight.*

Scott tried to think of an escape plan while, at the same time, keenly listening to what was going on in his bedroom. For a moment he caught a glimpse of himself in the mirror mounted on the inside of the closet door. His short brown hair was disheveled, but his intense green eyes lit up as he prepared to strike. Being almost six feet tall and fairly strong might help, he thought. The grey beings looked to be short in stature and had slender bodies, but still, there was no way of knowing how they might fight or come after him. *Maybe I can make a run for it before they break into the house. Wait, are those footsteps in my room?*

Suddenly the doorknob of the closet door started to turn. The hair stood up on his arms as a prickly heat swept through his body. There was a strange buzzing sound coming from the other side of the door. He grabbed the doorknob to keep it from opening, his hands were sweating. Suddenly, the closet light flickered, popped loudly, and went dark.

Chapter 2
The Skies Above

Hovering above Scott's house, a spaceship lit up with crimson-colored lights, lowered a white tractor beam of light to the earth below. That beam of light allowed grey alien beings to be transported back and forth between the ship and the ground.

The ship was commanded by a captain who was referred to as the "Master" by his workers. The Master had been telepathically communicating with those workers, the grey beings, on the ground. He could hear their thoughts, and they could hear and respond to any of his thoughts he wanted them to hear. *What do you see,* he asked those creatures with the wispy alien bodies and ashen faces, who were peering through Scott's windows.

We can see a boy inside. We can't see his face, but we think he is the one. We are about to go in, was the answer the Master received.

The Master watched all of the action from within a large room on his spacecraft that had a miniature three-dimensional representation of everything that was happening below. He could see Scott's house and his band of grey followers trying to open Scott's window.

The Master was seated in the control center of his ship. The control room was bathed in cherry red light to protect his sensitive eyes from the damaging effects of full-spectrum light. A flash outside one of the windows caught his eye and then disappeared. At first, he turned away to shield his eyes from the brightness, then, when it was gone, he looked again and saw his reflection in the glass. The pupils of his eyes were obsidian black, but the part that should have been white was pink, looking as if the eyes were sickly and inflamed. His skin was greyish-white. Although his head and massive muscular upper body looked to be human, there were large wings protruding from his back, and those wings created a constant, rhythmic swishing sound as they moved back and forth. He thought to himself: *I am a pitiful looking creature. How could this have happened? Why did they do this to me? I used to be young and powerful; now I look old and decrepit.*

The Master started to feel an uncontrollable anger and wanted to strike out at that boy who was living in the house below, but inside his head were five distinct voices that made it almost impossible for him to give the command. Those five voices tormented him every day and rarely gave him a moment of peace. Each voice was very different from the others, in tone and personality, each telling him what to do.

Kill him, kill him, kill him, kill the boy now, was an instinctive voice that seemed to be the loudest in his mind.

A second voice was more gallant but still supported the argument of the first. *You have searched for these gifts for many years. They belong to you. Lure the boy outside where you can fight him to the death.*

Then, a mysterious voice came up with a darker strategy: *Don't be foolish. Don't risk your life. You can simply conjure up a lightning bolt and blow him away. You have all the power and so many ways to kill him.*

But a fourth voice—a voice of intellect—cautioned: *No, you can't do that. If you destroy the boy, you might destroy the gift you covet. Be logical. Don't let your emotions carry you away.*

And, finally, the commander felt a tear well up inside him when a fifth voice, a soft and gentle voice, pleaded inside his brain: *You can't hurt him. He is only a boy. You can't kill an innocent child.*

But the Master's contradictory thoughts were interrupted by the telepathic voices of the grey beings on the ground. *Danger approaches from the Eastern skies. Prepare for an attack.*

Chapter 3
The Earth Below

The closet doorknob stopped turning. As he waited in the darkness, Scott's heart was racing so fast that he wondered if he was having a heart attack. After taking a moment to calm his mind and reassure himself, he gripped the bat in one hand and held the knife, like a dagger, in the other. With a sudden burst, he threw open the door and sprung out of the closet, ready to fight.

But no one was there. His bedroom was empty. The grey beings had vanished. The low rumbling sound was becoming softer, and the closet light had come back on. The window was open, and a cold wind was blowing in, but the intruders were nowhere to be found. Scott ran over to the window to see where they'd gone, but there was no trace of the creatures, only the silence of the night interrupted by a few dogs barking off in the distance.

As he leaned out the window, Scott noticed, floating directly over his house, was a saucer-shaped craft, thin, round, and dark red. The lights of the ship had a reddish glow that looked like smoldering embers.

Suddenly, there were three bright lights in the Eastern sky, racing toward his house at an incredible speed. Those lights quickly took the form of three approaching ships, each glowing with a greenish cast. All three ships appeared to be aimed directly at the larger crimson red vessel. Within moments, the pursuit progressed into spinning and darting maneuvers as if the ships were in a dogfight. The red ship fired bolts of lightning at the smaller ships, and the green ships returned fire with rapid bursts of light, but there were no explosions or indications that any of the firepower had connected with its target.

Then, a loud sizzling sound came down from the sky. It lasted a few seconds and as soon as it went silent, the red ship was gone. In an instant, all that was left was a wide streak of reddish light followed by the three smaller green ships in pursuit.

The ships moved with such remarkable speed that they soon resembled colored stars off in the western sky. And as quickly as they appeared, all of the ships vanished into the darkness.

But then something else caught Scott's eye. Even though the saucer-shaped ship and the mysterious grey creatures were gone, they had left behind something that looked like a picture on his bedroom window. At first, it appeared to be etched into the glass, but as Scott looked closer, he could see that it was made up of silvery-white particles of light coming down from the sky, almost like it was made of shimmering starlight. The picture was composed of three distinct images bordered by a series of five mysterious letters along the bottom.

What does this mean? Is this a message or a warning? Scott quickly grabbed a pencil and a pad of paper and tried to recreate the images, hoping that it might provide a clue as to why the aliens had, once again, come to the skies over his house. His hand was almost too shaky to get accurate reproductions, but he was determined.

As he sketched the images of the hologram, he noticed that the largest of the three images depicted a man who looked like a mythological figure with a large, muscular body and a long beard with wings protruding from his back. The second image looked like an ancient stone carving of a human figure with starlight raining down over him. The third image appeared to be a three-dimensional representation of the solar system with a landscape of rolling hills in the foreground.

Along the bottom, below the three images, were five mysterious symbols that Scott assumed were some kind of runes.

Then, the picture, the hologram, slowly began to fade. It gently turned into glowing particles and disintegrated into thin air.

Scott finally felt like he could breathe again, but his heart was still pounding. The chills he felt running through his body, and the drawing he was holding in his hand, told him that this was no dream. His bedroom window, once latched tightly, was wide open and a cool breeze was blowing in. *Why are they watching me? What do they want from me?*

He found himself glancing at some of the posters on his walls, posters of galaxies and rocket ships and an autographed picture of John Glenn. He had always been fascinated by the stars and even wanted to be an astronaut, but now it felt like whatever it was, out there in space, was tormenting him in a frightening way.

Scott crawled back into bed. Since he knew he wasn't going to sleep, he concentrated on the images that made up the hologram, racking his brain in hopes of some clue that might help him solve the mystery of these unusual visitors.

Chapter 4
The Images of the Hologram

On the following day, Scott waited on his front porch for his friend, Christina, to come join him so they could walk down to the library together. Scott would often think of his grandfather when he sat on the porch because that was something they used to do together. Grandpa Austin was an aviation buff who spent much of his life flying a wide variety of aircraft. He was also a great storyteller, and the two of them would sit out on the porch drinking lemonade while Grandpa Austin shared stories about his amazing flying adventures; everything from flying in the war to the time he tried to fly through the eye of a hurricane.

Scott inherited everything in his grandpa's shed which was packed to the brim not only with tools, but propellers and instrument panels and parachutes and everything imaginable from just about any craft that ever was able to fly. The family called it a work shed, but it was the size of a double garage.

Scott was eight when his grandfather died. The house was left to his mom, so Scott's family, excluding his father who had divorced his mom when Scott was five, moved in soon afterwards. Scott quickly became best friends with the Latina girl who lived across the street, Christina Rivera. Scott loved being around Christina. She had a wild imagination and a crazy sense of humor which helped him lighten up when he became too serious.

She bounded out of her house, full of energy, with her long brown hair flowing behind her. She was wearing blue jeans with a white top and a blue jean jacket. "Okay, what's this big mystery you couldn't tell me at school?" asked Christina.

Her brown eyes always gave her away. They could be soft and compassionate, but they could also sparkle when she laughed or teased or became playful. Today, they looked at him with intrigue, as if she was excited to delve into a complicated mystery.

"I'll tell you on the way to the library."

The library was in Stonebridge, their hometown, just down the hill and about a half mile from where they lived. The settlement was named after an old stone bridge, built centuries ago, which crossed over a river that passed through the center of town. Stonebridge was only about eight blocks long and usually very quiet and peaceful.

As they walked toward town, Scott recounted the events from the previous night and showed her his drawing. Christina listened carefully to every word until they got to Main Street.

"Let me see that drawing again," Christina said.

As she carefully studied the sketches, Scott looked at the old brick storefronts of Main Street. There was no indication that anyone had seen anything out of the ordinary the night before. In fact, everything seemed completely normal. There was the market, the Blue Moon Diner, the hardware store, the local police station, Joann's Antique Store with Abigail, the old tabby cat, lying in the front window, and the Bijou Movie Theatre. And, down the street, cars steadily rolled in and out of Earl's gas station.

Christina finally broke her silence. "The three images are arranged in the shape of a pyramid. I wonder if that's a clue." She continued to study the drawing. "The figure at the top has the face of one of those Greek gods."

"Yeah, I thought so too, but his body is half man and half dragon," Scott added.

"It looks like he is holding a lightning bolt, getting ready to throw it."

"Like Zeus?"

"Yeah, kinda like Zeus." She studied the images more intensely. "These shapes on the left," continued Christina, "look like a diagram of the stars and planets or maybe a couple constellations over some rolling hilltops." She thought about it for a moment. "Those look like the hills and the fields behind your house."

"What?" Scott stopped in his tracks.

"Maybe it's your address."

Scott looked at her in disbelief.

"Maybe it's like a map showing where you live, so they know where to find you."

He felt a chill run through his body. "Great. Like I'm not paranoid enough already. You make it sound like they're coming to get me."

"Well, you told me about those dreams where you go onboard alien ships. Maybe they aren't dreams at all, and this," as she pointed to the drawing of the solar system, "is how they find you."

They started walking again, passing the art gallery with paintings in the window. One painting was of an old farmhouse in the snow. Another canvas depicted a Victorian house with Halloween pumpkins on the front steps and fall leaves swirling in the wind. Something about that autumn scene added to the uncomfortable feeling in his body.

"Yeah, but this time was different."

"What was different about it?"

"For one thing, I was definitely awake. It wasn't a dream. And there was this giant ship with red lights that almost looked like burning embers."

"It was different from the ones you've seen before? The green ships?"

"I don't know. I think so. I'm not really sure because when I wake up from those dreams—or whatever they are—I'm so groggy I don't remember much of anything, but the green ones seemed friendly. The red one felt scarier."

They passed the coffee and dessert shop, *Mystic Delights*, and picked up the aroma of hot chocolate and warm cinnamon rolls. That caught Christina's attention. "It always smells so good when we walk by here."

The sounds of an acoustic guitar came from inside, accompanied by the voice of an old folk singer.

"And I heard the guy who's playing there now is really good."

"All right, all right," said Scott reluctantly. "I can take a hint. We'll get some hot chocolate after we're done at the library."

Christina smiled. When she smiled at Scott, her smile was so warm that for a brief moment he was able to forget all of the unsettling things that had happened the night before.

"Does this mean we're not working on the ship today?" asked Christina.

"No, not today. I really need to see if we can find out anything about these drawings at the library."

"What about Bugman?" asked Christina referring to Scott's younger brother, Brett, who earned his nickname because of his interest in insects. "Did you tell him *why* we're going to the library and not working on the air car?"

"No. I didn't tell Brett about any of this, and I probably won't for a while. I think he's getting a little freaked out by all of my stories."

"Well, they are a little strange."

"I know. I know. Come on, let's check out these images at the library."

* * *

After several hours of pouring through books about folklore and Greek Gods and indigenous art, Christina's brown eyes lit up. "You're a star baby," she said in a loud voice, catching the attention of the librarian and several of the locals.

"A what? I'm not sure I like the sound of that."

"Look at this picture. It looks a little like the drawing you have on the right side at the bottom. The one that looks like a human figure with starlight raining down on him."

Christina handed Scott the book opened to a page she had marked, and he examined it closely. "Well, I guess there are some similarities to the drawing." Then, he read the description. "But this is from an American Indian petroglyph."

"Yeah, but it's the only thing I've found that even comes close. They say it's from American Indian folklore. It's the symbol that they used long ago to represents a star person."

Scott read the description: "One of the legends of Indian mythology is what has become known as the story of the star people. On warm summer nights when Indian women fell asleep under the stars, they would sometimes become so mesmerized by the beautiful starry sky, they would go into a trance. Then, according to folklore, one of those stars would come down to earth and seduce them. The offspring from that union between the Indian woman and the star was referred to as a star person. They would look like a completely normal child but would sometimes be blessed with special powers. He or she would be raised by the mother until the age of five."

"Then what happened?"

"Shhhhhh." From behind her desk, the librarian shot them a disapproving look.

"Then what happened?" whispered Christina in a softer tone.

"Then the star father would come down from the sky, steal the child away and take that child back to the heavens."

He handed the book back to Christina.

"Maybe the Indians assumed it was stars coming down because

                    Star People: Mystery of the Hologram

they didn't know about UFOs back then. Maybe they were really experiencing alien abductions. So, that's it," said Christina in a teasing manor, "you're a star baby."

"What?" said Scott in disbelief. "First of all, my mom's not an American Indian."

"Minor technicality."

"Second, she doesn't sleep out under the stars," argued Scott.

"Maybe she was on a camping trip."

"Third, I'm older than five..."

"Only in earth years."

"...and no one has come to get me. And fourth, I have an earthling father."

"But maybe the rules have changed as our civilization has evolved," suggested Christina. "We hear about alien abductions all the time on TV and in the tabloids."

Suddenly, the librarian was standing right behind them. "If you can't be quiet, I'm afraid I'm going to have to ask you to leave."

"He's having trouble getting used to some of the customs on our planet," whispered Christina to the librarian.

There was no forgiveness from the librarian who acted like she'd heard it all before. "Well, he'd better learn pretty quickly, or he'll be out on his ear."

"What else does it say?" whispered Scott as soon as she was gone.

"That's all they have about the star people. After that it goes on about aliens and something called genetic manipulation."

"What's it say about that?"

"Oh, I don't know. Something about how aliens might have conducted genetic experiments on our planet where they combined the genes of humans with the genes of their own race." Christina looked back down at the book, and read aloud, "... possibly to create a super race or to create spies that look like humans or maybe even to create a race of slaves. Some extraterrestrial experts think that genetic experimentations, or cross-breeding, is one of the main reasons that aliens come to earth."

"Yeah, I've read about that in some of those Sci-Fi magazines. And before you even say it, I'm not a genetic experiment gone wrong."

Christina smiled and looked as if Scott took the words right out of her mouth. "No, you're a star baby," she said with a big grin.

"We need to get going," said Scott as he gathered up the books. "It's getting late."

As they passed by the front desk on the way to the exit, Christina whispered to the librarian who looked up from her book. "Sorry we interrupted the silence."

"Glock. Glock," said Scott to the librarian as he walked out the door.

"Glock, glock? What was that?" asked Christina with a laugh once they were outside.

"Glock, glock means goodbye in alien speak."

"See I knew it, you are a star baby, although that sounded more like a chicken to me."

"You just don't understand the complexities of our language."

Chapter 5
The History of Flight

In the work shed in the backyard of his house, Scott, Christina and Scott's younger brother, Brett, were working on a project that was somewhat unusual: building a homemade flying machine. The craft consisted of a large board, about eight feet by ten feet with rounded corners and a hole cut in the center. Above the hole was an electric motor, and that motor was attached to a large propeller mounted below the board. On the underside of the ship, there were four twelve-inch risers that served as legs for the craft and made room so the propeller wouldn't come in contact with the ground. It was a very, very simple flying machine, but Scott figured that if it worked, they could make improvements before any future flights.

"I'm still not sure about this propeller in back," Scott said as he gently tapped one of the blades causing it to spin.

"Why?"

"Well, if that's all we have moving us forward, we're not going to be able to go very fast," said Scott.

"Let's worry about that after we get the ship off the ground," said Christina.

Scott felt frustrated whenever Christina and Brett doubted that the hovercraft would ever become airborne. Sure, it was a crazy idea—

after all, how many people had ever built their own flying machine—but Scott was really, really good at anything related to building and mechanics. He had spent countless hours in the shed, with his grandfather, taking things apart, rebuilding and even designing their own inventions from scratch. His grandfather had taught him to become a master craftsman, so when Christina or Brett doubted whether or not the machine would work, it felt like they were questioning his abilities.

When Christina saw Scott's reaction to her doubtful comment, she quickly changed the subject and turned her attention to Brett. "What have you got in the jar?" she said, referring to the glass jar Brett was holding up to the light.

"It's a praying mantis. I put some ants in there, so she'd have something to eat."

Brett put down the jar and watched as Scott worked on the homemade flying machine. "I still don't know if it's gonna work," repeated Brett for what seemed like the thousandth time.

Scott looked at Brett with annoyance. Sometimes he wondered if they were really related. They didn't look alike at all. Brett had brown eyes, brown hair, and pale skin. Unlike Scott's thin body, Brett had a short, thick build and was very strong for his age. He was the eleven-year-old warrior who would relentlessly fight when engaged in sports or games. On the positive side, Brett was extremely loyal, but he could also be stubborn and opinionated, which were traits that often irritated Scott.

"Then, you don't have to ride in it."

"Okay, okay," caved Brett. "Can we really try it tonight?"

"I think so," said Scott while examining the electric motor. "We have to wait until it gets dark."

"How come?"

"We don't want anyone to see us," added Christina. "That might get us in trouble."

As Scott triple checked the tightness of each bolt to make sure everything was secure, he said, "I think we're ready to go. All we have to do now is wait for the sun to set."

                    Star People: Mystery of the Hologram

"That's like three whole hours," complained Brett.

"Let's meet back here after dinner," suggested Scott. "Then we'll see if it will really fly."

As Scott set the wrench down on the workbench, he saw the plans for building an air car pinned to the bulletin board and it reminded him of how the three of them got started on the project.

* * *

It began on a cold winter's day, about four months earlier. Scott was out in the shed going through some of the old *Popular Mechanics* magazines that had belonged to his grandfather, when he ran across an advertisement for an "Air Car." The ad was in the March 1958 issue, and it claimed you could "build your own air car by using materials around the house."

Scott started to dream for a moment. *Could that really be possible? That would be incredible.* But then he thought: That was almost six years ago, and the company is probably out of business by now.

Then, in the next stack of magazines, Scott found a small pamphlet titled: "Instructions for Building Your Own Air Car." Apparently, his grandfather had found the exact same advertisement, mailed off five dollars to the company and then tucked the instructions away inside the stack of magazines. When Scott found the step-by-step plans, he called up Christina, and she came over a few hours later.

"How exactly does it work?" asked Christina looking at the sketches in the pamphlet.

"Kind of like a hovercraft. It has a propeller mounted underneath the craft. That propeller is powered by a lawnmower engine, and if the propeller spins fast enough it will create a cushion of air that will lift the craft off the ground."

"Would that really work?"

"Well, if you built it exactly the way it says to do it in the instructions, I think it would be too heavy to ever get off the ground, especially with a person on it. And if it really worked, everyone would be flying around in air cars, but if we made some changes…”

“Do you think we could redesign it so it could actually get off the ground?”

“Maybe if you could find the right—”

“Right what?” asked Christina.

“Well, the right parts.” Scott took the instructions from Christina. “It says to use a lawnmower engine, but what if we took the electric motor out of my dad’s golf cart? Ever since the divorce, he never golfs anymore. That golf cart has been sitting in the garage for years. I’m not even sure why we store it for him. Anyway, that motor would be quieter and much more powerful.”

“But what about the propeller?”

“Well, that’s kinda interesting. With all the aviation stuff my grandpa collected—there *is* a propeller.”

Christina’s eyes lit up. “There is?”

“But it’s much bigger than the one in the diagram. It’s almost six feet across.”

“Where’d it come from?

“Knowing Grandpa, it might have even come from a real hovercraft.”

“Do you think it might work if we used those things?”

“I don’t know for sure, but if it did, we’d probably only be able to get a couple feet off the ground.”

“Yeah, but think how cool that would be. It would be like having our own car, but we’d be flying.”

For a moment Scott let himself imagine. “Even a foot off the ground would be amazing as long as no one saw us.”

“We could fly at night, and we wouldn’t tell anyone. Even if we just flew in the fields behind your house, it would be so awesome.” Christina gave Scott a look he couldn’t resist. “I think we should do it!”

“But what if we spend all that time building it, and it never gets off the ground?" As soon as he said that, Scott quickly told himself to shut up. He realized that building an air car would be a way to spend a whole lot more time with one of the few people who actually was a true friend.

"We won't know if we don't try," said Christina.

"Okay, let's try it."

"Are we going to tell Bugman?"

"We almost have to," said Scott. "Brett's going to see us working on something and will want to know what it is, and he's out here in the shed all the time."

"Will he tell anyone?"

"No. He won't. Brett can keep it a secret."

Chapter 6
Test Flight

F inally, all of the planning and building of the ship came together, and the perfect moment for a test flight had arrived. Scott's Mom was away for the evening, and no one seemed to be out or about in the neighborhood. As the three of them carried the ship out of the shed, Scott realized how rudimentary it looked. It was simply a large piece of plywood with a motor on top and a propeller underneath. Mounted on the board was a wooden seat and a couple of handles, designed to allow the rider to hold on and steer the craft by shifting their weight.

"It's so heavy," whispered Christina as the three of them carried the craft out from the old work shed and onto the large back lawn behind the Harrison's house. "I can't see how it will ever get off the ground."

"If the propeller spins fast enough, I think it might work."

It was agreed that Scott would go alone on the inaugural flight.

Seeing that it was already getting dark, Scott said, "I'll need lights, so I can see where I'm going."

"I'll get a flashlight from the house," Brett announced. He ran into the house and returned a few minutes later with a large flashlight.

Scott could tell the others were skeptical. "I can see it working in my mind. I really can. I think it'll work."

"Okay, let's give it a try," said Christina.

Scott turned on the electric motor and the large propeller under the craft slowly began to turn. At first the propeller just kicked up swirls of dust and dirt and leaves.

He slowly increased the speed of the engine, and the propeller rotated faster. Brett and Christina stepped back out of harm's way in case the ship lurched or lunged sideways rather than moving upwards. They turned away to keep the dust from getting in their eyes but kept peeking back to see if something might happen.

Despite the increased speed of the spinning propeller, the ship stayed on the ground. Scott felt a momentary sense of despair.

Then he closed his eyes for a moment and imagined how fantastic it would be if this ship really could fly. He focused his attention on visualizing the ship not just lifting off the ground but soaring all around the neighborhood. He even conjured up the impression of what it would feel like if he was airborne and what that feeling of exhilaration would be like in his body.

Then he opened his eyes and accelerated the motor to a much higher speed. The propeller started to spin so fast that it became a blur. It didn't seem possible that the small electric motor could make the propeller turn so rapidly, but it did. For a moment, nothing happened, but then, the ship started to gently lift off the ground.

At first the homemade craft only rose about a foot in the air. As soon as it started to move, Scott began to lose his balance and quickly reached for the handles and readjusted his position.

He glanced at the others, but as the craft lifted a couple more feet in the air, he had to focus on piloting the ship. It wobbled as if it were out of balance. He shifted his weight and when it stabilized, he revved up the motor a little faster and the craft slowly elevated to about twenty feet above the ground. He could hear Christina and Brett squeal in disbelief.

As he rose higher and hovered above his house, Scott found the sensation of flight both mesmerizing and scary. His body trembled with excitement and nervousness. One moment he was thrilled and exhilarated by being able to fly, but the next thought that ran through his mind was the fear of falling if the homemade flying machine, for some reason, should suddenly stop working and rapidly drop to the ground. That thought scared him to death.

Scott had always felt a strong pull towards outer space. His life-long dream was to become an astronaut and explore the universe. And even though he couldn't explore the universe on this flight or even in this homemade flying machine, just being able to lift off the ground and see the world from above was a dream come true.

After a few moments of anxiety, Scott was able to push down those fears and appreciate what he was experiencing. The magical feeling of being weightless and floating in the air was something he had experienced numerous times in his dreams, but he never expected to actually be able to achieve that sensation in real life, *until today.*

As he looked down from above, Scott could see the neat rows of the vegetable garden and his mother's colorful hydrangea and rose bushes along the fence. He thought about the countless nights he had spent in his backyard watching the skies through his telescope. Behind their property, on the other side of the fence, was the grassy field where he would often see deer grazing.

Before moving the ship forward and starting his journey, Scott waved to his brother and Christina. Then, he noticed something in the distance that he hadn't been aware of when he lifted off. There were flashes of lightning along the far horizon in the western sky. Scott knew better than to fly if there was an electrical storm, but he wasn't aware of the storm until now when he was already up in the air and high enough to see it.

It wasn't uncommon for storms to pass through in the summertime, but the path of those storms often missed the Stonebridge area altogether. There was a pretty good chance that it would be too far north to cause any problems, and it would probably be an hour or so before the storm would arrive even if it did come in his direction. Scott thought about it and felt a little queasiness in his stomach, but the excitement of being in flight took over and he wasn't about to stop now.

The craft gently glided over the rolling hills above Stonebridge. From this new vantage point, he could see the small cluster of houses with big yards and enormous horse chestnut and maple trees on each side of the street. Then, he passed over a couple of parked cars and looked down at the glowing house lights and streetlamps below.

He wasn't sure where to go, so he headed towards the center of Stonebridge. Along the way, he saw the dirt bike path he had ridden down hundreds of times, on his way to school. Then there was the Jensen farm with acres of fruit trees and a creepy scarecrow whose job it was to protect the vegetable garden.

At first Scott felt like he needed to hold on tightly and to carefully steer the ship, but once he got out in the open and away from all the lights, his body relaxed, and he started to feel a sense of peace as he looked up at the stars. The moon was in the crescent phase, and whenever there was a crescent moon, Scott would always make a wish. *Why do I need to make a wish tonight? Sailing this ship over the countryside is already a dream come true.*

From the Jensen farm, Scott passed over the Ulysses S. Grant Elementary school, which brought back lots of memories. There was the upper baseball field where he'd played many games. The game he remembered most was last year, where he came within two outs of pitching a no-hitter. His coach always said that when Scott was "on," he was the most accurate and hardest thrower of any of his pitchers, but Scott would often get nervous when he tried to pitch. He was afraid he'd let his teammates down if he messed up, and that fear sometimes caused him to throw a lot more bad pitches than good ones.

He was a reluctant athlete. He didn't live for the games like many of his friends. He mostly played sports so he wouldn't be picked on for being the brainiest boy in the class. He learned at a young age that the tough guys didn't bully the boys who were good in sports because the athletes could fight back, so that kept him off the radar of the troublemakers.

Just as he turned away from the school, there was a brilliant flash of light followed by a loud crash. In what seemed like only a few minutes, that storm which had appeared to be so far off in the west was closing in on him. Another lightning bolt lit up the sky, followed by a loud explosion of thunder. With the lightning and thunder came the rain and gusty winds that started to blow the ship off course.

I have to get out of here. I have to get home. It isn't safe to fly in stormy weather. He tried to turn the ship in the direction of his house, but a powerful wind spun the ship around and blew it about fifty feet off course. Scott knew the dangerous effect high winds could have on the flying machine. If a strong gust of wind was able to take hold of the ship and flip it upside down, it would be certain disaster.

Another flash lit up the sky, quickly followed by a crack of thunder. The sound of the thunder was sharp at first, but the echo continued to rumble far off into the distance. Then, more lightning bolts, and they were coming so close to the ship that Scott almost felt like they had been aimed in his direction.

Scott realized that with the growing intensity of the storm, he was in a very dangerous predicament. Could it be that his dream of flying—which had finally come true—was also going to be the death of him?

Chapter 7
The Summer Storm

Hovering in his spaceship, hidden in the clouds above where he wouldn't be seen, the commander of the crimson ship and the Master of the grey beings had returned. That commander, with his wings beating rhythmically, looked over a miniature three-dimensional model of Stonebridge and the surrounding area. The model, located inside the command center of the ship, depicted a perfect representation of everything below the ship but on a much smaller scale. It included a layer of stormy clouds and the Master's own red ship hovering just above those clouds. Below that, was the town of Stonebridge, the rolling hills, the school, the Harrison's house, and Scott trying to stay airborne while being tossed around by the violent winds.

You can't escape me this time. The Master filled up his lungs and blew air in the direction of Scott's ship. The blast of air delivered by the Master created a corresponding gale force wind below the clouds that sent Scott and the ship hurtling across the countryside. Every action the Master took—as he worked with the model—directly affected what happened to Scott and his ship flying below the clouds.

The Master rubbed his hands together and conjured up a bolt of lightning. He reached back and fired the lightning bolt at Scott's ship, narrowly missing his target.

* * *

The panic inside Scott had made his body start to tremble. Then, he got an idea. He remembered Miller's Pond. Ever since old man Miller passed away, the farm had been deserted and fallen into disrepair. There was an old vacant barn there that could give him a place to ride out the storm. Many of the kids from Stonebridge would go fishing at Miller's Pond in the summertime, and when the sun got too hot, they would go into the barn to eat lunch and cool off in the shade. The old doors had fallen off the barn and now it was home to bats and raccoons, but it would be a safe hideout until the storm passed. Scott figured that if he turned around and rode the wind instead of trying to fly into it, he could be at Miller's Pond in minutes.

Knowing it was his only hope, Scott made a sweeping turn. The wind grabbed hold of the ship and swept it in the direction of the Miller's farm. Another crash of lightning and thunder rocked the craft. He knew that being up in the air with an electric motor made the craft a likely target as each lightning strike sought out a destination where it could release its intense electrical charge. He didn't want to think of how explosive, and how deadly, that would be. He needed to get out of the sky and take cover immediately.

With each burst of lightning, Scott felt his neck and shoulders tense up. His stomach was feeling upset, and the rain had made him wet and cold. By riding the wind, the ship was propelled faster than he thought it could ever move, but the plan was working and off in the distance, he could see the old barn through the driving rain.

But there was another problem: trying to steer the ship and land in the barn at this speed would be like trying to park a car in a garage when the car was traveling sixty miles an hour. Not only were the air currents moving him too fast, but the ship was rocking and tipping with each swirl of wind.

Scott took a moment and quieted his mind so he could really focus on the maneuver. When he could imagine it in his mind, he knew he was ready. By leaning all of his body weight to one side and pushing into the squall, he quickly spun the ship around so he was facing directly into the wind and then accelerated the ship as fast as he could make it go. That force, pushing directly into the storm, slowed the craft to a more controllable speed where he was able to navigate the airship into the barn. It meant that the craft had to go in backwards, but to get out of the thunderstorm, he was willing to do whatever he needed to do.

Despite slowing the ship down by accelerating into the wind, the ship landed with such force that it bounced three times before coming to rest in a wet pile of hay.

Once Scott was safely under the cover of the old wooden structure, there was an incredible sense of relief that went through his body. He knew that these storms moved fast, and in twenty or thirty minutes the air would be still, and it would be safe to fly home. In the meantime, the rain pounded on the leaky old roof of the barn and the bats fluttered up in the rafters. It was very dark and spooky in the broken-down makeshift hanger, and every few seconds, the bright flashes of lightning continued to light up the sky outside the shelter.

* * *

The Master watched on his miniature three-dimensional model as Scott's ship landed inside the wooden structure. *You think an old barn can protect you from me?* He rubbed his hands together and produced another bolt of lightning. As he started to take aim at the barn, he saw three spaceships come flying into his three-dimensional model. The ships were above the clouds and coming straight towards his vessel.

"Master, prepare for attack. The enemy is approaching," was the message the commander heard from one of the crew. The Master abruptly stopped his attack. As the three spaceships approached, the winged commander wanted to look out the window and size up his enemy, but he had to cautiously shield his eyes from their green lights. He put his hand up to protect his eyes and squinted as if he was trying to look into the sun, but it was too bright. He quickly extinguished the lightning bolt between his hands and shouted out orders: "Abort mission. Raise the shields. Prepare for flight."

* * *

Scott waited in the barn until he noticed that the rain had started to soften, and the explosions ceased. Within minutes, the storm quickly died out, creating the safe window to head back home.

He had to manually turn the ship around and drag it out of the barn before he could take off again. He checked to make sure there wasn't any damage from the hard landing and was a little worried about whether the craft would start up after such a tumultuous journey, but the motor fired right up. Taking advantage of the break in the weather, the flying machine rose up from the soggy grass then floated up above the barn and out over Miller's Pond before heading back home.

On the return flight, Scott couldn't think about anything except wanting to get home safely. He flew the ship as fast as it would go. He felt drained from all the tension, and it was a huge relief when he spotted his house and was able to bring the ship down onto the large back lawn where Christina and Brett were waiting for him.

What Scott had hoped would be a quiet ride in the country turned out to be one of the scariest experiences of his life. He didn't want his brother or Christina to know that he was afraid, but he could tell that he wasn't the only one who had been scared. He could see it in their faces. It was hard to know for sure because it was so dark, but he thought he might have seen Christina brush away a tear. After he touched down, no one said anything. Scott tried to act like everything was okay. It wasn't. It felt like he had aged ten years in that one night. As much as he wanted to be able to fly, he never wanted to feel that much fear again.

Chapter 8
The Rebuild

As summer started to heat up and everyone was out of school, Scott, Christina and Brett would often hang out on the front porch of the work shed. For about a week, Scott didn't feel like talking about what happened on the night of the storm, so things had been much quieter than usual until one day when Brett spoke up.

"Hey Scott. I was wondrin' if one of these nights we might be able to fly the ship again."

Christina silently looked up from the magazine she was reading.

Scott could feel himself being pulled in two directions: his life-long dream of being able to fly was pushing up against the fear he continued to feel after his terrifying first flight. He remembered something his grandfather had told him about having courage when he was in the war: "If you let fear run your life, you won't have any life at all." Over the last few days Scott had been trying to convince himself that he wasn't going to give into the fear, but he was struggling. He knew, at some point, he would need to face what he was battling inside.

Christina didn't say a word. She just waited and watched for Scott's reaction.

After a long hesitation, he said, "Yeah, Brett, I guess we could fly again, but we need to make a few improvements first."

"What kind of improvements?" Christina blurted out and eagerly jumped up and came over and sat next to Scott. She sat so close that he could feel her shoulder and arm leaning against his.

"Well, for one thing, when I was up there, sometimes I thought I was gonna fall off."

"Why don't we put sides on it?" suggested Brett. "That way we can't fall off, and it'll look more like a real spaceship."

"That's a good idea, Brett," said Christina. "That would also make it less likely for people to see us."

"And we need lights. Something brighter than a flashlight."

"Okay. We could add those," added Christina.

Scott thought about other fixes for a moment. "I think if we made it more aerodynamic, it'd be easier to steer."

"Can we make it curved and shaped like a racecar?" asked Brett.

"No. We don't have the right saw to do that. We have to mostly use straight edges."

"What if it was shaped more like an arrow, and we put sides on it?" Christina jumped up, hurried into the shed and came out with a pencil and a pad of paper. She quickly sketched out her idea. "Like this. Sort of a wedge-shape. That would only require straight edges and it would still be aerodynamic."

Brett looked over her drawing. "Yeah, that'd be cool!"

"We could do that," said Scott looking at the drawing. Then he hesitated for a moment. "Yeah, but what are we going to use for the parts?"

With Scott's concern, much of the excitement started to lose momentum.

"There must be something in the shed," said Christina. "With all of your grandpa's old airplane parts in there, we could almost build our own plane."

"I can look around," said Scott, "but I'm just not sure if there's anything that would work to make it like our drawing."

* * *

Later that night, after Christina had gone home and Brett had gone to bed, Scott was turning out the lights of the work shed when something caught his eye. At first, he thought it must be reflections of light shining through one of the windows. But the neighborhood was mostly dark, and no lights were coming in from the outside. As he looked closer, there were two small lights. They were perfectly round and a light green color. At first, they were spinning around one another, but once he paid attention, they floated to the back of the work shed, to the exact area where he had found the propeller for the craft.

Scott felt more intrigued than afraid of the glowing spheres. His intuition told him that they were trying to tell him something. He didn't want to turn the overhead lights back on because he thought that might make the orbs disappear. Instead, he grabbed a flashlight off the shelf, switched it on and walked over to where the green lights were slowly floating up and down.

It appeared that the orbs wanted him to look at something in the back corner of the shed which was buried under a couple of detached closet doors and an old ping pong table. Scott pulled the table out of the way. The orbs continued to move up and down, almost touching the doors, indicating that those needed to move as well. Under the piles of junk were several lightweight sheets of metal that were strong but pliable. They had an amazing metalflake finish that sparkled in the light, a finish like he had never seen before. He also observed that, as he held the metal panels in his hands, they felt warm to the touch. It was the perfect material for building the sides and top of the ship.

Hidden below the metal sheets was a set of four wheels, battery-powered lights, and a small electric motor. Scott's imagination took off once he realized these were exactly the kinds of parts he needed to properly finish the ship. In his excitement, he had forgotten about the orbs. He looked up and all around, but they were nowhere to be found. He searched the shed, but there was no trace of the mysterious green lights that had led him to find the parts he needed. The orbs had vanished.

* * *

It was exactly two weeks later when the construction was finished, and the flying machine was ready for the second test flight. Scott knew that his mother was going out on a date, and it would be the perfect time.

Scott and Brett's mother, Judy Harrison, a forty-four-year-old single working mom, was quickly getting ready when the doorbell rang. As Judy breathed in, tightened up her body and zipped up her red dress, she gave instructions to the boys.

"We're just going to dinner and the movies, so I shouldn't be late. If there's an emergency, you can always call your grandma—"

Scott interrupted her: "Mom, I know, I know. You tell us this every time you go out."

She looked at herself in the mirror and fixed her reddish-brown hair. "I just want to make sure that you're all right."

As she walked back into the bedroom, the doorbell rang again.

"Brett, can you get the door? That should be Steve."

The boys looked at each other with horrified faces when they heard the name Steve. They whispered to each other "Mr. Spiffy" as they mimicked some of Steve's mannerisms such as fixing his hair in the mirror, picking at his teeth, or brushing the dandruff off of his shoulders.

Brett opened the door.

"It's just Christina."

Christina gave Brett a "thanks a lot" look and then joined Brett and Scott in the family room.

"Hi, Chris," Judy hollered from the bedroom. "If you want to stay for dinner, you can. I ordered a pizza for the boys." The doorbell rang again. "Now that must be Steve."

They followed Judy into the living room where she opened the door and gave Steve a quick kiss. The kids all looked at each other and cringed when they saw the kiss.

Steve was one of those guys who tried really hard to be cool. His real name was Steve Speferelli, but Christina came up with his nickname, Mr. Spiffy, because he was so fastidious about his appearance. Christina once said that he should have been born a cat so the constant grooming would have been more socially acceptable. Even though it was eighty degrees outside, Mr. Spiffy was wearing a scarf. Scott figured that the scarf was supposed to get people to really notice him when he drove around in his new convertible.

As they walked out the door, Judy said, "Okay, be good. I should be home around eleven."

Christina, Scott and Brett ran to the window where they could see their mom and Steve get into the sports car. After glancing at himself a couple of times in the rearview mirror, Steve fired up his new Triumph Spitfire. He let out the clutch too quickly. The car lurched forward and then stalled. Both passengers jerked back and forth. Steve's long flap of combed-over sideburn hair dislodged itself from the top of his head, flew sideways and was left dangling off the side of his head, revealing a smooth bald head underneath.

"Guess he hasn't figured out how to use a stick shift yet," said Christina.

As soon as their mom was gone, the three of them were on their way out to the backyard. They opened the work shed where they kept the ship and sized up their redesigned craft. They had been working hard. The vessel now had a wedge-shaped streamlined body. There were sides and a partial top with a large moonroof opening so they could lean over the edge and look down at the scenery or look up at the moon and stars. The ship was painted a dark blue color so that it would easily blend into the night sky. They had also added three seats, small windows in the sides and back of the craft, wheels, headlights, and a door so they could easily climb in and out.

The ship didn't look much like the original design Christina had drawn out on the paper, but it still looked cool. The three of them found that by searching through the plethora of airplane parts that Scott's grandfather had collected, they had everything they needed.

"I can't believe all the things you found in the shed," said Christina. "It was almost like your grandpa bought a kit with all of the parts to build a flying machine."

"I'm not sure there are any kits like that," Scott said with a laugh. "But I think my grandfather had gathered all the parts and was building one himself. How else would all of this stuff have been there and how could it fit together so easily?"

"But then why didn't he ever tell you about it?" asked Christina.

"I don't know," said Scott. "Maybe he got all the pieces together but passed away before he could build it."

As they were rolling the craft into the backyard, Scott said: "I've been giving it some thought, and I think I came up with a name for it."

"For the ship?" Christina asked.

"Yeah."

"What is it?"

"Well, you know how the first manned rockets ever launched by NASA were named after the Mercury Project." The other two looked at him with a little uncertainty. They didn't know nearly as much as Scott when it came to space exploration. "You know, there was the Gemini Project, the Mercury rockets, then the Apollo program."

Christina nodded her head in a way that indicated she had no idea about these things but understood Scott was the expert.

"Since this is our first ship, I think we should call it the *Mercury One*. We'd be naming it after the first series of manned spaceships built by NASA."

"Was the *Mercury One* the first one that carried an astronaut?" asked Brett.

"Actually, that was the *Mercury Three*, which, by the way, was also called *Freedom Seven*."

Brett and Christina rolled their eyes in unison.

"Shouldn't we call ours the *Mercury Three* since our ship will have people on it?" Brett asked.

"I thought about that, but since this is our first air ship, I think it should be the *Mercury One*."

They all agreed that Scott's idea was a pretty good one, especially since they'd spent several weeks trying to decide on a name and the best thing they'd come up with was Brett's idea of *PT 109*, the name of a naval warship they'd seen in a movie on TV.

Everything seemed ready for the newly rebuilt and redesigned craft to be taken on a test flight. Scott opened the door and looked over at the others. "Are you ready?"

Brett didn't hesitate for a minute. He jumped into his seat in the back. Christina seemed a little more reluctant.

"Wow. What are those things?" Scott asked as he moved his hand like he was swatting at something flying around his head.

"What?" asked Christina.

"I keep seeing these flashes of light flying around me, and they move really fast. They're here for a fraction of a second and then they're gone."

"What are you talking about?"

"They're small glowing balls of light, about the size of shooter marbles. They're so fast, I can't even see what they are, but they look like glowing orbs, and they keep darting around me. I saw them once before in the shed."

"Orbs? You're getting a little weird on us now, Scott," said Christina. "It's probably just mosquitoes. There's a lot of them out this time of year."

Christina held up her arm as she climbed into the ship. "Look, I'm so nervous, my hands are shaking."

"Everything will be okay." It took Scott's best acting job to convince her. His hands were shaking too, but he was careful not to let anyone see. Even though he was excited about going up again, Scott was still struggling with the fearful memories of his last flight.

Christina reluctantly got into the craft and took a seat in the front. There was one seat in the back of the craft and two seats in front. The control panel and the steering wheel were on the left side in front, just like the set-up in an American automobile.

Scott climbed in last and closed the door. His heart was pounding, but he knew he had to face his fear. Inside, he was wondering if his queasy stomach was his own anxiety or if it was his intuition telling him that there truly was danger lurking out there.

Chapter 9
Under the Light of the Milky Way

Scott gave the others a hopeful look and then turned on the motor. Because it was an electric motor and they had surrounded it with insulation, the craft was now very quiet. He wanted to appear positive for the others, so he called out, in a cheerful voice, "Okay everybody, here we goooooo."

This time the take-off was very smooth. The *Mercury One* gently rose up about six feet in the air and hovered there for a moment. Then, Scott accelerated the motor, so the bottom propeller turned a little faster, and the ship began to climb until it reached a height of about 30 feet.

Next, he turned on the smaller electric motor that ran the second propeller, the one that would make the ship move forward. When that propeller got up to speed, the ship started to float straight over the Harrison's house. Since the second propeller located in back was much smaller and the ship was carrying more weight, the *Mercury One* moved slowly, only about 10-15 miles per hour. Scott made a wide turn and then steered the craft directly above the street, between two rows of horse chestnut trees. Beneath them, the streetlamps gave off a soft glow that lit up the world below. Once the ship cleared the trees, it gently glided out towards the town of Stonebridge.

The ride was incredibly quiet and peaceful. The lights of the town were illuminated and twinkled in the air of the balmy summer night. There wasn't a trace of wind and, on this night, no storms. Even though it had rained earlier in the day, the sky had cleared and was full of stars. The glow of the moon was minimal because it was buried behind some wispy clouds near the horizon.

It was only a matter of minutes before Scott tested the limits of the *Mercury One* to see how high and how fast it would go. The craft could only rise up about 50 feet off the ground, but since it was dark, that was high enough. Unless someone was really paying attention, Scott figured that it was unlikely that anyone would see or hear them. The rear propeller only gave them minimal thrust. They couldn't go very fast, but that didn't matter. Christina and Scott didn't want a speedy rocket, they just wanted to feel what it was like to fly.

Everything seemed calm as they floated over the countryside. It was very different from the fast-paced existence of the world below. It felt very safe and peaceful to be away from the constant motion and busyness they witnessed every day.

Brett was the first to break the silence. "This is amazing!!!"

Both Christina and Scott finally started to relax and breathe again.

"I can't believe it," Christina added. "This is so cool."

Scott was starting to put his last journey behind him. "It's just like those dreams I have where I can fly."

The three of them looked down at the streets and houses as they drifted over Stonebridge. The redesigned craft seemed to float so gracefully that the sensation was mesmerizing.

"Does it fly any better now that we added all the upgrades?" Christina asked.

"Yeah, much better. I've got a lot more control, but it is *really* slow. This is about as fast as we can go."

The craft flew over the rooftops of the shops in town. Abigail, the antique store cat, had somehow climbed up onto the roof, and she was meowing at the strange object in the sky as if she were sounding out a warning to anyone who'd listen.

"Is that Abigail?" asked Christina.

"I think it is," said Scott as he looked out the moon roof.

"It's all right, Abigail." Christina called out, trying to reassure her. "You know us. We're friendly." That didn't work; however, and Abigail continued calling out as if there was an alien invasion happening right before her eyes.

As they moved on and flew over the retirement home, they could hear music playing. On most nights, the old-timers would sit out on the front porch in the summer, playing cards and sipping cool drinks, but tonight was Thursday, and every Thursday evening was dance night. Scott imagined the couples inside practicing the fox trot.

After gliding over Stonebridge, they headed out towards the countryside and the lights of the town gradually faded away. For the next few minutes, it was much darker as the *Mercury One* moved away from civilization. The quiet calm of the starry night lulled Scott into a state of total serenity. It almost felt like he was floating on a big raft down a gentle, lazy river. In flight, there wasn't a care in the world. It felt free and calm, completely removed from the frenetic world below.

The moon was lurking behind the clouds, and the stars were brilliant. The Milky Way stretched out across the night sky, and Mars smoldered in its orangish-red glow.

"What is that over there?" asked Brett, pointing at the horizon. "It looks like a big television screen."

Scott stuck his head out of the moonroof. "It must be the drive-in theater way out on Highway Two. That's the road that goes into Boston."

"Hey, it *is* the drive-in," said Brett. "You can see the screen from here."

"My turn to drive." Christina quickly climbed over Scott so she could switch seats with him. Scott scooted into the other chair. As the two changed places, it was the first time the ship had bobbled, but it

                    Star People: Mystery of the Hologram

only rocked for a moment and then the flight was smooth again.

Scott gave her a puzzled look as if to say, "What are you doing?"

"I wanna see what's playing at the movies."

Christina steered the craft in the direction of the movie theatre, and a few minutes later the *Mercury One* was buzzing over the parked cars at the outdoor theater. After a long wide turn, Christina headed straight for the giant movie screen. On the screen, dinosaurs were chasing after a small group of humans who had probably invented some kind of machine that allowed them to travel back to prehistoric times and, as luck would have it, dropped them off in a dinosaur-infested location.

"Look, it's Tyrannosaurus Rex," observed Brett. The dinosaurs kept getting larger and larger as the *Mercury One* got closer to the screen. "And he's getting *really* big!!!"

Concerned that the ship was headed for a collision with the giant screen, Scott pulled Christina back over into the passenger seat and slid underneath her into the driver's seat. "What are you doing? Are you crazy?" Now that he was back in control, Scott made as sharp a turn as he could to avoid the screen, but the *Mercury One* still came uncomfortably close.

Christina and Brett were laughing.

"Just having some fun," Christina replied. "Don't worry. Nobody saw us. They're all too busy watching the movie. I wanted to buzz the people in the drive-in."

"It looked like we were going to be eaten by a T-rex," Brett said with a laugh.

"No more crazy driving. You almost hit the screen, and we don't want to get reported."

"I wasn't planning on getting so close, but this thing doesn't turn very well, does it?"

"No. I told you that. It moves very slowly, and the turns are really wide." Scott hesitated for a moment. "All right, enough craziness. Let's go out in the country where we can practice flying, and no one will see us."

"All right," Christina agreed. "Let's go out by Miller's Pond. No one will see us out there."

Scott piloted the craft out to the abandoned farm. When they got there, they hovered over the barn and deserted farmhouse and then above the nearby creek where the soothing sound of water rushing over stones could be heard beneath them. Along the edges of the creek, flashes from the fireflies lit up the bushes and trees.

"Look at the fireflies down there," Christina pointed out. "They're everywhere."

The creek fed into Miller's Pond which sat about a hundred yards from the barn where Scott had taken refuge the night of the electrical storm.

The pond was perfectly still, and one whole side of it was overgrown with cattails and willows. Bullfrogs occasionally called out to each other in deep voices, but there was also another sound coming from around the edges of the water. That sound was the much higher voices of the smaller frogs, singing in unison, welcoming the coolness of the night.

"Do you think if I lean far enough out the moon roof, I could catch a firefly in my hand as we fly over the pond?" asked Brett.

"Maybe if I cut the power to almost nothing and we fly really low," answered Scott. "But if you lean that far out on that side, Christina will have to lean out on this side to counterbalance the weight shift."

"Let's try it," said an excited Christina.

Scott took the craft down low and flew just inches above the surface of the water. Christina reached out of the ship and brushed the top of the lake with her hand. She gently parted the water with her fingertips, creating a wake that spread out over the perfectly smooth surface.

"There's one," said Brett as he focused in and tried to catch it in midair.

"Did you get it?"

Brett sat back in the ship and slowly opened his hand. There was nothing there. "Its light went out right before I was about to grab it, and it disappeared. I guess I missed."

Beyond the pond was a secluded clearing, a round grassy area that was surrounded on three sides by an old forest of hardwood trees. It seemed like the perfect place for a landing and a place where no one would see them. Scott steered the ship in that direction and descended. The landing was a little rough as the ship bounced before coming to rest, but the sturdy wheels seemed to handle the impact.

As soon as they were on the ground, Scott jumped slightly. "Did you see that? More of those glowing lights."

"Fireflies?"

"No."

"The orbs?" Christina asked half-amused and half-intrigued.

"Yeah," said Scott. "The orbs. Did you see 'em?"

"I did see a flash or something, but I think they seem to be more interested in you."

Scott shook his head, not sure what to make of it.

"Let's go over and get a closer look at the fireflies," Christina suggested, abruptly changing the subject.

"Yeah, I want to catch some and take 'em home for my insect collection," added Brett.

But before they could get out of the craft, Scott noticed that the sky had suddenly become filled with crimson light.

"Hold on," warned Scott as he felt an uncomfortable sick feeling in his stomach. "I don't think anyone should go outside right now."

Scott looked up. Even though it was dark, the sky had a reddish hue to it.

"Why not?" complained Brett.

"Shhh. Everyone be quiet and don't move," whispered Scott.

Scott could see the smoldering lights of the same ship that he had seen flying over his house last spring. It was hard to make out the form of the ship in the darkness, but he recognized the disc shape and the crimson color.

"What is it?" whispered Brett.

"There's a spaceship up there."

Christina grabbed his arm. "What do we do?" She gave Scott a frightened look that he interpreted as *get us out of here, and fast.* Scott tried to fire up the motor. No response. He tried again, but it stayed silent.

"The motor won't start."

"Why not?" asked a nervous Christina.

Scott frantically tried working with the controls again, but the motor wouldn't respond. "We have no power. Everything's dead."

"Try it again!" urged Christina.

Scott tried the starter and then shook his head when, once again, there was no response.

"Let's try to make a run for it," said Christina. She tried to open the door of the *Mercury One*, but it wouldn't budge. "It won't open!"

"We're trapped!"

Chapter 10
The Wild Ride

Just as Scott was trying to manage the sick feeling in his stomach, a loud hissing noise crackled above them, and then that sizzling sound quickly began to fade as it moved off in the distance. He had heard that sound before. It was the same sound that occurred when the crimson ship fled from his house on the night that the hologram appeared.

Scott looked up again and scanned the sky. "I don't see it anymore."

The red glow was gone, but the colors in the sky seemed to be changing.

"Good, then let's get out of here," exclaimed Christina. "What was...," she started to ask, but before she could get the words out, everything around them suddenly became flooded by an eerie green light. It was as if someone had just flipped on a switch and about a dozen very intense green spotlights shone down directly on the *Mercury One.*

Then, they started to hear a strange high-pitched ringing sound. It came from directly above but rapidly moved closer until it seemed to drop down almost right on top of them.

As the sound grew louder and the green lights became brighter,

Brett was the first one to speak, "What's going on?"

Scott looked out of the moon roof to try to get a better view. Hovering above them was a mysterious craft, about one hundred feet in length, and shaped like a diamond. It was illuminated with brilliant green lights. "I don't know. I think... I think I can see the outline of some sort of ship right over us. It's hard to see with all those lights," he said as he pointed upwards and tried to trace the general shape of something floating overhead about thirty feet above them. "It's a different ship, not the red one."

"What do you think it is?" asked Brett.

"I don't know. There aren't any manmade planes or hovercrafts or blimps or anything that look like that," said Scott. "It looks like... it might be... a...a real UFO."

"Try the motor again," urged Christina.

Scott tried. "It won't work."

"Keep trying."

The motor wouldn't start.

"What do we do?" asked Christina, and just after she uttered those words, she let out a brief startled scream when their ship mysteriously began to move without the assistance of the motor.

The *Mercury One* started to slowly rise up from the ground, being lifted by some mysterious force.

"Now what's happening?"

"It's like we're being pulled in by some magnetic field. There are no wires or arms or anything between us and their ship, but somehow, they are lifting us up in the air," observed Scott as he alternated between looking out the windows of the craft and out of the moon roof. "We're somehow locked into their ship and can't go anywhere. They have control of our ship."

"Why are they doing this?" asked Brett. "Where are they taking us?"

Christina looked out one of the windows. "So far, just straight up in the air."

Scott studied the situation. "I don't get it. There's nothing holding us up. We're just suspended in midair. How can they do that?"

"What do you think they'll do to us?" asked Brett.

"I don't know."

"I hope they don't drop us," Christina was starting to look worried. "We're getting awfully high."

"If they do, I'll try to fire up the motor."

"What if it doesn't work? They already shut it down. We would crash down to the ground."

The upward movement of the two ships had now taken them about a thousand feet in the air before they came to a halt. The view below had changed dramatically. As they got higher, Miller's Pond looked no bigger than a drop of water; the round clearing in the woods where they had landed their ship seemed to be about the size of a fifty-cent piece. The deserted barn had become too small to see altogether.

Suddenly, the two ships stopped moving and paused in mid-air. Four large robotic arms emerged from the alien ship, reached down and firmly latched onto the smaller craft.

"They just grabbed hold of us with these big clamp-like things," observed Brett. "We're their prisoners now!" Brett had always seemed fearless, but all of the color in his face had disappeared, leaving his skin looking completely white.

"This is getting really scary, Scott." Christina grabbed his arm. He could feel her hand trembling.

Scott didn't panic. He stayed calm and tuned into his intuition. "I...I...I think we'll be okay. I don't think they'll hurt us."

"Are you sure?" Christina grasped the door handle on one side and now started to hold Scott's hand. "We're awfully high."

"I think we'll be okay. They're just curious." Scott wasn't convinced that what he was saying was true, but he had to try to calm the others. His intuition told him that they would be all right, but he was starting to experience some of the exact same feelings he felt on the night of the storm. His stomach was tied up in knots.

Once the two ships were firmly locked together, the alien vessel shifted into another gear and took off at a super high speed. Although the *Mercury One* seemed to be securely attached to the alien ship, Scott, Brett, and Christina held on as tightly as they could. As the two ships picked up momentum, the ride was smooth but incredibly fast. Everything around them was a blur. It was unnerving because their homemade craft had never gone higher than just above the treetops and had never gone faster than about fifteen miles an hour.

"I don't know how fast we're going, but all I can see below us are streaks of light," observed Christina. "We're moving so fast; I can't even tell where we are."

"Is this light speed?" asked Brett, squirming in the back seat.

"I don't know," answered Scott, "but we're *really moving*."

After a couple of minutes, the alien ship slowed down enough so that Scott was able to make out objects outside the windows again.

"Where are we?" asked Brett as the ship reduced its speed.

"Look," Christina pointed, "It's the Statue of Liberty. We're flying over New York."

Scott looked at his watch and mumbled half to himself. "How is that possible? It's only 9:00. How could we get to New York that fast? That only took about two minutes."

"I don't feel so good," said Brett looking as if all the color had left his face.

Scott tried to distract him. "There's the Empire State Building. Remember, Brett, that's the building that King Kong climbed up in that movie."

"Yeah, yeah. I remember."

After a few moments, the ship switched back into the blazing hyper speed mode and everything outside became a blur again.

"Wow, this is a hard on my stomach too," said Christina.

"Are we ever going to see our home again," asked Brett, "or are we going to be their prisoners forever?"

"I don't think so, Brett. I think we'll be okay. I just don't know what they want from us." Scott was starting to feel calmer, like everything would be all right, but he was puzzled by why an alien ship would come and capture them. *What would they want with us? Why take us instead of someone more important like a world leader?*

When the two crafts slowed down again the flight had taken them to a new destination.

"Look, there's the Capital building and the White House." Christina pointed out the sights as they flew over them. "The lights are on at the White House. That means the President's there." Christina looked out the window on the other side of the ship. "And there's the Lincoln Memorial and the reflecting pool. I was there with my parents last summer."

Scott was more impressed with the aeronautical abilities than the sights. "Wow. That only took us about two minutes to go from New York to Washington D.C." Scott observed looking at his watch. "That's amazing."

"Scott, look down at the water in the reflecting pool," Christina pointed out the window. "In the reflection, you can see the ship that's driving us."

Scott looked at the reflection. All the lights of the ship had been turned off, but the gigantic diamond-shaped craft looked enormous in comparison to the smaller *Mercury One* locked in below it. The shadow of the alien vessel looked ominous as it moved over the surface of the water. "Wow. It's gigantic. It's amazing."

"It's also really scary, Scott," added Christina. "What do they want from us?"

"If they wanted to hurt us, they could have done that by now. For some reason they are just showing us around."

"I just want to go home," said Brett.

"I think we'll be okay, Brett."

Then, the large ship switched back into the hyper speed mode.

"Oh, there goes my stomach again," said Christina as she crouched over.

When the ships started to slow down, Brett asked, "Where are we now? It feels cold in here all of a sudden."

Christina looked down. "I don't know, but it's really foggy down there. Wait a minute. That looks like Big Ben and the Houses of Parliament. We're in London. I've never been to London before, but we learned about all this stuff in geography class."

"What's that castle thing down there?" asked Brett.

"That's the Tower of London. That's where they kept the prisoners. I just finished reading this book about the Tower. Anne Boleyn was beheaded there."

"Who's Anne Boleyn?" asked Brett.

"She was the queen of England a long time ago. She was married to King Henry VIII."

"He was the guy with all the wives," Scott added.

"And she was beheaded?" asked Brett.

"Yeah, they cut off her head with a French sword, and they say that her ghost still haunts the place." Christina hesitated for a moment. "But, you know, that was kind of weird."

"What?"

"Well, as soon as I saw that it was London, I started thinking about Anne Boleyn and the Tower, and then suddenly we were there."

"At the Tower of London?"

"Yeah," said an intrigued Christina. "How did they do that? Do you think they can read our minds?"

"I don't know," said Scott.

"I'm going to think of a place and see what happens. I'd like to see where the queen lives," said Christina and as soon as those words were out of her mouth, the ship was circling Buckingham Palace. "Wow, that was kind of eerie. They knew where to take us before I even said it."

The excitement of seeing another part of the world and the test to see if the aliens could read their minds took away some of the fear.

"I'm going to think of a place," said Scott, and immediately, the ships sped off at an astonishing speed that felt even faster than before.

The speed was too intense for them to talk or move or even look at one another, so the three of them just sat in their places and held on.

As the ships started to slow down, Christina observed the change in temperature. "Okay now the air feels really warm. Did you think of the desert?"

"Sort of," said Scott as he pointed out the window. "That's what I thought of."

"The Pyramids of Egypt."

The visit to the pyramids lasted only a few seconds before the ships sped off again and didn't stop until they reached a row of stone sculptures that stood like guardians along the coastline of a small island.

"Oh, my God, it's Easter Island?" said Christina as they slowed down to look at the statues in the shapes of giant human figures carved in stone. "Who thought of that?" she asked.

"Not me," said Brett. "I never even heard of this place before."

"We learned about this in geography class, but I wasn't thinking about it," replied Scott.

"I like the big heads though. They're really cool," added Brett as he looked out the window at the stone sculptures.

"It's where I'm from," said Christina.

"You're from Easter Island?" asked Brett.

"No, not Easter Island," Christina clarified, "but I'm from Chile, and Easter Island is a part of Chile just like Hawaii is a part of the U.S. My family moved to the house where we live now when I was two."

Scott noticed a hint of a tear in her eye.

"I've been back to Santiago a bunch of times but never to Easter Island."

"Sorry to interrupt all this, but we gotta get home," said Scott looking at his watch. "We're going to get in trouble. Mom's going to be there any minute. If we get caught, it's all over. Let's all think about going home, and maybe they will take us there."

Chapter 11
The Appearance of the Star People

O h, here we go again," said Christina holding her stomach.
"Where are they taking us now? I just wanna go home." Brett shouted out as the speed started to build.

The ships accelerated, and the three of them braced themselves for the pressure that came with such high-speed travel.

About ten minutes later, the ships slowed down again.

"Wait, that looks like Stonebridge down there," observed Christina.

"We're home!" said Brett looking out the window. "What do you think they'll do with us now?"

"I think they'll just let us go," said Scott. "Why else would they take us back here?"

The aliens landed both ships in the large field behind the Harrison's house, first setting down the *Mercury One* and then landing their own much-larger ship nearby. Scott didn't hesitate. He jumped out of the ship, his body tingling with excitement, and walked briskly towards the alien ship. Christina and Brett followed cautiously behind him.

Brett looked around and said, "How'd they know where we lived?"

"They can read our minds," answered Christina. "But what's Scott doing? He's going right up to their ship."

Scott had moments of doubt where fear would creep up his spine and try to convince him to run, but something in his gut told him it was okay.

Christina and Brett held back as Scott approached the alien vessel and tried to get a closer look. Christina called out in a loud whisper: "Scott. Scott, come back. What are you doing?"

Scott was silent. He waited to see if the aliens would come out from their ship.

"Scott, we don't know if they're safe or not," warned Christina.

There was an incredible silence all around them, absolutely no wind and no sound. It was as if everything and everyone in the area had been placed in some sort of mesmerizing sleep. Scott noticed that all of the lights in the neighborhood had gone dark.

"Scott," whispered Christina. "We don't know if they're friendly. Don't you think you should stay back a little ways?"

Scott just stood his ground outside the ship and waited.

Finally, the door to the alien ship opened. A ramp dropped down from the door to the ground, and then three figures appeared in the doorway. They moved very slowly, as they came down the ramp, and walked as if they were barely touching the ground. Scott wondered if the lightness about their bodies might have been from a gravitational differential that was far less than what they were used to on their home planet.

All three aliens had large heads and slim bodies. Their skin was greenish-brown and rough, almost like that of a lizard. The aliens had thin lips, narrow mouths, and enormous almond-shaped eyes. Their large eyes were green in color, but the green was so intense that it looked like their eyes were glowing. They had no hair and wore no clothes. It was impossible to tell from their bodies whether the aliens were male or female. The only noticeable difference in the three was that one looked older—his skin was more wrinkled and had a grey cast—and he had a long scar running down the side of one of his cheeks.

Their arms and legs were long and thin, and all of the movements they made were slow and very fluid. In the center of each of the alien's foreheads, about an inch above the center of their eyes, they each had a star-shaped jewel. Sometimes those jewels would momentarily glow in different colors.

"Look, they have stars on their foreheads," observed Brett out loud. "People with stars… they're star people."

Scott looked back in time to see Christina grab Brett's arm in a way that told him not to speak for a minute or two, at least until they established some sort of connection.

For several moments after that remark, everything and everyone was quiet. Scott studied the extraterrestrials, and they studied him.

The shortest of the three aliens made a high-pitched sound with its mouth and four more aliens came from the ship. These four aliens were smaller—children perhaps—and their skin looked younger and had more of a silvery color. The four nodded to the one who had called to them as if they were accepting their instructions and then began a transformation where their bodies started to morph into different shapes. The conversion happened quickly and looked like a painful process, but after about a minute, all four of the beings had shape-shifted into four healthy beautiful deer, two with a full set of antlers and two without. After the transformation, each deer took off, bounding at full speed, one in each of the four directions.

"What just happened?" asked Christina.

"Apparently, they can shapeshift," answered Scott. "I read about that in a Sci-Fi book once."

"What does that mean?" asked Brett.

"They can somehow rearrange their atoms in such a way where they can turn into animals," Scott whispered back to Brett.

Scott's heart was beating fast. He was excited and wanted to know more. He turned back to the aliens. "Thank you for the ride. It was amazing… the best ride I've ever had…in my whole life."

He waited for a reply, but the aliens were silent. The only change that happened was something about their eyes. Their eyes seemed to brighten and then grow dim almost as if the brightness reflected understanding of what Scott said, and the dimness was their frustration at not being able to respond.

"Do you speak English?"

One of the taller aliens looked over and appeared to silently communicate with the others. He seemed to specifically address the oldest-looking one, the one with many age spots and a large crescent-shaped scar on his face. The elder bowed his head as if he had been given a command and was following orders. He went back into the entryway of the ship and emerged with a blanket which he wrapped around his body.

The elder alien, cloaked in the blanket, started to undergo what looked like a difficult transformation. As he went through the shape-shifting process, it took a little longer than the others who had turned into deer. He had a look of profound sadness on his face. As his form changed shape, it eventually turned human. First, he turned into a red-haired baby but then began to rapidly age until he looked to be about eight years old. He had pale skin and lots of freckles and still—even in human form—had the scar on his face. Although the alien had taken human form, he maintained the green eyes which Scott sensed contained eons of wisdom.

"Where are you from?" asked Scott.

No answer. There was only silence as the two aliens stared at him. The alien with the scar—who had turned into the red-haired boy—seemed to need a few minutes to settle into his new eight-year-old body.

Scott suddenly got an idea. "Wait there. Don't go anywhere," Scott said to the aliens as he hurried towards the house. "I want to give you something." Before he went into the house he turned to Christina and Brett and said: "Don't let them leave."

Brett and Christina slowly walked closer to the aliens. Scott could still hear their voices as he entered the kitchen. "Okay," Christina said nervously to Brett. "What do we talk about now?"

"I don't know," said Brett. "Why did you take us to the island with the big heads?"

"He means Easter Island," Christina clarified.

Still, there was no answer.

Scott quickly returned holding a couple of things that he had brought from the house. He walked up to the aliens and held out an English dictionary and a box of French/English language tapes.

"Those are Mom's language tapes," Brett started to object.

"She never uses 'em. It'll help them learn to speak English." Scott turned to the aliens, "Here, you can take these and learn our language. Don't worry about the French part. There's about a dozen tapes in there and it will tell you about everything from history and culture to entertainment and religion," said Scott as he read aloud from the label.

For a brief moment, the bodies of the three aliens lit up in a faint reddish-pink color. Scott wondered if that color appeared because they were appreciative. Or were they just curious, he couldn't tell for sure.

"Look, they're glowing," whispered Brett.

One at a time, the three aliens stepped forward and placed a hand on the book and box of tapes. The alien that transformed into a human was the first to put his hand on the box and the other two followed his lead.

Finally, the alien who had transformed into the red-haired boy spoke. His voice sounded weak and hoarse as if he was trying to speak for the first time. "There. It is done," he said, as he pushed the dictionary and language tapes back in Scott's direction as if he wasn't interested.

"Don't you want to at least read them or listen to them?"

"It is already done," repeated the boy.

"Wow, they learned all that in a couple of seconds. Their minds are about a thousand times more sophisticated than ours," observed Christina, as she and Brett slowly walked forward to join Scott.

Then, the red-headed boy spoke again. "We don't speak or use language. We communicate only with thoughts. We read thoughts and send thoughts. As our minds evolved, we no longer had the need to talk, so we lost the ability to speak because our vocal cords were seldom used. In our normal form, we can only make a few sounds," he explained.

As Scott listened to him, he noticed that the aging process seemed to still be underway. The boy looked to be about ten years old now.

"They use telepathy to communicate," Scott whispered to the others. "They can read our minds."

Scott was intrigued and wanted to see how gifted they were. He wanted to test their telepathy. He looked around for a moment, trying to come up with an idea, and then he noticed his grandfather's workshop. "What was my..."

"... grandfather's name?" the red-haired boy finished the question before Scott could get the words out. The two aliens—and the transformed alien boy—started to glow in a cool, electric blue color. "Austin."

"Why did they turn blue?" asked Brett.

"We turn blue when we go into a heightened state of focus, when we are reading thoughts. We had to scan back through Scott's lifetime because he was trying to see if he could mentally block us from getting the right answer."

"Was that true, Scott?" asked Christina.

"I wanted to see if I could prevent them from reading my mind."

"I guess you got your answer," quipped Christina. "They got it right."

"What happened to those..." Scott didn't want to use the word *aliens* in case that was somehow inappropriate, "others who turned into deer?"

"They are keeping watch for us and will tell us when your mother returns. As deer, they blend in, and no one would think twice if they should see them. That is not the case with our natural bodies," answered the redhead.

"How do they change like that?" asked Scott.

"We can command our atoms to take different shapes or forms."

Scott thought for a moment about what to say next. He noticed that the young boy was continuing to age and looked to be about twelve.

"I'm Scott." He turned and gestured to the others. "That's Christina and Brett. What are your names?"

The tall alien stepped forward as the boy spoke. "If we shorten our names to make it easier for you to understand and to pronounce, he is called Zocuul. He is the leader of this expedition. He is known as a keen observer or what you on earth would call a tracker."

Then, the other alien stepped forward. This one was slightly shorter than the others.

"Zula. She is the kind and gentle one."

"I am Zin," said the alien who was transforming into the red-haired boy. He continued to age and now looked like he was about 16 years old.

"Do all of your names start with Z?" asked Brett.

"The first letter of our names indicates the planet we are from."

"So why did you take us to the island with the big heads?" asked Brett.

"Those carvings are sculptures of our ancestors," answered Zin who was looking as if he was now in his mid-twenties. "That island is like our art gallery, our sculpture garden."

"So those ancient statues were made by aliens, not earthlings?"

"Do you think it would have been possible for a primitive society to move eighty-ton stones by themselves? Earthlings did not have the technology or the ability back then to build many of the wonders that are attributed to ancient civilizations," answered Zin looking now to be about thirty years old.

Scott thought about the implications of that statement. He looked over at Christina who, based on the surprised look on her face, may have also been considering what they had just been told.

"So, this isn't the first time you've come to our planet," asked Christina.

"We have visited many times over many millenniums."

"What's a millennium?" whispered Brett.

"A thousand years," answered Christina.

"Where is your planet?" asked Scott.

"Our planet is Zelmoria, in the constellation you refer to as the Scorpion. Our sun star is known as Antares, the heart of Scorpio," said Zin who had aged even more and was looking as if he was about 50 years old.

"A binary star," Zin added.

"So, it has two stars or two suns," said Scott.

"Yes," said Zin whose hair was starting to turn slightly grey, and his hairline was receding. His body didn't look quite as youthful. His skin wasn't so vibrant, and his facial scar was more pronounced.

"You are Antarians," observed Scott, and before they could answer, Scott followed it with a suggestion: "Maybe someday you could take us to your planet."

Christina pulled Scott aside and whispered, "What? Are you crazy?"

One of the deer bolted back into the center of the group. Zin, now with pronounced streaks of grey in his hair, looked at the deer and spoke. "Your mother approaches."

Zula let out a gentle high-pitched call that sounded a little like the cooing of a dove. Within seconds, the other three deer returned. All four of the deer morphed back into their alien shapes as they boarded their craft.

"We must hurry," said Zin who now looked to be about sixty years old.

Scott looked at his watch and noticed that it had stopped. He tapped it a few times in an attempt to make it work, but that didn't help. "Before you go, can I just look inside your ship, just for a minute?"

"You have already been on our ship, many times," answered the now grey-haired elder. "We've been training you."

Scott had no concrete recollection of being on their ship, but, at the same time, was suspicious that it might be true. It made him feel a little uncomfortable. *What did that mean? Was that what was happening in his dreams?*

"You are very important to us, Scott Harrison. We need you," said Zin whose hair had turned completely white. His mid-seventies body started to look weak and frail. "We will be back for you."

Scott felt a little uneasy when he heard this. *What are they saying? How could I possibly be important to them? What do they want with me?*

Zin came forward. "If you will allow me, I want to activate a part of your mind that has been mostly dormant for much of your waking life. You may have sensed that there was something different about you, but this will bring more clarity. If you will allow me, I can help you unlock a door within your mind."

The alien man—now weaker at age eighty—held his hands a couple inches above Scott's head, and a beam of energy, in the form of light, was emitted from the palms of his hands.

"Wait, is this safe?" asked a nervous Christina even though the alien had already started the process.

"We are a kind and loving race," answered Zin who seemed to age even more as he gave away his energy. "This will eventually give Scott insight about why he is here in this lifetime."

When the light stopped coming from his hands, Zin put his hands down by his side and closed his eyes and sent a message to Scott: *Focus, and you can hear our thoughts.*

Scott turned to Brett and Christina. "Wow. That was pretty bizarre. I could hear his thoughts in my head."

"What'd he say?"

"Focus, and you can hear our thoughts," answered Scott. "Did you hear him say that?" Scott asked Brett and Christina. They both shook their heads and looked at him like they didn't know what he was talking about.

We need you to hear the thoughts we send from our alien forms. There are too few of us left for any of us to become human again. Again, Scott heard their voices in his head. He looked at Christina and Brett. "Did you hear that? That time it was all three of them speaking at the same time."

Christina and Brett shook their heads.

"They said there are too few of them left for any of them to ever become human again."

"What does that mean?" asked Christina.

As soon as she asked that question, Scott heard the answer. *We can change into animals and change back, but we can never change back and forth from human form. Once we become human, we can only survive for a few minutes.*

"If they become human, they can't change back, and they can only survive for a few minutes," Scott repeated their message and then turned back to the aliens. "But why?"

"When we turn into humans, our hearts can't change back into their natural form. It becomes a human heart forever. And since we live so much longer than humans, it is the equivalent of a human heart that has beaten for centuries. It is worn out and has no life left. So, the body rapidly ages to match with the failing heart, and then both the body and the heart die together," answered Zin.

As soon as Scott heard the response, his mood changed. "No, you can't let that happen."

Scott looked over at what was once a young vibrant red-headed boy who was now quite elderly. His hair was white and his skin wrinkled. His body was stooped over. Then, in a moment, Zin collapsed.

"What's happening?" asked Christina with sadness in her voice.

"He's dying," Brett said as he burst into tears.

"Isn't there anything we can do?" asked Christina.

Scott listened for their thoughts. "They say there isn't," answered Scott feeling as if everything about that wonderful night and amazing ride had gone away in a second as he watched Zin dying in front of him.

A few moments later, Zin took his last breath.

The two aliens looked very distraught. Their green eyes had lost their excitement and their alien bodies, glowing in a grey color, made them look like dark shadows. The tall alien walked over, gently lifted

Zin off the ground and held him in his arms.

He was old and was dying. He volunteered to do this. He had to become human to activate your memory so you could communicate with us, said the two voices in Scott's head.

Scott didn't know what to say. He was shocked. He didn't want the alien to die.

We must go, said the voices in Scott's head. *We will be back. We will come for you. Look for us to return when the moon is full. And again, when a second full moon returns a month later.*

"But wait..." objected Scott.

We must leave. Your mother approaches.

The aliens boarded their ship, and the door closed behind them. A familiar ringing sound indicated that the engine had been fired up and was gaining momentum.

Scott, Christina, and Brett backed up so they would be a safe distance from the ship when it took off. In just a few moments the ship was off the ground. It wasn't a high-speed liftoff; it was gentle, and the ship rose smoothly. It made a long, fluid, arching turn to get pointed in the right direction, and then it pulled away in a flash. The departure left a streak of white light almost like the transient trail of a shooting star.

As Scott watched them fly away, he said: "I can't believe it. I don't know what all this means." He felt like he was in a daze and couldn't think straight.

"Come on, we have to hurry and put the ship away before your mom gets home," said Christina grabbing Scott's arm and interrupting his moment of bewilderment.

As the three of them began to push the *Mercury One* back inside the shed, a car turned onto their street, and they could see the headlights approaching.

     Star People: Mystery of the Hologram

Chapter 12
The Watcher of the Skies

On the night following the alien encounter, Scott had set up his telescope in the backyard and was looking at the heavens. He was always excited when there were cosmic events like comets, meteor showers or an orbiting spacecraft. On the evenings without those special occurrences, he would often spend many hours focusing on the planets of the Earth's solar system. He liked Saturn because he could see its rings through the telescope, but his favorite planet was Mars because it was so mysterious and fascinating. Even looking at the earth's moon was something he could do for hours. He felt a mystical connection to the moon and always dreamed that he might be able to fly there in his lifetime.

But on this night, Scott couldn't think about anything else but the previous night's alien visitation. As he kept going over every detail of what happened, his mind kept returning to the moment when the alien died. The only other person he'd known who'd passed away was his grandfather, Austin, and the loss was so painful that, after all these years, he still felt sadness in his heart. His thoughts would go back and forth from the dying alien to the last time he saw his frail grandfather. All of that sadness came right back to him when Zin took his final breath.

In his final days, his grandfather told him that he would accomplish great things during his lifetime. Scott always figured that grandfathers were supposed to say things like that to their grandkids, but Zin said something like that as well. The aliens said they were very interested in him, but why? That thought went round and round in his mind. *What was it about me, that would interest the aliens? Why did Zin have to die on behalf of me? Why did they say I was important to them? What would they do when they came back?* He was a little excited about seeing the Star People again, but something felt ominous about the way they said they were so interested in him.

* * *

Christina quietly came into the backyard and watched as Scott looked into the telescope. *What do I do now,* she thought to herself? Until last night, Scott was an enigma. He talked about weird things like alien ships visiting in the night. And while those stories were interesting, she could always dismiss those tales as being Scott's wild imagination. But now, she was in the middle of it. The strange friend of hers, who lived across the street, suddenly seemed to be more tuned in than anyone she knew.

Furthermore, on the night of the storm, when she thought something had happened to Scott, she realized that her feelings for him were a lot stronger than she ever imagined. *But I'm not sure he even notices me or likes me as anything more than a friend.*

As Christina approached, she softly said, "Hey."

Scott jumped a little when he heard a voice behind him. He turned around and smiled.

"Are you looking for a planet in the vicinity of Antares?"

Scott laughed. "I'm afraid that's too far away even for the Haystack Observatory," he said, referring to the observatory they once visited together on a school field trip.

"I can't believe what happened last night," said Christina.

"Me neither. I was so wound up I couldn't sleep. I kept watching out the window just in case the aliens came back and landed their ship in the field behind our house again."

"I know what you mean. I didn't sleep either. Even now, when I think about it, I keep wondering if it was some sort of dream. But we couldn't have all dreamt the same thing, could we?"

"No, it was all real." He motioned towards the telescope. "Wanna look?"

"What is it?" asked Christina as she closed one eye and looked into the eyepiece.

"Venus."

"It's very cool, but what are all of those little people doing down there?"

"Very funny."

After gazing at Venus for a few moments, Christina went back to the occurrences of last night. "What do you think they wanted? And why did they pick us?"

"I don't know. I wanted to ask them so much more, but then we got interrupted when my mom came home."

"It was amazing the way they shapeshifted."

"And the way they glowed in different colors," added Scott.

"Everything about them was so cool, especially those stars on their foreheads."

"Everything except for the one that died."

"I know. I can't stop thinking about that. I wish it hadn't happened. I didn't want him to die. It was so sad."

"It hurts when I think about it."

"Yeah, I know. Me too."

"Brett's been pretty bummed as well. He doesn't know what to make of any of this. Until last night, he thought he just had a really weird brother, but now he can't ignore it anymore. He's caught up in it too."

"Do you feel different after they—what did they do again—open your mind or something?"

"No. I don't think so. The only difference I've noticed so far was that when I asked them something, they would give me information."

"What's that like?"

"It was like," Scott hesitated, "I would ask questions, and these voices would give me the answer. It was as if they were guides, whispering in my ear, telling me what I needed to know."

"Wasn't that kind of scary? After all, you were hearing voices in your head."

"No. It wasn't scary. I feel like the Star People are good. I don't think they would hurt us."

"So, can you read our minds now as well?"

Scott put his fingertips on his temples and pretended to read Christina's mind. "You are thinking that your neighbor, Scott, is the smartest person you know."

"Wow!"

"Impressed?"

"That's totally..." she hesitated as she thought of the right word, "inaccurate."

Scott laughed. "No, I can't read anyone's mind. And even then, I'm not reading their minds, I'm hearing their thoughts. It's like they're talking, and I can hear their voices in my head."

"I wish we could go back up tonight and make contact again."

"I know. Me too, but we can't," said Scott. "It's my grandma's birthday."

"Your grandma?"

"On my Dad's side. I don't know what happened to my Mom's mom. I never met her," said Scott. "Anyway, my mom went to pick her up and then we're all going to *Mystic Delights* for dessert."

"But it's so hard having to wait."

"Well, I think my mom's going out with Mr. Spiffy tomorrow night so we can fly then."

A car approached and turned into the driveway at the Harrison's house.

"Looks like my mom and grandma are here. I gotta go." He picked up his telescope to take it inside.

"I guess I should apologize," said Christina as they walked towards the house.

"For what?"

"There have been times when you talked about all of your outer space alien stuff when I gave you a hard time."

"Yeah," Scott shrugged. "You're not the only one. Remember, I told you about that time in eighth grade when I read my composition to the class? The one about dreaming I was on another planet."

"Oh yeah, I forgot about that. *Everyone* laughed at you."

Scott shrugged his shoulders again as if it didn't bother him too much anymore. "They always have. So, I just stopped talking about it. Whenever I did, everyone thought I was crazy."

"Well, you're not crazy. I learned my lesson last night." Christina looked down and paused for a moment. "So, I'm sorry I've been giving you a hard time about all this stuff, and I'll *try* not to make fun of you anymore." Christina emphasized the word "try" to suggest that there were no guarantees.

"Don't worry about it," said Scott opening the back door to his house. He hesitated and then looked down as if he were trying to come up with the right words. "There's one more thing."

"What's that?"

"I've been having this dream."

"The one where your body turns into dust?"

"No, not that one," said Scott. "In this dream I'm flying."

"Flying?"

"Yeah, but not in the *Mercury One*. I'm not even sure what kind of craft it is," he said shaking his head. "I'm only about fifty feet up in the air, and I'm watching myself, on the ground, running."

"Wait. You're watching another version of yourself?"

"Exactly, and that other Scott, the one on the ground, is being attacked by a spaceship from above. That spaceship is firing—I don't know what kind of weapons they're using—but when they strike the ground everything bursts into flames."

"So, you're running for your life?"

"Right," Scott hesitated. "Only I don't make it."

"What?"

"One of those missiles hits me and I go down."

"Are you all right?"

"I don't know. That's all I can ever remember, but you know how my dreams are. Sometimes they come true."

Chapter 13
The Sighting

On the following night, as soon as his mom and Mr. Spiffy were gone, Scott, Christina and Brett were preparing the *Mercury One* for another flight. Scott had learned from his grandfather to always make sure everything was tightened, tuned, and adjusted before you start up a machine. One of the most important checks was to always make sure that the batteries which powered the motors were fully charged so the ship wouldn't run out of power and leave them stranded miles away from home.

On this night, the air was still and full of the scent of honeysuckle vines which grew up along the fence that separated the Harrison's backyard from their neighbors. The sunset colored the clouds in pinks and oranges, but that color was rapidly disappearing as the last traces of daylight were quickly fading. In the sky above, bats darted and fluttered erratically catching gnats and mosquitoes in midair. As darkness approached, the hooting of an owl emerged from the woods nearby, interrupted occasionally by a dog barking off in the distance.

As Brett climbed into the *Mercury One*, he asked: "Can I drive tonight? I'm the only one who hasn't had a turn."

"That's true," said Christina settling into her seat and looking at Scott. "Even the aliens have had a turn."

"Okay, Brett, but let me go first. We'll take it out to Miller's Pond so no one will see us, and then I'll let you drive."

Gently, the *Mercury One* left the ground and they headed out towards Miller's Pond.

* * *

Earl Stubbs, owner of the gas station in town, and his two friends were out in a field with flashlights collecting crickets for fish bait when, as he was reaching down to grab an unsuspecting cricket, Earl thought he heard something pass overhead. It was so dark that he couldn't see well enough to know what it was, but he definitely felt a gust of air rush over him.

"What's that?" Earl said to himself as he looked up in the sky trying to discover the source of the strange sound and the burst of wind that had just passed over him. He was certain that he saw some sort of craft move overhead and then fly away from him in the night sky.

Earl pointed to the sky and yelled out to his buddies: "Hey, did you see that?!?"

At first, his friends, Ray and Gordon, didn't know what Earl was so excited about.

"What?" Ray asked. Ray was portly, bald, had a very round face and big lips. He usually wore a baseball cap and wide suspenders to hold his pants up.

Earl pointed at the flying object that was moving away from them. "O'er there...going that way...in the sky. It's one of them flyin' saucers!"

"A flying saucer?" said Ray in disbelief. "Earl, what are you talkin' about?"

"Look, o'er there." Earl pointed with his flashlight, but the flashlight beam was too weak to cast any light on the ship which was moving away from them now. "It's going that way."

"What exactly did ya see?" asked Ray.

"I dunno. First, I heard somethin', then I looked up and seen what I think was a flyin' saucer. It's headed for them fields that way," said Earl pointing again.

"I didn't see nothin'," said Gordon. Earl's other friend, Gordon, wore thick, black-rimmed glasses, an orange plaid shirt and baggy jeans that were rolled up at the cuffs. Despite his glasses, Gordon never saw things very well, even in broad daylight. He had a habit of stepping in things that everyone else would walk around.

"Me neither," added Ray looking up in the sky.

"We gotta go check it out," exclaimed Earl.

"What?" said Gordon in disbelief.

Earl knew that almost anything out of the ordinary made Gordon feel uncomfortable, but he wasn't going to be deterred.

"Let's follow it," said Earl. "Come on. Quick, get in the truck."

The three of them jumped into Earl's 1958 cherry red Chevy pick-up truck and took off in the direction of the sighting. Earl was excited and accelerated like a wild man.

"I think it's long gone by now, Earl. We should just turn back and let things be," said Gordon in a high-pitched voice.

"What happened to your voice? It got really squeaky," observed Ray.

Earl remembered how Gordon's voice got about an octave higher whenever he got scared.

"I don't know," said Gordon sounding like a soprano.

Earl wasn't interested in the small talk. He kept watching the sky, sometimes forgetting to look where he was going.

As the truck bounced and bumped over the rugged terrain, Ray hung his head out the window of the pick-up truck and pointed up at the sky. "Well, what the hell. I think I actually *do* see something up there."

"Where?" asked Gordon as he fumbled under the seat for his glasses which had fallen off his head when the truck hit a large bump. "I can't see nothin' without my glasses."

"Yep, Gordon, it looks like one of them flying saucers from outer space," Ray said with authority as he looked out the window keeping an eye on the craft. Earl chuckled to himself because while Ray pretended to be an expert on everything, in reality, Ray didn't know a whole lot about anything.

Ray looked over at Gordon and shook his head. "What am I tellin' you for? You're so blind without your glasses, it could smash into the front of the truck an' you still wouldn't see it."

Earl kept watching the skies. "Look, it's doin' maneuvers or somethin' over'n that field. Let's get on over there."

"Oh, I dunno," said Gordon in a shrill voice. "I don't like that idear. Don't like it one bit."

Earl went after the craft as best he could. He was able to follow it on a couple of dirt roads, and then, when there were no more roads, he drove across open fields, almost bottoming out on the bumps along the way. Finally, Earl hit a bump that was too much for the old truck to handle. It landed with a loud crash and came to an abrupt stop. The engine was still running, but the wheels wouldn't move. The three of them hopped out of the truck to survey the damage.

"Now Earl, see what you did," blurted out Ray. "You've gone an' busted an axel or somethin'."

"Looks like we ain't goin' any further," added Gordon, wiping the sweat off of his forehead with his shirtsleeve and adjusting his dirty glasses.

"The heck we ain't," said Earl. "I'm goin' after 'em on foot. You guys with me or not?"

"Not me. I'm close enough right here," said Gordon. "They might have a ray gun or somethin'."

"Gordon, you've been watching too many of them science fiction movies," said Earl.

"Earl, you dim bulb! You're gonna get yerself killed!"

"That's a chance I gotta take. I know they've come for me. I can feel it. They come lookin' for intelligent life, and now they found it. I gotta go."

Ray and Gordon tried to hold Earl back, but Earl was determined. He shook them off and took off running in the direction of the ship. As Earl sprinted off across the field, he looked back and saw his friends in the distance, standing beside the pick-up truck with their arms crossed and shaking their heads in disbelief.

The field was wet from the afternoon rain showers, and Earl could feel his heavy black army boots kicking up mud and splashing through the wet grass. He slipped and fell a few times in his pursuit of the spacecraft but wasn't about to give up. Something inside of him told him this was an experience he must not miss.

* * *

Meanwhile, in mid-flight, Scott began to notice that something wasn't quite right with the craft. "Uh-oh."

"What's wrong?"

"I think the steering propeller is tilted too far back and needs to be adjusted. It should only take twenty seconds to fix, but I'm going to have to land to straighten it up. Hold on while I take it down."

The *Mercury One* plummeted quickly and hit the ground with a thud.

"Wow, that was a rough landing," Christina remarked. "Almost felt like we hit something."

"Sorry about that. I'm still trying to figure out how to land this thing. I think I cut the power too quickly. That's why we dropped so fast and hit the ground so hard."

Scott jumped out. "This will only take two seconds," he said as he focused intently on what needed to be repaired. He identified the problem, and with a few quick turns of a wrench, the propeller was adjusted, and Scott was back aboard the ship. In less than a minute, the *Mercury One* was airborne again.

* * *

Earl ran across the fields as fast as he could, always trying to keep an eye on the mysterious spacecraft. As the ship started to descend, Earl had finally caught up to it and was standing directly underneath the ship. But when he stopped and looked up, the craft dropped so abruptly that it came down directly on top of him. Earl, with his heavy boots stuck in the mud, couldn't get out of the way and before he knew it, it was too late. He felt something hit his head and then everything went dark.

Chapter 14
Disoriented and Delusional

As Earl lay unconscious in the field, he had delusions of being on board an imaginary spaceship. In his dream, he was greeted by aliens and taken on their ship. His captors wanted to touch him, examine him, and ask him questions, but Earl couldn't make any sense of what he thought was the sound of squeaky extraterrestrial voices. All he knew was that he was hearing someone talk, but it was hard to tell who it was or where it was coming from. At first, the voices seemed to be off in the distance, but they gradually got louder as if they got closer to him.

"Look, Gordon, we gotta make sure that Earl's okay. He's our buddy."

"He was a fool to run off after a spaceship like that. He could have gotten himself vaporized."

"I know that, Gordon, but the flying saucer's gone now, and we gotta check on Earl. Let's walk out there and find him."

"Oh, aw right. If he had half a brain in his head, we wouldn't be in this mess."

"Is that him over there? It looks like he's hurt."

Earl heard footsteps approaching.

Gordon whispered: "Are you all right, Earl?" Then, it got quiet for a moment before the voice spoke again. "We shouldn't get too close in case he's radioactive."

"What? What are you sayin'?" mumbled a confused Earl who was hearing voices but still wondering if it was the aliens who were talking to him.

"We're askin' if you're all right," Ray said as he and Gordon knelt down beside Earl.

"What? Speak English, you little green creatures," Earl shouted, "and stop stickin' me with that probe."

"What?!?" said Ray and Gordon in unison.

"Stop stickin' me with them needles."

"He's delirious. Let's see if we can sit him up," said Ray.

"Now, look," said Ray. "There's the problem. He's been lyin' on that there rock. An' it looks like a sharp one too, pokin' him right 'n the back."

For a moment Earl was aware that his body was being moved, but then everything went black again. He could still hear voices but wasn't sure where he was.

"We gotta wake him up." Ray gave Earl a good shake and tapped him on the cheeks. "He's out cold. I think you're gonna have to give him mouth-to-mouth."

"Now that's just not right."

"Why not?" asked Ray.

"Well, 'cause..." There was a long pause. "'Cause Earl always liked you better than me."

Earl had moments when he struggled to stay awake but felt his mind drifting. Then, he heard the voices again.

"Tails it is, Gordon. Get to it."

Still in a delusional state, Earl looked up and saw what he thought was some alien creature with his mouth open wide and his thick wet lips about six inches above his face.

"Keep your slimy, green alien lips off of me, you weird little monster," Earl exclaimed as he started to wake up.

"What's he talkin' about?" Gordon asked.

"I don't know," said Ray. "Maybe he thinks you're one of his dates."

Gordon gently patted Earl's face, and Earl began to come back to reality.

"Come on, Earl, wake up." Gordon gave him a shake and Earl finally snapped out of it. "Earl, it's us. Ray and Gordon. Are you okay, buddy?"

"Ray, is that you? Gordon?" Earl hesitated, "You ain't gonna believe what jus' happened. I was abducted by a UFO!!!"

* * *

After the UFO incident in the field, the three men hitchhiked back to Earl's gas station where Earl made an important phone call. The other party was interested, but if he wanted to share his story, he needed to convince his friends to make the hour-long drive into Boston.

"To Boston? Tonight? You must still be delirious," argued Ray.

"No, Ray, I ain't delirious. I just got off the phone with Channel Eight News and told them about the whole thing."

"The flying saucer?"

"Yep, and the abduction," said Earl.

"What'd they say?" asked Ray.

"They told me to get to the station as fast as I could, and they're gonna put me on the eleven o'clock news."

Chapter 15
Ron Covington

The morning after Earl's "alien encounter," he was back at his gas station in Stonebridge, pumping gas and cleaning windshields as he did on any normal day. Then a car drove in that he had never seen before. Earl knew what all the locals drove, and when a pink and white 1958 Rambler sedan, with New Jersey license plates, pulled into his station, he wanted to see who had come to town.

A man stepped out of the car wearing an outdated grey suit with a white dress shirt and a thin red and black tie. The man quickly covered up his slicked-back hair with a fedora hat that looked a little too small for his head. He sported a thin black mustache and a smile that never seemed to quit. Earl noticed his pale white skin and assumed he wasn't an outdoorsman.

The man walked up to Earl with an air of self-importance. "Excuse me; I'm looking for Mr. Earl Stubbs."

"Well, you found 'em," answered Earl.

"Earl, I'm Ron Covington, with the *National Reporter*. My assistant called you earlier today."

"Sure, sure, I remember."

Earl knew about the National Reporter and sold copies of the tabloid at his gas station. He thought most of their stories were ludicrous, but he would still read all of the outrageous articles during those downtimes between customers.

"Earl, I've been driving since 3:00 a.m. this morning because I was so excited to meet—in person—the man who had a genuine alien encounter, and I was hoping you'd be willing to sit down and share your story with me."

"Sure. Sure, I can do that. Why don't you come on inside, and I'll tell you all about it," suggested Earl as he puffed out his chest and wiped his greasy hands off on his coveralls.

"Let me get my camera out of the car and then we're gonna make Earl Stubbs a name that's known in every home across this great country of ours."

As the interview progressed, Earl found Ron's style of questioning to be very confusing. Within each of Ron's questions, he seemed to embellish the real story and then he would follow the question up with a statement like: "But you can't say that you don't remember that it didn't happen, can you?"

To which Earl said: "Huh???"

Ron was able to rattle off his questions with lightning speed and his clarification didn't help much. "Wouldn't I be correct in assuming that since you don't remember saying it, but might have said it and wasn't sure, yet didn't deny it, that it probably did happen, and you just didn't remember to mention it, but you thought you did?" As Ron finished each question, he would nod his head so profusely that Earl found himself wanting to nod his head right along with him.

"Yes...I mean...no. I mean, I'm so darn confused, I don't even remember the question."

"Just nod your head, Earl, and that'll be confirmation enough for me."

Earl felt overwhelmed and befuddled.

"Earl, don't you want to be famous?"

"Well, I... I guess."

"So, I'll take that to be a 'yes' to everything we talked about."

Earl shrugged his shoulders.

"I'll take that shrug to be a 'yes' as well." He patted Earl on the back. "Great!" Ron winked. "Once this article hits the stands, Earl T. Stubbs is going to be famous the world over."

Chapter 16
The New Celebrity

It had been two days since the last *Mercury One* flight, and the summer heat was starting to set in. Scott was supposed to mow the lawn, but the lawnmower was out of fuel. He asked Brett if he wanted to walk down to Stonebridge with him. "Hey, Brett, I gotta get some gas for the lawnmower. Want to go to town with me?"

"Yeah, sure." Brett threw on a baseball cap to protect himself from the intense sun. As they walked along, whenever Brett saw a butterfly, he'd chase after it and try to catch it in his hands.

After several failed attempts to catch a butterfly, Brett finally gave up and asked Scott, "When can we go flying again?"

"Not for a couple of days. Uncle Jason is going to be staying with us this weekend."

"Again," moaned Brett. "All he does is sit on the couch and watch TV all day."

"Yeah, but he's leaving Monday night, and Mom has to take him to the airport in Boston. That's going to take her about three hours, so we can go then."

"Aw right!!!" They gave each other "fives" where they slapped hands and then Scott, with a turn of his head, indicated that they needed to keep moving.

"Come on, let's get the gas. I have to have the lawn mowed before Mom gets home."

As they approached the gas station, Scott handed Brett the money, "Here, you go pay for it, while I look at the comics."

Earl's gas station was called *Earl's Gas & Stuff* because Earl also sold "stuff" like coffee, candy bars, newspapers, comic books and hot dogs that seemed to rotate and spin for weeks in the hot dog warmer. But it was the only place in town to buy comic books.

When Scott and Brett went inside to give Earl the money, they didn't pay much attention to the crowd that had gathered around Earl and his magazine rack. They were all buying newspapers and asking questions. Scott wasn't too interested in that because he wanted to see if there were any new *Superman* comic books.

"Hey mister," said Brett interrupting Earl posing for a picture.

When Earl saw Brett, he stopped immediately and leaned down to talk to him. "What's up little buddy? You wanna autograph too?"

"A what?" said Brett with some confusion. "No mister, we just want a gallon of gas. We need gas to mow the lawn."

Scott came up and joined them as Brett carefully counted out the coins, but Earl waved him off in mid count. "That's okay little buddy," he said with a wink. "You and your brother can use that change to stop by the candy store and get yourselves somethin' on the way home."

"Gee thanks, mister," said Brett.

"Yeah, thanks, mister," added Scott.

Chapter 17
The Shirley Show

On the set of *The Shirley Show*, the studio lights were so bright that it was difficult for Earl not to squint. It felt funny to be wearing makeup. He really wanted to scratch his nose, but the make-up lady told him not to touch his face. For a moment, he thought about the millions of people who watched *The Shirley Show* on television every afternoon and felt a shiver of fear run down his spine. Earl was glad that he was wearing a dark-colored flannel shirt; that way, no one could see what felt like two large swimming pools forming under his arms.

Earl thought Shirley was a real nice lady. She was a black woman who Earl guessed to be in her late thirties. She took time to personally sit down with Earl before the show. She even gave him a few pointers. He caught just a slight hint of a Midwestern accent which she told him came from her time in Chicago. He never would have guessed that she was originally from New Orleans where she insists that she "filled herself up with southern hospitality."

During the commercial break, Shirley settled into her seat, gave Earl a wink and a smile and reassured him that he would be great. Then, a woman with a clipboard jumped up in front of them and did a countdown from five to one. When she reached the number one, she pointed at Shirley. The audience applauded and as soon as that settled down, Shirley introduced her guest.

"With us today is a man with an extraordinary tale. A few nights ago, Earl Stubbs, from Stonebridge, Massachusetts, was out collecting crickets in a wheat field when he saw something pass overhead in the night sky. He followed the object, which he described as a flying saucer, and then wound up being abducted by the space aliens who were on board that ship."

She turned toward Earl. "Earl we're so glad to have you with us today, and we're all just so excited to hear your story."

"Thank you, Ma'am." Earl realized that this was a lot more difficult than he ever imagined. He thought he would love being on television, but at that moment, Earl felt like he wanted to run away as fast as he could. He kept trying to reassure himself. *You're okay. You're okay.*

Shirley tried to set the scene for her audience. "So, you were out in the field when you saw a strange object in the sky."

Earl shifted nervously in his seat and thought for a moment. "Well, first I heard a whirring sound coming from up above, and then I felt this eerie breeze all around me. Then I looked up and there was this spaceship goin' overhead."

"What did it look like?"

Earl looked upwards and tried to recall what he saw at that moment. "Well, it was hard to see because it was pretty dark that night, but I could tell it was some kinda UFO."

"What did you do next?" she asked with genuine interest.

"I yelled over to my buddies, Ray and Gordon—Gordon's the one with the lazy eye—to get in the truck 'cause we were gonna chase it."

"That was very brave."

Earl puffed out his chest a little bit. "Thank you, Ma'am."

"Then what happened?"

"We drove after it as far as we could, an' when I couldn't follow it in the truck no more, I set out on foot."

"Oh, my."

Maybe this will be okay. She is a very nice lady. Stay cool. Stay cool.

"And where did you say all of this took place?"

"Jus' outside of Stonebridge, Massachusetts."

Shirley leaned in as if they were telling secrets. "Now, tell us, Earl, were these aliens friendly?"

Earl became a little choked up. Shirley saw this and gently reached over and touched his shoulder.

"I'm afraid that they were..." Earl hesitated. He took out a handkerchief and dabbed at his eyes, "...a little too friendly."

"What do you mean, Earl?"

"I'm a little embarrassed to say that they uh...they...touched and probed and pinched my body."

A disgusted gasp came from the audience.

Wow. I didn't expect such a strong reaction. Those people in the audience must really feel for me.

Shirley was gentle, but she wasn't going to back off. "Okay, Earl, bottom line, why do you think the aliens chose you?"

Earl thought about it for a moment. "I think they wanted me for reproductive purposes."

Another disgusted gasp swept through the audience.

"As you know, we always like to get members of the audience involved in the show. Does anyone have a question for Earl?"

Several hands in the studio audience shot up.

Shirley jumped out of her seat, ran over to a woman in a yellow and white polka dot dress and held the microphone in front of her. "Do you think the aliens wanted you more for your mind or for your body?"

Earl was slow to respond. Shirley had made him feel at home, but he wasn't expecting questions from the audience. "Well, now, that is a good question. It's real hard to say which one has more value."

Oh no. Did that sound too conceited? Earl started to squirm in his seat.

Shirley looked over at Earl and caught him dabbing his face with a handkerchief.

He was starting to feel a sense of panic.

"We're going to take a quick commercial break, but we'll be right back."

Chapter 18
The Brotherhood of Aliens

Uncle Jason's visit was uneventful: lots of television and a few board games with Brett and Scott. Then, the night came when it was time for Jason to go home. As soon as Judy and Uncle Jason left for the airport, Scott called Christina.

Brett and Scott rolled out the *Mercury One* and waited for her to arrive.

It was a calm night, and in the distance, there was the sound of a great-horned owl hooting from one of the nearby trees. Then, from another direction, another owl answered the call. Scott loved the outdoors and always paid close attention to nature. Tonight, he noticed the crickets singing in synchronistic rhythm.

After saying hello to Christina, Scott suggested "I'll go first, and then you and Brett can drive."

"So, where are we going this time?" asked Christina.

"Not to the drive-in."

Christina and Brett smiled at each other.

As the motor and propeller started to increase in speed, the ship started to rise. It gained elevation and then hovered above the roof of the Harrison's house.

"I think we'd better go out to the country again," said Scott. "It's a good place to practice our flying, where no one will see us. Brett's been wanting to fly the ship. He can try it out there."

The craft lifted higher into the air, gliding smoothly between the trees and then out over the rooftops of the neighborhood houses. It was a hot, still, lazy summer evening, with a half-moon lighting up the sky. There were coyotes howling off in the distance, and it was the time of year when the cicada bugs would sing out from the tops of the trees.

They passed over Stonebridge where it appeared that nobody was aware of anything passing overhead. As they headed out to the country, a falling star streaked across the sky in front of them. Christina said the star meant good luck. Off in the west, Venus glowed at the edge of the horizon.

Scott had read that on this night, if they timed it right, they might be able to see a comet in the northern sky, not far from the pointer stars of the big dipper.

"I brought the binoculars because I thought we might be able to see that comet I was telling you about. That is, if the moon's not too bright," said Scott. Once they got away from the city lights, he spotted the faint outline of a star-like object with a small luminous tail. "I can see it now."

"Let me see," said Christina taking the binoculars from Scott. "Where is it?"

"It's that object that looks kind of like a blurry star," said Scott pointing about thirty degrees above the horizon, "in the northern sky."

"Oh yeah," said Christina as she looked through the binoculars. "Wow. It's pretty cool. You can see the tail a lot better with the binoculars."

While Christina and Scott took turns looking at the comet, Brett spoke up. "Hey, what are all those people doing down there?"

"Where?"

"In that field down there? They weren't there when we flew over the other night."

Scott and Christina popped their heads out of the moon roof to take a look.

"It looks like they've set up some sort of a camp," observed Scott.

Christina looked down through the binoculars. "It's definitely a camp. I can see tents and campfires, but why would people come to Stonebridge to camp? There's lots of better places to do that. They could go up to Twin Falls or Emerald Lake. No one comes to Stonebridge to camp. And that isn't even a campground. It's just an empty field."

"Can you see what they're doing?"

"It looks like some of them are just sitting back in lounge chairs and looking up at the stars. A few of them have telescopes and binoculars. And there's one area where they are setting up some equipment."

"What kind of equipment?"

"I can't tell. It's too far away, but it looks like scientific equipment, like they're doing some kind of scientific research."

"Maybe they're looking at the comet," suggested Scott. "Maybe it's an astronomy group."

"That's a lot of people for a geeky astronomy group," quipped Christina. As soon as the words came out of her mouth, she said "sorry." They all knew that Scott fit into that category.

"Well, I don't know why they're there, but we'd better turn off our lights 'cause I don't want anyone to see us."

* * *

In the fields below, Earl pulled up to the camp in the tow truck from his gas station. As soon as he got out, there was a man waiting to greet him.

"Are you Earl?"

"I am."

"Earl, I'm Paul," said the short, thin, balding man. He was wearing white linen pants, sandals, and an orange and black shirt with a repeated pattern of ancient geometric symbols. Earl found the design of the shirt to be very intriguing but couldn't understand why anyone would wear white pants for camping.

"We're thrilled to have you joining us tonight, Earl. Come with me and I'll introduce you to the others." The two of them walked by several tents as they headed to what looked like a meeting area for the group.

"I'm glad to be here, but I have to confess, I don't really know much about your organization."

"Well, like I said on the phone, we call ourselves the Brotherhood of Aliens because we feel like we have a connection to aliens from other planets and other galaxies. In a sense, we believe that we are all related, and, someday, our alien brothers and sisters will come and meet us and possibly take us away in their spaceships."

"Okay. All right," Earl wasn't sure how to respond, but he didn't want to let on that he wasn't particularly knowledgeable about such things. "When's this all gonna happen?"

"We don't know when or where, but we want to be ready, so we travel around the country to any place that's become what we call a hot spot."

"A hot spot?"

"That's a place where there have been recent UFO sightings or activity."

"So, you guys go camp out wherever the UFOs are?"

"Right, and we do that in hopes that someday we can be reunited with our brothers and sisters."

When they reached a small group of people who appeared to be in charge of the Brotherhood, Paul pointed out the leader of the group.

"Roselda, is our leader."

"Is she the one with the red hair?"

"Yes. We affectionately refer to her as the Queen of the Brotherhood. She's been our leader for 23 years."

Roselda looked to be in her mid-to-late forties, a little hefty and tall. She was wearing a suit that was a mix of silver and gold, adorned with lots of shiny sequins, glitter and sparkly jewelry. Earl always liked things that sparkled and thought her outfit was amazing.

"Roselda, this is Earl Stubbs. Earl, meet Roselda Starchild."

As they shook hands, Earl spoke first. "I'm mighty pleased to meet you, Roselda."

"Earl, thank you for coming." Roselda had a very calm manner and a soothing voice. "We were all hoping that you'd share your alien experience with us."

"I'd be mighty glad to. I can show you right where it happened. It's just over that way 'bout quarter mile or so," Earl said pointing off in the distance.

"Will you take us there?"

"I sure will. You all jus' follow me." Earl loved the fact that he had become sort of a celebrity. He also liked Roselda because she seemed so mysterious and otherworldly.

While they were walking, a young member of the brotherhood asked Roselda if she thought they would have another sighting tonight.

Roselda looked up to the sky. "I think so. Yes. Yes. I do. I can feel their presence. They're out there...just waiting for the right moment."

Earl tried to fit in with the group and wanted to look important. "I can feel it too. Sure can."

One of the members of the group was carrying a piece of electronic equipment and attached to that was a sensing device that made intermittent clicking noises.

"What's that for?" asked Earl.

Paul quickly jumped in. "It senses intergalactic particles. It starts to make a clicking sound whenever it senses dust or particles from outer space. It tells us if aliens are near or if they've been to the area."

Roselda interrupted: "I don't believe we need scientific instruments to detect these things. All you have to do is be open, and you can sense their presence." She turned to Earl and started walking again. "Please show us the way, Earl."

"It was right over here."

Seven other interested members of the Brotherhood—leaders in the group—had come along to visit the site. The group tromped through the long summer grasses and out into the field where Earl had been a few nights earlier. Earl suddenly came to a stop, surveyed the area and then walked about fifteen more paces. "The place it happened was right 'bout where I'm standin'. See where the wheat grass is flattened down?"

"What does the meter say?" Paul asked the technician with the electronic sensor.

"It's been going crazy ever since I turned it on. The reading is off the charts," answered the man with the scientific equipment.

The group examined the area looking for any evidence that might have been left behind.

After searching the area and not finding any visible trace of the aliens, the group started to head back to camp. As they were walking, Roselda spoke: "I can feel so much eco-intergalactic energy tonight." For a moment she was quiet and then started to tell a story. "Once, when I was spirit-traveling through the universe, I experienced this exact same feeling on the moon of Io..."

"Huh???" Earl didn't know what else to say, and his response came out much louder than he had hoped.

"...and then twelve glorious spaceships came and swept me away."

Roselda's story was abruptly interrupted by a member of the brotherhood who had been running and caught up to the group. "Roselda, we just had a sighting. There was something in the western sky, but as soon as we spotted it, it turned out its lights and we couldn't see it anymore."

"Were you able to get any pictures?"

"No. It happened too fast, and it was too far away."

"Let's have everyone double up on watch duty tonight."

"Yes, Ma'am," said the messenger, and he was off as fast as he had appeared.

"I'll be watching the skies tonight. I know they're out there." Roselda opened her palms and lifted them to the sky. "I can feel it. Tonight is very special. There is something about the energy out there that is calling to us tonight."

Chapter 19
The Labyrinth

The night of the full moon finally arrived, and it was coming up with a blaze of light over the horizon. But there were also storm clouds moving in from the northwest with flashes of lightning in the distance.

After a long period of silence, Christina asked, "They did say the full moon, didn't they?" as she watched the golden moon rising higher in the sky.

Brett was trying to catch moths that were darting around the porch light in a glass jar. "Got one," he interrupted. Then he examined it and let it go. "But that's not the one I wanted. I wanted one of those big ones with the black spots."

"Yeah, they said they would return on the night of the full moon."

"Do you think they'll come here, or do we need to go to Miller's Pond?"

"I've been wondering that same thing," said Scott. "But it's not a good night for flying. The moon is full which makes us a lot more visible, and there's lightning in the sky over there. I don't want to fly on a stormy night again. It's too dangerous."

"So, all we can do is wait for them?"

"Yeah," said Scott softly. "They'll come."

It was about half an hour later when everything changed. The night became perfectly still and all of the lights in the area started to dim and then go completely dark. Then, it felt as if a heaviness dropped down from the sky and covered the whole area. There was not a sound, even the insects went silent.

"Can you feel that?" asked Scott.

"I feel really sleepy," said Brett sitting down on the steps. "And the porch light went out on me."

"They're coming," said Scott with excitement in his voice.

They waited in silence for a couple of minutes. Scott was scouring the night sky to see if he could see a ship approaching but spotted nothing. Then, the grass in the field started to sway even though there was no wind. Out of nowhere, the Antarian ship appeared and dropped softly to the earth where the grass had parted. This time there was a soft green glow rather than the intense green lights that had been present in the past.

The door opened and Zula motioned for the three of them to quickly approach the ship.

Zocuul emerged from the ship holding what looked like a large thin black television screen that was about three feet across and two feet high. He held it up and then the two aliens started to glow in a violet color. The glow seemed to begin faintly at the core of their bodies and then become more radiant. It was at that moment that Scott noticed that their bodies were slightly translucent. He couldn't see through them, but he could see to the inner core of their bodies from which the violet color seemed to be emanating.

After glowing for a few moments, the alien holding the screen gently let go and it floated in the air just above where his hands had released it.

"Look, they can make things fly," observed Brett.

Scott hesitated, closed his eyes, and tuned in to the voices he could hear in his head. "They just told me that they created a new way for us to communicate," he said to the others. "They want the two of you to know what they are saying."

Suddenly the screen became illuminated. A million tiny stars appeared on the screen, and those stars quickly became letters that formed the words Scott had spoken:

They just told me that they created a new way for us to communicate. They want the two of you to know what they are saying.

Zula waved her hand in front of the screen and Scott's words vanished. Quickly, she transferred a different thought to the message board.

If you are willing, we must leave now. We don't have much time. Will you join us on our ship?

Scott looked at the others and they nodded in agreement.

As they climbed on board, Scott curiously glanced around. "Something about this looks really familiar," Scott whispered to Christina referring to being inside the ship.

"So, you recognize it?" asked Christina.

"Sort of. But it's like going back to a place you haven't been to in years. It feels like reliving a distant memory."

Christina elbowed Scott when they passed by the control room. "Look at that. "In the center of the control room was a three-dimensional floating model of the universe. It represented the stars and planets and moons with dozens of ships and satellites all in motion, moving exactly as they do in real life but on a much smaller scale.

"That's like your drawing of the stars and the planets. You know, the drawing you made with the runes on it, from the hologram," whispered Christina to Scott. "That must be how they navigate. That drawing really *was* your address."

Scott knew she was right but didn't know what to say. Instead of being able to take a tour of the ship, Zula guided them directly into a room that seemed to be designed for passengers. The room had several rows of seats facing a giant window, much like a picture window.

Their attention was quickly distracted by Zula who was motioning for the three of them to take their seats.

They all sat down in reclining seats and were strapped in place. The seat belts were automated: all the passengers had to do was sit in the chair and the seat belts automatically strapped them in. The language board had been moved to the passenger room. It read:

We must move quickly tonight. There is much to see.

Once they were strapped in, Zula left the room and within moments, they took off with galactic speed. Everything outside the window became a blur. The flight seemed to last only a couple of minutes, but that wasn't a surprise since they had experienced the amazing velocity of the Antarian ship in the past.

When they reached their destination, the ship gently set down. Outside the window, all the lights had gone dark, and it appeared that time had stopped.

"Where are we?" asked Brett looking out the window. "It looks like the desert."

"I think we're in Egypt," said Christina. "It looks like the pyramids, over there."

In the distance, the pyramids were glowing in the moonlight.

Before they could get out of their seats, Zula appeared holding four unlit torches. The harnesses that had held them in their seats automatically released. With a wave of her hand, Zula motioned that they needed to hurry.

"She is asking us to come with her so she can show us something," said Scott after he tuned in to her thoughts.

Zula made her high-pitched call, and the four smaller shapeshifting aliens came forth. This time, in the desert, they changed into coyotes and then charged off in the four directions.

Zula held her hand over one of the torches and her hand began to glow in an orange color. As the glow became more intense, it started emitting sparks which ignited the flammable material at the end of the torch.

"Did you see that!" exclaimed Brett, but Christina gave him a "not now, we'll talk about this later" kind of nudge.

Zula held out her burning torch and the kids took turns lighting each of theirs from the flame.

There were very few people around, and it seemed that the few people who were in the area were in a deep state of somnambulism.

"What if someone sees us?" asked Christina.

Scott knew that he needed to translate for Brett and Christina who weren't able to hear Zula's thoughts. "She says they put a wave of sleep over the entire area, and there is an energy field that disables all earthly electrical and mechanical objects."

Zula led the group to the ruins of an ancient temple not far from the great pyramid. The walls of the temple were made up of gigantic rectangular sand-colored stone blocks. Scott could almost feel the energy of the ancient people who had gathered there long ago. Whatever roof had been erected in the past had decayed or fallen to the earth over time, leaving the starry sky exposed.

They walked to the back of the temple, and Zula placed a purple crystal stone into an indentation in the side of a giant rock—almost as if she were putting a key into a door—and then an opening appeared. They followed Zula into the passageway. It was a long dark stone corridor with only the torch lights serving as illumination.

Eventually the passageway turned into an extensive underground labyrinth with what seemed like dozens of corridors going in all directions.

"Where are we?" asked Brett starting to look a little nervous.

"I think we're under the pyramids," whispered Christina.

"If anything happens to Zula, we'll never find our way out of here," added Scott referring to the complex maze of tunnels and corridors.

After a lengthy walk with several turns and directional changes, Zula stopped in front of a wall that was made up of smaller brick-sized stones. She pulled out five golden rectangular bricks—that appeared to be gold bars—turned each of them over and reinserted them in the different holes from which they came. Essentially, it was a puzzle, and the right movement of the bricks allowed them entry to the next underground passageway. A large wall dropped down into the earth, opening a secret hallway.

Zula looked at Scott and sent another message.

"She says if man ever figures out all of the mysteries and secrets we built into the pyramids, they will be amazed at what they find," said Scott as he verbalized the thoughts of Zula.

"I'm not sure I've gotten used to the idea that aliens built these," confessed Christina as she followed Zula. "But she seems to know her way around."

Another long hallway led them to a corridor that climbed up inside what Scott assumed was the center of the pyramid. As they ascended, they passed a large chamber along the way. Inside it was a golden sarcophagus surrounded with what looked to be items for the afterlife. There was everything from treasure to sacrificial items: gold coins, jewels, rotting tapestries, clothes that had faded and decayed and trays of what was once delicious food that had since turned into piles of black dust.

"This must be the tomb of a pharaoh," suggested Christina but no one responded.

Scott listened to Zula's message for a moment. *For these people, it was all about the afterlife. They wanted to have everything they needed when they crossed over.*

"Do you think we could take some of those gold coins?" whispered Brett so that Zula wouldn't hear.

"You'd probably be cursed for life if you did," warned Christina.

"And knowing this place, it might be booby-trapped to make

sure that grave robbers didn't steal anything," added Scott.

At the top of the tunnel, Zula motioned for the others to stop and wait. She pulled out a large tuning fork, struck it on a rock, and it produced a high-pitched tone. As the sound reverberated, a wall that looked like a thin veil of smoky glass started to vibrate and then broke into thousands of pieces revealing another passageway into a large room.

Again, with a hand signal, Zula motioned for the others to follow. Each person in the group stepped gingerly from stone to stone to reach a small stairway that led up into their final destination: a chamber inside the top of a pyramid.

At the top of the stairs, Zula pulled on a lever and several panels in the ceiling opened, revealing the starry skies above. It had been carefully engineered so that specific stars and constellations could shine through.

"Wow, this is amazing," said Scott looking up at the openings in the ceiling. "Look at all the stars."

"Forget the stars," said Christina, "Look at the artwork on the walls."

The walls and ceiling were covered with pictures of pharaohs and gods and goddesses. In addition to the larger figures, there were thousands of smaller symbols and animals. Scott could see dozens of shapes: serpents, falcons, lions, stars, boats, and suns, all carved into the walls and meticulously painted in vibrant colors.

"Where are we?" asked Christina.

Scott listened for a minute. "We are inside the top of the great pyramid," said Scott translating for Zula.

"I didn't know people could go into the top of the pyramids," said Christina.

Scott listened to Zula's response and then shared it with the others. "She says that no one has discovered this room yet. They, the Star People, put some kind of protective barrier around it to confuse any of man's scientific instruments and make it appear that there is no room here, only solid rock."

Zula motioned for the three of them to look at a specific wall in the chamber.

Brett got there first and studied the artwork. "This looks like one of those pharaoh guys, but his body looks like it's in a cocoon," observed Brett.

"I've seen drawings like this before," said Christina as she looked at the second picture in the series of hieroglyphs. "It's the body of a woman with beautiful wings."

"I like this one," said Brett moving down the wall to inspect the next figure. "It's the head of a crocodile, but the body of a man."

"So, why is she showing us these things?" Scott asked Christina.

"That's a good question. What do these paintings have in common?" Christina muttered to herself as she studied the hieroglyphs.

Scott knew that Christina loved challenges and was brilliant at solving puzzles. She quietly studied all the shapes on the wall. A moment later she said: "They're all parts. I mean, they are all parts that normally don't go together like a man inside a cocoon, a man's head on a lion's body, a woman with wings. These aren't normal life forms we find on this planet. They don't exist like this in nature."

Scott looked over at Zula who nodded.

For a minute everyone was silent, studying the pictures.

Finally, Christina broke the silence. "Ew, I just had a weird thought. It kind of made a shiver go through my body."

"What's that?"

"Remember in the library, we were talking about how aliens were said to have been doing genetic manipulation?"

"Yeah."

"Well, what if this is it?" suggested Christina. "Maybe these are their experiments. The aliens were combining DNA from different beings to create new life forms. Maybe they tried to combine the DNA of a man and a lion, and this is a record of that. Maybe this pharaoh guy in a cocoon represents the incubation period. Maybe these drawings were records of their experiments."

Scott wanted to say he thought Christina's idea was ridiculous, but Zula's voice, in his head, quickly interrupted him.

"That's exactly it," confirmed Scott reading Zula's thoughts.

There was a moment of acknowledgment by Zula—as if to say Christina was right—followed by a look of shame as if she wasn't proud of what her ancestors had been a part of.

Zula pointed to another wall. The group moved over and started to inspect it closely. It was made up of five distinct images.

Brett looked at the first object in the artwork and said, "Hey, there's one of the aliens—with a star on its forehead—standing by what looks like one of their ships,"

"Is that your race?" asked Scott. "A Star Person?"

Zula nodded to indicate that it was.

"Okay," said Scott, studying the second image. "Then, there is a giant fire-breathing dragon flying across the sky."

The dragon had an S-shaped body, a silvery grey color with hints of iridescent bronze, but the scales on his chest were a speckled metallic blend of purples and magenta. Its head was brown and the wings protruding from his back were striped with gold and black. Its wings were riding the wind. It had a short, forked tongue and was releasing a powerful burst of flames.

Christina was less interested in the dragon and had already moved on to the third figure. "She's beautiful."

It was a painting of a woman who appeared to be an Egyptian princess. Her skin was tan, and her brown eyes were captivating. All of her features were perfectly proportioned.

"But there's something else about her," said Christina. "I get a sense that her heart is beautiful as well. She looks so kind and compassionate."

"I know what you mean," echoed Scott. "She has a loving heart. You can almost feel it."

Zula nodded enthusiastically.

The fourth figure drawn on the wall was much more difficult to describe as that person was partially hidden behind a cloak. His face and eyes were peeking out from underneath the cape, but Scott felt an uncomfortable feeling when he studied the elusive figure. The man's body was twisted as if he were spinning and disappearing, under the cover of his cloak, all in a single motion.

"I'm not sure about this person who looks so mysterious and is hiding behind his cape," said Christina. "He looks like some sort of wizard or sorcerer."

Zula nodded, paused a moment, and then pointed to the last of the five images.

"Now this looks like a warrior," Scott continued. The drawing revealed a bearded man with a strong muscular back and robust shoulders. He appeared to be in battle where he was single-handedly defeating a dozen weaker men all with a single, powerful blow.

"He's very handsome. He looks like Adonis, the Greek god of beauty," remarked Christina.

"Not exactly," Scott said, reflecting Zula's response. "Not a Greek god, but one of the bravest of Greek warriors. A demigod." He studied the muscular figure until he was interrupted. "Zula's telling us to follow the lines."

There were lines running from each of the five images they had just evaluated, and all five of those lines converged at one point within the heart of a solitary figure.

"Wow!" remarked Scott. He moved over to the large image where the five lines joined together. It was a painting of a very powerful figure with a human head, muscular arms and shoulders, with dragon's wings, holding a bolt of what appeared to be lightning in his hand. Over the entire picture was a hint of red color almost like a cloud or aura that surrounded him.

"I think I see what she's trying to tell us," said Christina as she stood next to Scott. "They put those five things together and created this."

"And he's got dozens of little grey aliens around him," added

Brett. "Like an army."

When they studied the picture a bit closer, Scott and Christina looked at each other as if they both, at the same time, understood what all of this meant.

"That's him. That's the figure you drew the night you saw the hologram."

Then Scott looked at Zula. "Is this what I think it is?"

Zula looked away as if she felt shame.

"Is it true?" asked Scott looking at Zula. "Did your people create a genetic monster?"

Zula looked uncomfortable and then reluctantly nodded.

"I don't get it," said Brett. "You mean the aliens put all these things together and created this creature?"

"That's exactly what she's saying," said Christina.

"And this being is interested in me?" asked Scott.

"What?" said Brett who had never been told anything about the night the red ship appeared, or the drawings Scott had recorded on paper.

Zula hesitated for a long time and then motioned that it was true.

Scott sat down on the ground for a moment. It felt like his heart had stopped, and he was going to faint. Suddenly, everything was making sense, but it made him shiver all through his body.

Christina put her hand on Scott's shoulder. "But this monster isn't really out to get Scott, is it?" she asked Zula.

Again, there was a reluctant pause before Zula indicated the genetic creation was, indeed, interested in Scott.

Scott thought about having a genetically generated life form that was after him. *How could this be? Why would this creature be out to get me?*

Zula kept things moving. She motioned for them to come with her and pointed to a fourth wall. On the fourth wall was a bolt of lightning, striking an object and creating a massive explosion. In front of the fourth wall was a pedestal, and on that pedestal was what appeared to be an ordinary black rock.

Zula took the rock and handed it to Scott.

"What is it?" he asked her.

Christina and Brett looked at Scott waiting for him to get the answer from Zula.

"She says it's a fire stone, and it will help protect me from someone named Zarco."

"Zarco. Who is Zarco?" asked Brett.

Zula moved back to the third wall and gestured towards the genetic creature the aliens had created. As she pointed at the drawings on the wall, Scott narrated her thoughts.

"Z for Zartrel," Scott explained as she directed their attention to the drawing of the alien with the star on his forehead, "who was one of our smartest elders with an extraordinary mind. They took his DNA because of his incredibly powerful intellect."

Zula moved to the picture of the flying dragon. "'A' stands for actron. An actron is a fire-breathing dragon from a planet in the constellation of Draco. The actron DNA was used to give Zarco the ability to fly."

"But there's no such thing as dragons," objected Christina.

Scott translated once more: "That DNA came from the bone of an actron, a dinosaur-like creature living on a planet that was going through a period like we once had here when dinosaurs walked the earth."

"Draco means dragon, right?" asked Christina.

"Yes," answered Scott for Zula. "That is why that constellation was given that name. It is an area where some of the planets are still inhabited by dinosaurs and dragons."

"So, it is sort of like a pterodactyl?" asked Christina.

"Yes, but bigger, more powerful," interpreted Scott.

Scott looked at the next picture in the row. It was of the beautiful woman with the kind heart. He translated for Zula. "This is the

Princess daughter of the Pharaoh Radjedef, who was called the son of Ra. Ra means the sun. The 'R' in the name Zarco is for Princess Ra. She was the granddaughter of the Pharaoh for whom the great Pyramid was built. The R in the name Zarco represents her DNA."

"At least she appears to have some compassion," added Christina.

"Our ancestors tried to create a creature with a kind heart, but the aggression of the dragon and the anger of the sorcerer were too overpowering," said Scott, speaking for Zula.

"So, it *is* a sorcerer," remarked Christina.

"Yes," Zula pointed to the sorcerer as Scott interpreted. "'C' is for the cloaked one, the mighty sorcerer. Not much is known about him, but his powers give him the ability to conjure up storms: lightning, thunder, meteors, anything related to weather and climate."

And then Zula pointed to the human figure that looked like a warrior. "'O' is for Orion," Scott explained for Zula, "the bravest warrior ever known."

"Do you mean the Orion that the constellation is named after?" asked Scott. He heard the answer to his question: "Yes."

"But Orion was a mythological figure," objected Christina.

Scott waited and listened for Zula's answer. "He was, but many mythological figures were based on real heroes, especially heroes who were unrivaled in their bravery and accomplishments. Orion was a demigod, with a human mother and a Greek god for a father, who was known for his perilous adventures.

"So, if you put all of that together, it spells Z – A – R - C – O. Zarco," said Scott for Zula. "Zarco is a mix of five beings. Each letter represents one of the five elements that went into his genetics."

"Zarco is a combination of bravery, sorcery, compassion, the wisest of your race and a dragon's ability to fly," summed up Christina. "But if this was done thousands of years ago, he must be dead by now."

Zula became silent and looked up at the stars through the opening in the roof. A dark shadow passed over them momentarily blocking the star light, leaving a red cast in its wake.

Scott waited and listened for the answer to Christina's question. "She says that answer comes later. We had to understand this first. But she also says we must go."

Scott wasn't the only one who was uncomfortable about the fly-over. Zula's expression also became more anxious. Scott kept looking up to see what had just hovered over them, but Zula quickly got his attention as she motioned for them to leave.

"She says we must go *now*," added Scott feeling uneasy about what had been revealed to him.

The group retraced their steps. Zula put the various ancient security systems back in place. Once outside, they sprinted back to the ship, keeping an eye open for any danger lurking overhead. There was an ominous red glow, but as Scott scoured the sky, he couldn't locate the crimson ship. Nevertheless, he could feel the presence of the enemy and wondered if it was in hiding, waiting to strike.

 Star People: Mystery of the Hologram

Chapter 20
The Cave

Once everyone was safely back in the ship, the message board was put in place allowing Scott a break from speaking for Zula.

Scott started the questioning. "You're telling us that your people came to Egypt thousands of years ago."

Yes, we have come many times, but what happened here dates back to 2589 B. C.

"Why did your people come to Earth?"

It was to crossbreed.

"So, it was to breed aliens with humans," confirmed Christina.

"We've heard about that." Scott took a moment to decide how to word what he would say next. "The people who've studied these things say they weren't sure what the aliens were doing with genetics. One guess was to create offspring that would look like humans so they could infiltrate our society as spies. Another theory was to make a race of slaves to do things like build the pyramids."

It was none of those things. We had the technology and the engineering to build the pyramids. We didn't need slaves for that. Slaves couldn't have done that work.

"What do you mean?"

Some of the limestone blocks that make up the pyramids weigh as much as eighty tons. Most weighed about 5,000 pounds. How many slaves would it take to move a rock that size?

As Scott did the numbers in his head, he unintentionally spoke just loud enough for the others to hear. "Okay, if each man could pull 50 pounds, and the block was on a ramp or being rolled on logs, it would take 100 men to move each block." Scott thought about it for a moment. "But that's a lot of people to line up and coordinate."

And at the rate the pyramids were built, they would have had to put twelve blocks in place per hour.

"That's impossible," said Scott. "Even with modern technology and modern machinery, we couldn't build them that fast."

Exactly.

"But why would the aliens want to build the pyramids?" asked Scott.

We didn't. Our ancestors came to Earth–not to make slaves or spies as Scott suggested–but because there is a genetic abnormality in our DNA that was wiping out our race. We had to do something, or our race would die out. So, we came to Earth and made a secret deal with the Pharaoh Khufu, the grandfather of Princess Ra. We would build him a great pyramid for his burial site and in exchange he would allow us to cross our DNA with the DNA of his people.

"Do you have that genetic abnormality?" asked Christina.

No. The illness affects about ninety percent of us. I am one of the fortunate ten percent who don't have that condition.

"So, some of you are surviving?"

About one in ten of us live past childhood. Most of our race has died out. The crossbreeding didn't work well. We have tried with earthlings for years, and when we attempt to cross DNA with a human, it is only successful about one time in a million attempts.

"What happens when it works? What does it create?" asked Christina.

It creates what we call... the gifted ones. They look like normal humans, but they are blessed with many talents.

"But what about Zarco? Why would your people create a monster like that?" asked Scott.

At first our scientists were just trying to mix our DNA with human DNA to see if that might preserve our race, but then they became fascinated by the possibilities. They got out of control and tried to create a super being.

"So, Zarco was an attempt to make a super being."

Yes.

"But if this was done thousands of years ago, why isn't he dead by now," asked Scott.

The incubation period for a creation like that is very slow, and our lifespan is almost a thousand earth years.

"But that still doesn't add up. Zarco was created over four thousand years ago."

Yes. We discovered that for some reason when we combined those five gifts—the warrior, the Antarian, the sorcerer, the dragon, and the human—that made him immortal. Not only was he brutalizing our people, but he couldn't be killed.

"Wasn't there anything you could do?"

That is what we will show you next.

Zula pressed a button causing the engines to fire up. The seat belts automatically locked everyone in place and the ship took off.

It was only a matter of minutes before the spaceship landed and the seat belts released.

As Scott stepped out of the ship, it became apparent that they had come to a warm muggy area. The bright full moon and the thick humid air hit them immediately.

They were on a deserted beach. There were small waves gently rolling up on the sand, but otherwise, it was totally silent.

Zula made her call to the four sentries. Again, they came from the ship. This time they turned into birds that looked like falcons.

"What are those?" asked Christina.

"Caracara birds," answered Scott for Zula as each of the cinnamon brown caracaras took off in opposite directions to keep watch over the visitors to the island.

Once again Zula used sparks from her hand to light her torch and the others, in turn, used that flame to light their torches.

If it wasn't for the uncomfortable feelings inside him about what he was learning, Scott would have loved walking on this beautiful beach in the moonlight. He reached down and grabbed a handful of sand and let it run through his fingers. It was very fine sand, much softer than the sand he'd felt when he had gone to the beach in the past.

After a few steps, the shapes of several enormous statues could be seen along the shoreline. As they got closer, those figures became clearer. It was the stone statues the Antarians once referred to as their "sculpture garden." Each statue consisted of the head, neck and torso situated in such a way where they could gaze inland towards the island.

"We're on Easter Island," said Scott.

"The place with the big heads," added Brett.

"The islanders call these statues Moai," said Scott channeling the information from Zula. "Each of the Moai has energy and watches over the island. These are their sculptures. Their artwork. It is like their art gallery."

"That one kinda looks like Zin," added Brett pointing to one of the statues.

Scott noticed that Christina was crying.

"Something about being here, being on this beach, is bringing up such strong emotions in me," Christina said, wiping her eyes. "I don't know what is happening, but I'll be all right."

After walking along the shoreline for a while, Zula stopped, closed her eyes and focused. Then she pointed to a tall sea cliff that overlooked the ocean. They started walking inland, across the sand, and came right up to the base of the bluffs. Directly ahead, there was an old weatherworn trail that led them up the rock face to a hidden cave with an entrance that twisted in such a way that it made it almost impossible to discern that there was any opening at all unless you knew exactly where to look.

"We're supposed to go in there?" asked Christina.

"I'll go first," said Scott.

Brett followed Scott, then Zula and, lastly, Christina. The cave was dark and when they entered with the light of the torches, a few bats fluttered around and then flew straight at them as the velvety creatures tried to get outside and escape the intruders. When the bats were gone, the torches illuminated a cave that had been carved into the face of the cliff by centuries of pounding ocean surf. There were ancient carvings on the walls depicting what looked like great hunts, brave warriors, and bird-like figures.

Zula pointed to the sandy ground suggesting that there was something buried underneath the surface.

Scott got on his knees and started to dig in the area where Zula had pointed. His first thought was some sort of treasure that had been buried for centuries, but his hands quickly hit a cold flat surface. As he dug more sand away, he could see part of a picture.

Christina and Brett started helping to clear the sand away revealing a large mosaic, about three inches below the ground. It was made from colorful pieces of shells, coral, colored stones and crystals.

The mosaic was about six feet long and four feet across. As they cleared away the remainder of the sand, the beauty and the intricate detail of the artwork became visible. Many of the shell fragments and gems sparkled when they reflected the torchlight.

But the subject of the art was, by contrast, nothing beautiful. Even though he looked different, there was no doubt about the person depicted in the mosaic.

"There he is again," said Christina as she wiped more sand away.

"Zarco," added Scott, feeling even more uneasy.

"This is what he looks like now," Scott said conveying the

thoughts of Zula.

Zula looked at him as if to affirm that he got the correct message to the others.

"At least he doesn't look quite as scary," observed Christina as she studied the picture. "It looks like he's in an operating room and the Antarians are doing surgery on him. It looks like he is strapped down against his will."

Zula nodded.

"We were able to capture him," Scott translated for Zula. "We believed if we could extract those five energies from his body, it would take away his power."

"What do you mean by energies?" asked Christina.

Scott listened to Zula's thoughts for a moment. "We are all made up of energy."

"I thought we were made up of atoms," argued Christina.

Scott listened to Zula for a moment. "Our bodies are made up of energies. Not just the energy that keeps us alive, but also the energy that makes up our personalities or our character. For example, when someone is angry you can sometimes feel that energy. Or when someone is sad, you can feel that too."

"Okay."

"Well, what if those energies could be extracted?" Scott said for Zula.

"You mean like pulled out of a body," Christina clarified.

"Yes. That is what they did to Zarco," explained Scott. "Each of those energies—what they call gifts—the courage of the warrior, the compassion of the princess, the intellect of the Antarian, the ability to fly like a dragon and the magical powers of the sorcerer, are all energies that the Star People were able to partially extract from Zarco's body."

"I'm not sure I understand."

"DNA is used in genetics to create a being, but once that person is alive, the gifts live inside them in the form of energy. She says it is like when someone is angry. That isn't in their DNA; it is an energy they feel. Imagine you could reach into someone and pull that anger out of their being. That is what they did with Zarco, except it wasn't anger; it was things like courage and cunning. Does that make sense?"

"Kind of," said Christina.

Scott paused for a moment and listened to Zula's voice in his head. "She's explaining it in a different way."

"Okay," said Christina.

Scott nodded to Zula to let her know that he received her explanation.

"Imagine you have a great warrior—"

"Like Orion?" asked Brett.

"Yes, like Orion," said Scott. "When he is young and strong, he has the energy and is so skilled in battle, that he can take on twenty soldiers at a time and easily defeat them all."

"Okay, that makes sense," said Christina.

"But imagine him after fighting for three straight days, with no food or water. He becomes weak and tired. That is how Zarco is now. A shell of his former self. If a couple of soldiers should challenge him, he still has the strength and energy to win, but if twenty soldiers should attack, his mental and physical energy are too depleted to defend himself."

"So, it's like Zarco is a weaker version of what he once was?" suggested Christina.

"Yes," said Scott, "but it's not that he just lost his physical ability. It affects his emotions and intellect as well."

"So, they pulled out the same powers they originally gave to Zarco?" Christina asked.

"Yes, but they could only extract about ninety percent of each gift," added Scott as he relayed the information from Zula.

"What does that mean?"

"He has only ten percent of each of those energies left in him, but that still makes him extremely dangerous." Scott looked at Zula to make sure he was interpreting correctly. She nodded. "But he wants those gifts back—all one hundred percent—and he will stop at nothing to get them."

"Okay," said Christina, "I think I understand."

"She wants us to look at the mosaic again." Scott pointed to five small swirls of energy on the mosaic. "Each of Zarco's powers is represented by one of those five little colorful tornados. Each one is a different color because it represents a different gift."

"But what is this?" asked Christina.

From each of the five tornados there was a line drawn that extended to the bottom of the mosaic. Each line pointed to a picture of an object.

"This line goes from its tornado to what looks like an Asian village," said Christina.

"Then, there is a line that goes to what looks like some sort of tribal ceremony," observed Scott.

"Then one goes to a school with children," said Christina.

"An orphanage," said Scott. "Zula says that's an orphanage, not a school."

"And that line looks like it goes to the work shed in your backyard," said Christina.

"And this one goes to an airplane," said Brett.

"Those five objects are in the same position as the five runes on your drawing of the hologram," observed Christina, "and each one has a rune drawn right next to it." She turned to Scott: "Do you have that drawing with you?"

Scott pulled the drawing of the hologram out of his pocket, where he had been carrying it ever since the aliens had tried to break into his house.

"Show it to Zula," suggested Christina.

Scott handed the paper to Zula who studied it for a moment. Then he listened for her input. "She says the five runes in my drawing represent the five gifts. The images on the mosaic are a little different because each one is a record of where and when that gift was transferred into a person."

Scott examined the mosaic more closely. "That airplane is a Douglas C-47. I'm speaking for me now, not Zula. That was the same kind of plane my grandfather flew in World War II. That means Zarco's surgery probably happened in the early 1940's."

Scott paused and listened to Zula. "Nineteen forty-four, she says."

"Twenty years ago."

Scott hesitated. "Yes, twenty years ago."

"Can you ask her what those five pictures are supposed to represent?"

Before Scott could answer, from outside the cave, there was the sound of a bird's cry signaling a warning. Zula looked up when she heard that sound. Scott fell back a little as if he was hit by one of Zula's thoughts and her growing anxiety. "She says we have to get out of here." It was apparent that those cries were coming closer to the cave because they were getting louder. The squawking was forceful and shrill.

"We have to go," said Scott speaking for Zula. "Now!!!"

The four of them jumped up and ran out towards the entrance to the cave. Once they got there, they immediately froze. Standing outside of the cave, looking as if they were waiting for their next meal, were four full-grown jaguars. The eyes of the big cats reflected the fire from the torches. The closest of the big cats had its mouth open, flashing a huge set of sharp teeth.

Chapter 21
Running From Danger

"What should we do?" asked Christina.

"Don't run," Scott told the others. "If you run, they'll think you're prey, and they'll chase you."

"I'm scared," whispered Brett.

"Maybe if we go slowly back into the cave, we can look for sticks or rocks or something to use as weapons, but we have to move very slowly," suggested Christina.

"What if we go straight at them with the fire," suggested Scott. "Maybe we can scare them off with the torches, and then..."

Scott's words were interrupted as he felt Zula touch his shoulder, and she gave him a look that said, *listen to me.*

"She's telling us to get on their backs," said Scott.

"What?" asked Christina.

"Hurry, they will take us back to the ship," answered Scott.

Zula climbed on the back of one of the jaguars to show them. Scott followed her lead and approached another of the big cats. It crouched down a bit to make it easier for him to get on, so Scott hoisted himself onto the animal's back. Christina and Brett each climbed onto the other two large cats, and as soon as they were all on board, the jaguars took off at full speed running down the beach in the direction of the ship.

It was difficult to hold on because they had to wrap their arms around the necks of the sleek cats. Aside from the terror of the situation, the ride was exhilarating. It was unlike anything Scott had ever experienced. He could feel the driving muscles of the animal underneath him. With his cheek on top of the jaguar's back, the fur felt softer than he expected.

Christina's cat was running alongside them, and Scott could see its sharp teeth and the determination in its eyes. They were running at top speed, and the sand was flying up off the legs of the two jaguars in front of them.

But he couldn't enjoy the adventure for a moment because he knew that if the aliens were trying to move them out of there that fast, there was some sort of danger approaching. As they ran down the beach Scott became aware of something he hadn't noticed before. The sky out over the ocean had a distinct crimson cast to it.

"Scott look!" yelled Christina pointing out at the water.

What Scott hadn't seen was a gigantic wave building out in the ocean. It was hard to predict the size, but Scott figured the wave to be at least a hundred feet high. He felt fear move through his body.

He had never seen a wave of that magnitude and certainly not from ground level where it was almost like standing at the base of a mountain and looking straight up to the top. The breaker was moving rapidly in their direction and the crest was building, preparing to crash down over the entire beach.

The jaguars ran even faster as the giant wall of water closed in. As soon as they reached the ship, the riders were off the big cats in a matter of seconds.

"Run!!!" shouted Scott, speaking for Zula. "Get on the ship."

The jaguars shapeshifted back into their alien forms. Zula waited for everyone else to get up the ramp first and then followed closely behind as the gigantic tsunami grew closer.

The door sealed shut behind them and the ship blasted off the beach before anyone had time to strap into their seats. The sudden jolt of the lift-off knocked everyone onto the floor.

Even though the spaceship was able to get up in the air, they weren't fast enough. The top of the swell slammed into the side of the craft and sent everyone reeling. The power of the wave hit with tremendous velocity. To Scott, it felt like the ship shot sideways for what seemed like about a mile. But the ship stayed airborne and didn't get pulled into the enormous surge of water. Had they delayed a few seconds longer, the breaker would have certainly drowned everyone on the beach.

After the ship stabilized, Scott, Christina, and Brett rushed to the window to see the impact of the wave. It had plowed over the sand and slammed up against the cliffs. The cave that held the mosaic completely disappeared under the boiling surf.

For a moment, Scott wondered if he was in shock. As he looked down at the tumultuous ocean, he felt a surge of shivers move through his body.

Zula directed them to take their seats. For a few minutes, no one said a word. It took a few moments for their hearts to stop pounding and the nervousness to settle down.

"Are we safe?" asked Scott. "Can they attack our ship?"

The message board on the wall lit up.

No. He has the same technology as we do. We have force fields that repel them, and they have force fields that repel us. We can fire upon each other, but our anti-attack shields are so powerful that neither of us can beat the other with weapons. As long as we are onboard our ships neither of us can harm the other. It is outside of the ships where we— and they—are vulnerable.

"How do you know they are gone?" asked Scott.

They would be on our tracking devices.

"Good," said Christina with a sigh of relief. "Was that Zarco?"

Yes, and now you see. He is trying to destroy you.

"But why?" asked Scott.

Zula didn't answer. It seemed like she was not ready to talk about that yet.

Scott took a moment to compose himself and think about his next question. "Was Christina right about how you captured him and pulled out those gifts?"

Yes. Christina is very wise.

Christina smiled at Scott as if to say, "see they get me."

When we captured him, we extracted most of the essence of each of his five gifts. Remember he was made of five parts. Each of those parts gave him a gift or power: the warrior, the sage, the compassionate one, the magician, and the prowess of the dragon. We were able to pull out about 90% of each of those powers, but even at ten percent, he is almost unstoppable. But then something else happened. Something we had never expected. He started to age.

"So, he was no longer immortal?"

Until we removed those energies, he was immortal. Now he is getting older. So, he desperately wants those gifts back. He craves his immortality and will stop at nothing to get it.

"The ship is slowing down. Can I look out the window?" Scott asked.

Scott's seatbelt released, and he looked out. The ship was near Stonebridge and passing directly over the campers that they had observed several nights earlier from the *Mercury One*. As the ship flew over them, Scott could see the people below jumping up and down and waving. There were even a few flashes of light which he assumed were people with cameras trying to take pictures.

The ship gently landed in the field behind Scott's house.

You must go now. It is very late. We will return.

Chapter 22
Figments of Their Imagination

On the following day, at the Air Force command post in Colorado Springs, Colorado, Colonel Gregory Barnes entered an office that had a sign on the door that read:

Department of UFO Management and Public Perceptions
Colonel Gregory Barnes

After entering his office each morning, the Colonel always checked himself in the mirror to make sure everything was perfect. His crew-cut hair was too short to be out of place, but he always made sure his shirt was evenly tucked, zipper up and shoes were perfectly shined.

The second thing Barnes did each morning was look at the picture of himself and his wife. He would always close his eyes and send her some love since they were often separated for long periods of time, and he missed her.

The picture was taken at a Christmas gathering called the Officer's Ball. There was a military photographer there who captured Barnes and his wife on the dance floor. Even though they were the only black couple at the gathering, he remembered everyone being friendly and all of them having a great time at the party. Although Col. Barnes would never say it out loud, he always thought his wife was by far the prettiest of all the women there.

But Barnes' reverie was quickly interrupted by an abrupt knock on the door followed by the entrance of Brigadier General James Fulton, a seasoned 30-year veteran of the Air Force.

Barnes started to straighten up, but he was quickly waved off by the white-haired Fulton.

"Yes sir, what can I do for you, sir?"

"Colonel," said the crusty, old General with a smile, "You're going to love this one. It's seems like we're having another little UFO outbreak."

Barnes wasn't surprised by the news.

"And it seems," continued the General, "that they've invaded your neck of the woods."

"What?"

Fulton walked over to the television, switched it on and turned the set to channel seven. "According to this woman on *The Shirley Show*, they're having UFO sightings in Stonebridge, Massachusetts."

"What? That's only a few miles from our summer house," said Barnes. "My wife's up there right now."

"I thought that might get your attention," said the General with a smile.

The Shirley Show came back on the air after a commercial break, and the General turned up the volume.

"Welcome back. If you just joined us, we're calling this show 'UFO watch, day seven' because it was seven days ago when the little town of Stonebridge, Massachusetts, had its first UFO sighting. We just heard from Earl Stubbs who joined us a week ago and was also one of the witnesses to last night's sighting. Now I'd like to introduce Roselda Starchild who is queen of an organization called the Brotherhood of Aliens."

"The what?" mumbled Barnes incredulously.

"Welcome, Roselda. Thank you for joining us today. Tell us why *you* think that there might be intelligent life somewhere out there in the universe."

"Well, there are millions of planets and stars and other solar systems out there. Why should we think that this would be the only place, the only planet, with intelligent life?" Roselda looked calm and comfortable in front of the camera. She was very animated and used expressive hand gestures as she spoke. "It would be very egotistical for us humans to believe that we are the only life form in the entire universe that is capable of higher-level thinking."

While Roselda's glittery outfit might have looked ostentatious, Barnes thought she presented herself as being very bright and engaging.

Shirley seemed genuinely intrigued by these discussions about aliens. "And if there is intelligent life out there, why do you feel it is so important to make contact with these beings from other worlds?"

"Just imagine how much they could teach us, or maybe we could learn from one another. We should celebrate our connection and stop focusing on our differences. We are all brothers and sisters, made of the same atoms and the same energy."

"I see. And is that why you call yourselves the Brotherhood of Aliens because you consider extraterrestrial life forms to be brothers and sisters?"

"Exactly."

General Fulton smirked as if everything they said was ridiculous, but Barnes was fascinated by the discussion.

Shirley continued. "So, tell us a little more about your organization."

"Our mission is to establish peaceful contact and peaceful interaction with beings from other worlds."

"I see. And I've heard the phrase 'hot spots' quite a bit in the news lately, especially in regard to your group. What exactly are hot spots?"

"Those are places where there have been recent UFO sightings or activity. About three or four times a year we get reports that there may be a high level of alien activity in a certain area which we then refer to as a hot spot."

"So, Stonebridge, Massachusetts, is now what you would consider a hot spot?"

"Very hot," Roselda stated. "And when we discover a hot spot, we try to quickly get the word out to all of the members of the organization so we can gather in that area and make sure that if aliens do arrive, they will be greeted with love and open arms, not military force."

"Well," said General Fulton, "I've got news for you: the military is going to be there whether you like it or not." Fulton turned to Barnes. "Colonel, I want you to check out this Massachusetts story and see what's going on. I know it sounds like a bunch of loons—this Earl guy who was on earlier seems to have his pilot light stuck on low—but we'd better check it out just the same. The people out there don't know what to think, so we need to reassure them that this is nothing more than *figments of their imaginations:* weather balloons, light reflections bouncing off satellites, meteors breaking up as they enter the earth's atmosphere. You know the drill. Just make it clear that these *aren't* UFOs. Can't have that, as you know."

"Yes sir. I understand, sir. Figments of their imagination."

The two of them turned back to the television. Shirley paused for a moment before asking Roselda the next question. "And I understand that you have a more personal reason for wanting to meet up with these space aliens. Would you be willing to tell us about that?"

"Why, yes, of course. I am the product of what they call an intergalactic union," Roselda announced proudly.

The audience responded with a collective "ooooooooh."

"Now, what exactly does that mean?"

"That means that I am half human and half alien."

Gasps of disbelief came from the audience.

"So, which parent was the alien?"

"My mother is human. My father was the alien."

The General turned off the television and continued his orders,

"I'm authorizing two choppers and eight men. That's all we can spare right now. They're scheduled to leave tomorrow at 21:00, but I want you to go out there first and check it out. I've authorized a special flight to take you out there this afternoon. Just snoop around a bit and see what's going on. Find out what this is all about. Besides, it'll give you a chance to get some R & R with your wife."

"Well, I've been wanting to get back up there and see Marcia."

"Perfect. Then, this is your chance," said the General. "I'm not sure there's really a story here, but let's check it out just in case."

"I'll leave this afternoon, General," said Barnes.

The two men exchanged a quick salute as Fulton left the office.

Chapter 23
A Knowledgeable Source

Earl was starting to feel a sense of belonging as he walked through the Brotherhood Camp with some of the other members. He liked the fact that they welcomed him in and made him feel like he was an important part of the family.

He was also very excited about tonight's event. Roselda was going to lead the group in an evening meditation designed to reach out and communicate with the aliens who had been sighted in the area.

On the way to the community tent, Earl spotted Roselda, with her red hair, purple outfit and glittery crystal jewelry. She seemed to always have a crowd of devotees gathered around her, asking questions about her past encounters. But tonight, there was a voice Earl recognized from somewhere, but he was having trouble placing it. He couldn't locate the speaker because that person seemed to be trying to hide amongst the other members.

"Roselda, Roselda."

Earl was trying to remember where he'd heard that voice before.

"Roselda, I've heard that you gave birth to an alien child, and you've been hiding that child in your camper. Can you comment on that?"

As soon as he heard the question, Earl knew exactly who it was.

Roselda turned around with a puzzled look on her face, and Ron Covington quickly snapped her picture.

"What? I don't even own a camper. I sleep in a tent like most everyone else here."

Roselda started to walk away, but Ron wasn't about to give up. "Roselda, what about the rumor that you're here on this planet to steal government secrets?"

"What secrets?" asked a baffled Roselda.

"Military secrets so that your people can invade our planet and take over the world."

At that moment, Earl stepped in to help.

"Is he bothering you?" interrupted Earl. "He's a tabloid reporter."

"Please, can you make him go away?" she asked Earl.

Earl very gently put his arm around Ron and started to lead him away.

But Ron was persistent, calling out to Roselda, even as Earl escorted him out of the area: "I think the fact that you can't deny it, is just as good as saying that it happened, don't you? If *your people* won't let you talk, just nod your head and I'll take that as a confirmation."

Roselda shook her head and walked away.

As Earl led Ron to the exit of the camp, Ron turned to Earl: "Earl, you're knowledgeable about extraterrestrials. How'd you like to confirm that for me?"

"Uh... Gee, Ron, I don't know."

"Oh... all right then. I thought I could quote you as a knowledgeable source."

Earl liked the sound of that phrase but was a little confused. "Quote me as a source?"

Ron accepted Earl's line as a statement rather than a question. "Thanks, Earl. I knew I could count on you."

"What? Now wait a minute, I didn't say nothin'," argued Earl.

Ron pulled a shoe box tape recorder out of his briefcase and rewound the last thirty seconds. "You just said, and I'm using your exact

words here, 'Quote me as a source,'" Ron played back the tape recording of Earl's line where Earl did, in fact, say: "Quote me as a source?"

"Now, hold on..."

Ron interrupted Earl. "Earl, I respect you as a man of your word.
You're not gonna deny that you're a man of your word, are you?"

"No, but..."

Before Earl could finish his argument, Ron said, "Thanks, Earl,
you're the greatest," and rushed off into the darkness.

Chapter 24
The Mysterious World of Backyards

It was a few nights before Scott was ready to fly again. He needed time to process all that had happened at the pyramids and on Easter Island. In the days following their whirlwind adventure, he and Christina deliberated over every word that was shared by Zula as well as every detail of what they saw on the walls of the pyramid and the mosaic on the floor of the cave. There were still many unanswered questions. In particular, they wanted to know more about the five images at the bottom of the mosaic.

Finally, a night came when all of the conditions were right for flying. It was calm, not much moonlight, and Scott's Mom was across town playing bridge. Scott and Brett were rolling the ship out onto the grass when Christina came running up with a newspaper in her hand. Scott knew that Christina loved reading books, but she usually didn't bother much with newspapers unless it was something that really caught her interest.

"Scott, look." She handed Scott the paper.

The headlines read, "UFOs Spotted in Local Skies," with a picture that showed a faint streak of light across a starry sky. The subtitle read: "Thousands of tourists flock to Stonebridge to get a closer look."

"It's the night we were driven around by those aliens," said

Christina. "People must've seen their ship."

"What does the article say?"

"Well, you know all of those people who are camping out in the fields?"

"Yeah"

Christina hesitated. "They're all here looking for UFOs."

"All right!!! We're gonna be famous!" exclaimed Brett.

"No, we're not," said Scott. "We're not going to say anything about this, right?"

"But we could be in the paper or on TV."

"And we could be grounded for the rest of our lives when mom found out. And she'd take the ship away."

He looked at Brett, and Brett nodded reluctantly. "All right."

Christina had more to tell them. "And you know that Earl guy that runs the gas station in town?"

"Yeah."

"Well, it says that he also had an encounter with a UFO, a couple of weeks ago."

"Earl?" Scott said in disbelief. "Earl did?"

Christina pointed to part of the article. "It says so right here."

"Let me take a look."

Christina handed Scott the paper, and Scott read aloud. "'I was the first person in Stonebridge to see the UFOs, claimed Mr. Earl Stubbs.'" Scott scanned down and spotted the date of Earl's encounter. "Look at when he said that happened. That would mean that Earl had his alien encounter around the same time we did. Maybe the aliens have been here for a while."

Scott saw that Christina was holding another paper in her hand. "What does that one say?"

"It's my Mom's *National Reporter*."

On the cover of the *National Reporter* was a big picture of Roselda with a headline that read: "Intergalactic Baby Steals U.S. Military Secrets to Aid Alien Invasion." The subtitle read: "Knowledgeable source confirms story."

Scott read the title aloud and shook his head.

Christina filled them in: "It's about some weirdo lady, named Roselda, who says that she's a space baby."

"What's a space baby?" asked Brett.

"Someone who has a human parent and an alien parent," Christina explained and then added, "She's here too."

"In Stonebridge?"

"Yeah, looking for UFOs."

"What's so weird about her?"

"You mean besides that she thinks she's a space baby? Well, she says that someday a bunch of UFOs will come to our planet and contact her, maybe even take her away with them."

Scott handed the papers back to Christina. "Save 'em for me. I wanna read 'em later."

"And I brought something for the journey," said Christina holding up a plastic container.

"All right," blurted out Brett, "cookies or empanadas?"

"Cookies."

"Your homemade cookies are the best ever."

Scott started to turn on the motor but then hesitated.

"What's the matter?" asked Brett.

"Maybe we shouldn't go up tonight with all of those people watching the skies. Someone might see us."

"We have to go back up if we want to see the aliens," argued Christina.

"Yeah, but it seems a little risky."

"Maybe if we just go back to Miller's Pond, they'll find us there," suggested Christina. "You said you wanted to ask them more questions."

"That's true," said Scott thinking about his options.

"I think it'll be okay to fly around as long as we don't get too close to those people who are camping out."

"Come on, Scott, please," Brett begged.

"All right, but we have to be careful."

Scott started up the ship, and it gently lifted off the ground. There was something magical about flying over the rooftops and back-yards of the houses. It was a way to see the world from a whole differ-ent vantage point, almost as if you could look at hidden secrets that were all around you but you never knew existed. From the ground, all the houses in the neighborhood looked much the same. From the air, Scott could see what mysteries were hidden behind the walls and fences in the neighboring backyards. One backyard was set up with miniature model trains and tracks that went over bridges, inside tun-nels and through mountain gorges. In another backyard there was a vehicle that looked like half car and half boat. Christina once joked that Scott better ignore that yard or else an *aqua car* would be his next project. One backyard had a pond with a rope swing that would run from a platform in the treetops and then it would drop the rider safely into the water at the other end. The three of them had talked about how they might someday sneak in and try out the rope swing if they could only figure out how to not get caught. And, of course, there were the dreaded junk collectors whose backyards were cluttered with ev-erything from rusted refrigerators to decades-old stripped and beaten down never-to-run-again Chevrolets.

Tonight, the backyard that caught their attention was one with loud tango music. It was emanating from an old juke box housed inside a recreational room with large sliding glass doors that opened into the backyard. The owners had a black and white parquet floor that led out onto their patio where they were dancing under the soft moonlight.

Brett was the first one to spot them. "Hey, look at those people dancing down there."

Christina pulled out the binoculars and looked out her window. "They're doing the tango."

"I can hear the music all the way up here," said Scott although he didn't seem too interested.

"Uh oh."

"What?" asked Scott.

"The man is looking up here. I think he saw us."

"The lights are out. I don't think he could see our ship with the lights out unless he was really paying attention."

"I don't know. He's still looking this way."

"Okay, let's get away from here," said Scott. "We don't want anyone to see us."

* * *

In the backyard below, everything was perfect for dancing outdoors. The night was still and warm with just a little bit of moonlight. Col. Barnes was wearing his black tuxedo with tails. He prided himself on being a smooth dancer, always very disciplined in his steps. Marcia was wearing a low-cut dress with a slit up the side that showed off the shape of her legs each time she leaned back or made a sudden turn. Since it was only special occasions that allowed them to get together and do the tango, Col. Barnes was usually completely entranced by the music and the seductive dance. But tonight, Barnes—who always had to turn the volume of the music up high because of the hearing loss he sustained from being around loud artillery—was distracted. In fact, tonight Colonel Barnes' attention was partly on the dance steps and partly up in the sky above. So, when he spotted a ship floating right over his summer home, he was shocked.

"What the hell," he said as he stopped abruptly in the middle of the dance, let go of his wife, and squinted to try to get a better look at what he thought was a UFO. "What the hell? They have the nerve to fly right over my house," he said with amazement.

Within minutes Barnes was on the phone to General Fulton, giving him a report and asking for the men and choppers to be deployed as soon as possible.

* * *

Scott made sure they quickly left that area but never gave the dancing couple, or the man who might have seen them, a second thought. Once they left that neighborhood, they headed back towards Stonebridge.

"Scott, I want to fly over the antique store so we can see Abigail," said Christina.

"Why?"

"I brought something for her. I brought her a sardine from home."

When she pulled out a baggy with a sardine rolled up in it, Scott and Brett together said "ewww" when they smelled the fish.

Scott wondered how Abigail, the antique store feline, seemed to always be aware when they flew overhead. When the *Mercury One*—which was a very quiet craft—flew over humans, the humans almost never looked up, but Abigail was always watching. She would meow at them as if she were trying to warn the earthlings of potential danger from the skies above.

"Maybe she'll like us more and not get so upset when she sees us if we give her a treat."

Scott lowered the ship so they could get closer to the roof of the Antique shop, and there was Abigail meowing repeatedly as if she were saying, "aliens, aliens, aliens."

"There she is," said Christina as she launched the fish in the direction of Abigail.

The sardine bounced three times on the roof and then rolled to a stop. The cat sniffed at the aromatic fish and then looked up at the craft and wrinkled her nose as if to say, "couldn't you find something a little more appetizing."

"She's not eating it," observed Christina. "She seems more interested in us."

"Maybe it smelled too fishy," offered Brett.

"I guess it was a little smelly."

"A little?" added Scott. "I'm surprised she didn't throw it back."

Chapter 25
The Brotherhood Camp

On the following night, in the Brotherhood camp, cameraman, David Melies, was making preparations with reporter, Amy Sanders, as the two of them were assigned to cover the "alien story" to be broadcast on the eleven o'clock news.

Amy was a blonde with blue eyes in her early twenties. David thought she was stunning, but despite his physical attraction, he didn't like her lack of dedication. She was just getting started as a television reporter, but her real dream was to be a movie star. The news reporter stint was merely a way for her to get experience in front of the camera and hopefully help her get "discovered" by someone in Hollywood.

David wanted to move up in the industry as well—he hoped to someday be a foreign correspondent—but he was dedicated to his work.

The other difference between the two was that David was fascinated by UFOs and potential contact with other beings while Amy hadn't been as swept up by the alien fever as had many of the other locals.

When the camera started running, however, she was great at pretending. Before each take, Amy would pull a small pocket mirror out of her purse and triple check her make-up and hair. The one gift

Amy did have was that as soon as the camera was on, she became remarkably articulate. When David gave her the signal that he was recording, she would immediately smile and switch into her professional persona.

"Good evening. I'm Amy Sanders reporting from what the local people around here have come to refer to as the Brotherhood Camp. Originally, the camp was set up by a group of UFO enthusiasts, but over the last few days, the number of campers has grown from a couple hundred to well into the thousands. It seems that the desire to contact alien beings has touched a nerve in people across America. Apparently, there are a lot of people out there who feel that they have some connection to beings who are not of this earth."

In addition to all the dedicated campers, over the last couple of days, the Brotherhood Camp had been invaded by unscrupulous merchants who had moved in to try to make a quick fortune off of the influx of people. During her report, Amy stepped a little to one side to let David's camera reveal some of the booths that had been set up in the camp with the sole intention of making fast money. David thought it cheapened the atmosphere and was glad that Amy was calling them out. "And, of course, there is always the shameless commercialism that goes with an event like this..."

Amy read some of the signs as she walked down the row of booths while David tried to follow her with the camera. "Alien burgers, in the shape of flying saucers, $7.00 each, UFO identification guides $11.00, maps of the alien's celestial homes $7.50, and the biggest rip off of all, special UFO glasses that are supposed to help you see UFOs at night."

Working hard in the UFO Glasses booth were two men, each wearing a pair of the brightly painted glasses as they collected money from eager customers. The two men waved and tried to get their faces on camera. As Amy walked by, she picked up a pair of glasses from the display rack. "These are obviously just cheap dime store sunglasses that have been painted with glow-in-the-dark paint. And they want

$10.00 apiece for these." Even though David was trying not to give free publicity to these merchants whom he regarded as swindlers, he wasn't able to keep the sign for the booth out of his shot: **Ray and Gordon's Intergalatic Goodies.** David noticed the misspelling on the sign and chuckled to himself.

Amy set the glasses back down on the counter, and David zoomed in. The glass frames were painted with bright shades of glow-in-the-dark greens, pinks, oranges, and yellows. There was also a crudely painted flying saucer and alien on the far side of each lens positioned in such a way that neither object would obstruct the customer's line of sight as long as that person was looking straight forward. David assumed that the sloppy artwork—which looked like it could have been done at the local elementary school—was, no doubt, the work of the two proprietors.

The quality—or lack of quality—of the product didn't seem to be deterring the public as sales continued to be brisk while Amy was at the booth and even after she walked away. "That is all for now from the Brotherhood Camp. We'll check in with you again with another report during the 11:00 o'clock news. Signing off, this is Amy Sanders."

One of the vendors of the booth called out to the other: "Hey, Gordon, I've run out of UFO glasses. Can you get a few more boxes out of your truck?"

As soon as the camera was off, Amy turned to David and said, "This is the most boring assignment ever. What are we going to do for the next three hours?"

David didn't say anything, but, in actuality, he loved being there and, throughout his lifetime, had often watched the skies hoping he might see a flying saucer in person. He didn't share his thoughts with Amy because he was thrilled just to be spending time with her.

Suddenly some loud dance music started up from one of the buildings in a row of temporary structures and booths nearby. Amy turned around and lit up with excitement. "Wooo Hooo, a dance hall." She looked over at the guys selling UFO glasses and continued her thought in a voice that was loud enough for them to hear: "Forget these losers. We've got some dancing to do."

David wasn't excited about that idea. In the first place, the thought of dancing with the hottest woman he'd ever known, and had actually talked to, absolutely terrified him. And he wanted to be sure they didn't miss something important. "Shouldn't we get more footage or do some interviews or something?"

"Come on, David. Why do you have to be so serious all the time? No one ever watches our crummy little channel. And besides, who am I going to dance with if you don't come with me?"

"But what if there's another sighting?" he objected. "That could be our big break... the story of a lifetime... We could be famous or get a gig with one of the big networks."

"Yeah, right. Like there's ever going to be a UFO around here. Get real." She flirtatiously put her arm around him and walked him towards the ticket window. "This is the only excitement in this entire boring camp. Come on, it's my treat."

David's head was racing. The thought of dancing with Amy—especially if they played a slow dance—was too much to resist. But would she really like a mid-twenties guy with a beard who dances like a stiff old robot? "Well, I guess we could..."

Amy walked him over to the ticket window where the saleswoman said: "Welcome to Uncle Steven's Starlight Dance hall."

"I want two tickets," said Amy.

"That will be twelve dollars each."

"Oh, wow. I'll have to charge it to the station." She turned to David. "It is business, right?"

When they entered the dance hall, David thought it was kind of a rip-off. The building was no more than a large room that looked like a doublewide trailer. The walls and ceiling were painted black and covered with glow-in-the-dark images of stars, moons, planets, comets and other celestial objects. There were two spinning flashing lights with light beams bouncing all over the room. The room was packed with dancers, and the speaker system seemed to be playing 45rpm records at full volume.

When the song ended, David reluctantly put aside his camera equipment and Amy quickly pulled him out on the floor. The owner of the dance hall had either forgotten or was too cheap to install an air conditioner, so the air inside the makeshift disco was stifling.

The DJ's voice came over the loudspeaker: "Okay all of you Venus Hotties and Plutonian Studs, it's time to rock 'n' roll. They call me Uncle Steven, and I'm going to make sure that your evening is absolutely star-tastic."

Amy had all the moves of a fabulous dancer. She was all smiles and seemed ready to dance all night. David, however, was hoping she might like him as a partner even if all he knew how to do was something his friends used to describe as the robot shuffle.

Chapter 26
Trying To Make Contact

In another part of the Brotherhood camp, far away from the booths and crowds of people, the serious sky watchers and real members of the Brotherhood had gathered under the stars. Roselda was leading a large group in a meditation. Earl had joined the group and was sitting cross-legged on the ground next to Roselda.

"Fellow members of the brotherhood," Roselda said as she led the meditation, "we have to let our alien brothers and sisters know that they are welcome on this earth. We must concentrate and send rays of love out into the universe."

The members of the group were deep in concentration.

Roselda continued: "We want them to find us. We are their orphan babies, and they are the parents who can guide us through the galaxy. We are not so different. Made from the same molecules, we are children from the same source. Concentrate. Concentrate. They can feel your thoughts. Send them your kindness and your love, and when they receive our message, they will come. They will come."

Earl became aware of someone who arrived late and was stumbling around in the dark, trying to find a place to sit. The latecomer staggered around the group and ended up sitting next to him. Earl tried to ignore the distraction and stay focused.

"Hey, Earl?"

Earl recognized the voice but pretended he was too deep in trance to notice.

"Earl, it's me Ron."

"Go away, Ron."

"Good to see you again, Earl."

Earl put his finger to his lips to indicate that Ron needed to be quiet.

"Of course. Of course," said Ron and he actually was quiet for a couple minutes. Then, he whispered to Earl: "Wow! That's amazing! Is that for real, or is that just a gimmick?"

Earl tried his best to ignore the interruption. He just figured it was Ron trying to get another story.

Ron started tapping on Earl's arm. "Earl, look, look, look. You gotta see this!"

Earl didn't want to give Ron any attention, but he was curious to see what Ron was so excited about, so he opened his eyes a little. Ron appeared to have no interest in the meditation but was extremely focused on Roselda.

"That's impossible. She must be using mirrors or something."

Earl could see why Ron had become so excited. There was a glowing energy all around Roselda as if she were wrapped in violet light. Her body appeared to be floating a couple of inches above the ground.

Wow, Earl whispered to himself. He, too, was amazed. *Could she actually be levitating?*

"That can't be real. It must be some sort of trick." Then Ron looked at his watch and started to look unsettled. He whispered in Earl's ear: "Hey Earl, I've got another deadline in a few minutes. I really need another story, and I thought you might help me out."

"Nope, Ron. 'fraid you're outta luck."

"I've been thinking about it, Earl," Ron whispered. "And I bet you're one of those intergalactic babies too."

"What?!?" Earl blurted out with a start as he opened his eyes and came out of his meditative state.

"Oh, no you don't," Earl whispered back, "I'm not even gonna talk to you. You're not gettin' any more stories outta me."

A few of the meditators started to shush the two men.

"But you can't deny it."

"Leave me alone, Ron." Earl tried to ignore Ron and closed his eyes.

"Hey Earl, I hear the aliens are planning an attack."

"You can't trick me again, Ron. I'm just not that stupid."

"Shush," whispered the other meditators.

Earl tried to go back into trance.

"Hey, Earl, I hear that the brotherhood wants you for their king."

Surprised and flattered, Earl couldn't control his excitement. He blurted out, "They do???"

Earl immediately realized that he'd been tricked again, and he just gave Ron the confirmation he needed for his next story. Earl brought his hand up to his forehead as if to say, *how did I let him get me again?*

"Oh, No!" Earl argued, "Ron, when I said, 'they do,' I meant it as a question, not a statement." Then he overemphasized the phrase to make his point clear. "I meant 'they do?????,' not "'they do!!!!!'"

Even though they were speaking in whispers, several of the members of the circle continued to shush the talkers.

Ron was beaming. "Thanks for the confirmation, Earl. Got it right here on my recorder." Ron opened his briefcase which contained his two tape recorders. Earl noticed that the briefcase had two round holes cut in the top near the handle. Mounted flush with the top of each of the holes were two microphones, one connected to each recorder. Earl figured that the system must have been custom made by Ron so that he could record conversations without anyone knowing.

Ron closed the briefcase and disappeared into the night.

Chapter 27
The Flyover

After observing the ballroom dancers and flying over Stonebridge, Scott piloted the *Mercury One* back to Miller's Pond and waited, but the aliens never came. Brett took a turn flying and then it was decided that Christina would fly home. As Christina was steering the ship, she turned to Scott and Brett and said, "Let's buzz the camp."

"What?" questioned Scott.

"You know, let's fly over all those UFO people and get 'em all excited."

"Are you crazy?"

"What're they gonna do? They can't catch us."

Scott looked at Brett who seemed to like the idea.

"We'll turn out all the lights," added Christina, "so they can't see us, and then fly about fifty feet over their heads. If we're that high up, no one will know who we are. Then tomorrow, I bet we'll be in the newspaper."

"Yeah!!!!!" Brett chimed in.

"They'll never know who it was."

"I don't know." Scott was still reluctant. "What if somebody figures it out?"

"Look, the moon's gone behind those clouds," Christina reasoned, "so it's going to be too dark for them to see who it is. Besides, all those people down there'll be thrilled. They've waited their whole lives for something like this."

"Come on, Scott," begged Brett.

"Oh, all right, but be careful...and not too close...and make sure you turn out all the lights first."

As the ship floated over the countryside, it took a long sweeping turn, and then Christina switched off all the lights. At first the camp looked like a small city of sparkling lights. As they got closer, they could see hundreds of tents and a large compound of booths, amusement park rides and vendor kiosks.

"Okay, there they are." Christina lowered the craft. "Here goes."

Scott was still cautious. "Make sure you keep your heads away from the windows and inside the moon roof. I don't want anyone to see us or get any pictures."

There were cheers and screams that moved through the crowd as the ship flew over the Brotherhood Camp.

"Listen to all the excitement down there. They love it," said Christina.

Scott looked out one of the windows and could see the people on the ground holding up lighters or lit matches. The night sky flickered with dozens of camera flashbulbs. As the ship moved over the crowd, some of the children tried to run along with it, but they couldn't keep pace with the speed of the *Mercury One*.

* * *

The news of the flyover quickly reached the dance hall when a young teenaged girl ran into the disco and screamed over the music: "There's been another sighting!" David quickly grabbed his camera, and he and Amy ran outside and found the entire camp abuzz with excitement.

Amy grabbed the first person she could find, an elderly man, and asked him, "Where is it?!?"

"Gone now. You missed it," he replied. "I wouldn't have believed it if I hadn't seen it with my own eyes."

His wife wasn't so happy. She held up her glow-in-the-dark UFO glasses. "I almost missed the whole thing because of these damn glasses. I put them on, and everything went dark."

Amy turned to the man. "What happened? Where did it go?"

"Right overhead. You should've seen it," the old man said. "I've waited my whole life to see something like this. I can't wait to tell my grandkids."

David was trying to be calm, but inside he was fuming at the missed opportunity.

"Oh well," Amy said.

"Oh well?" protested David. "We missed the chance of a lifetime!"

"David, you're always so over-dramatic. Like anyone really cares about this stuff. All the UFO geeks are here, so they can't watch us on TV. Everyone else is out having fun on a Saturday night, not sitting around at home waiting for the Channel Eight News to come on. Don't worry about it. It's no big deal," Amy tried to reassure him. "So, come on. Let's go back to the dance hall. That was fun."

* * *

Later that night, Scott was lying in bed watching the 11:00 o'clock news, still too excited about the flight to fall asleep.

The anchor on the news, a respectable silver-haired gentleman named Bill Danville, started off with the main headline of the day. "Our top story tonight: The aliens are back."

Superimposed behind the anchor was a very poor-quality photo of a vague, dark object flying over the campers. The picture quality was so poor that the station had to draw a circle around it to help viewers find it on the screen.

"This is an actual photograph of an alien craft flying over the Brotherhood Camp earlier this evening. This photo was shot by one of the campers who was a witness at the scene. If you look closely, at the circled area on your screen, you can see that there is some kind of object in the sky. It is too dark to tell exactly what that object is. A copy of the photo has been sent to Air Force officials. Their preliminary finding is that the picture is a phony."

The phone rang in Scott's room. Scott had the phone right by his bed as if he had been expecting a call. He quickly grabbed the receiver and was careful to speak in a whisper. "Hello."

Christina was on the other end of the phone. "Scott, are you watching the news?"

"Yeah, I've got it on right now."

"Can you believe it? We really gave them a thrill. Who thought we'd ever be on the news?"

"Yeah, but I'm worried about this Air Force thing. What if they find something an' figure out who it is?"

"Don't worry about it. They'll never figure it out. We made sure that there were no markings on the ship to give us away. All you can see in the picture is a very faint black blob. The picture quality is terrible."

"Yeah...but still, I think we'd better cool it for a while. We better not go up again for a week or so."

"Yeah, you're probably right."

The camera zoomed out as Amy Sanders joined Bill at the news desk.

"Amy Sanders, the reporter from the field is with us in the studio now. Amy was at the Brotherhood Camp this evening, covering the story, when the flyover occurred."

Bill seemed excited to jump right into the interview. "Amy, we just looked at an amateur photograph of what was supposed to be an alien ship, but all of us at the station are wondering if you and your cameraman—who were actually there on the scene covering this story in person—were able to capture this incredible event on camera. Do you have any footage that you can share with us?"

Amy shifted nervously in her seat. "Um, well, we were covering another story and unfortunately missed the flyover."

"You have to admit, this is pretty exciting," said Christina.

Amy was doing her best to save face. "But we did get a fascinating interview with one of the campers who witnessed the event."

Suddenly Earl's face came up on the television screen.

"Scott, quick, look at your TV. It's Earl."

Scott looked over, saw Earl, and chuckled to himself. "Actually, I like Earl. When we go down to his gas station, he always takes time to talk to us and asks how we're doing. He's a really nice guy."

"Yeah, my dad has always said that about him too."

Earl looked a little nervous about being on camera, but he certainly seemed to enjoy the attention.

"Now, I understand, Mr. Stubbs..."

"Earl."

"Earl," Amy said, not missing a beat, "that you were the first person in this area to have an actual encounter with the aliens. Is that right?"

Earl nodded.

"And that you actually witnessed what happened tonight?"

"I sure did," said Earl looking straight into the camera rather than at the reporter.

"And can you tell us what you saw?"

"Well, there was this dark object movin' 'cross the sky not more'n fifty feet over our heads, but we saw it clear as day."

"We've all heard stories about your abduction from a couple of weeks ago," said Amy trying to move the interview along. "Do you think these were the same aliens you had your encounter with?"

"I can't say for sure," Earl looked up as if he was trying to make a comparison in his mind, "but the ship that flew over the first time looked pretty much the same."

"So, Earl, tell me, why do you think our little town has become such a hotbed of UFO activity?"

"Well...quite frankly, I'm wondrin' if they've come back lookin' for me. I understand that once they abduct a fellow, they often come back and try to get another specimen."

After Earl's answer, Amy appeared to be uncertain about what Earl meant by specimen and then looked mildly nauseated once she figured it out. After taking a moment to compose herself, she was able to continue the interview.

Christina quickly whispered, "Gotta go. My parents just got home. See you tomorrow."

Scott said goodbye and hung up the phone. When he looked back up at the TV, the interview was over, and Amy and Bill were exchanging some light banter to fill time before the commercial.

Bill, referring to Earl, said, "Boy, a story like this one sure brings 'em out of the woodwork."

"It sure does, Bill," agreed Amy. "Well, you have a good night."

"You too, Amy, and make sure that there aren't any alien ships following you home."

They both chuckled in what was obviously phony laughter.

Amy, put on her UFO glasses and added, "I'll be watching for 'em, Bill."

They both followed the exchange with more fake laughter.

Chapter 28
The Air Force Base Camp

Around midnight on that same evening, Col. Barnes was getting the base camp set up about a half mile from the Brotherhood Camp. Eight Air Force airmen and two helicopters arrived with all the latest tracking and radar detection devices.

Major Rodriguez, who was new to the UFO division, was working diligently to set up radio communications. "Colonel Barnes."

"Yes, Rodriguez."

"Our communications system is up and running and we have established contact with headquarters."

"Good work, Rodriguez."

Barnes took a moment to talk to his crew. "Men, we'll split the watch into eight-hour shifts and work in pairs. I want someone monitoring the equipment, and the skies, at all times. We're going to be ready the next time the aliens show up. Simmons and Rodriguez will take the first watch."

* * *

Hours later, just before dawn, Major Rodriguez and Airman Simmons alerted Colonel Barnes about a possible intruder.

"There's something moving out there, behind those bushes," whispered Rodriguez as he handed the binoculars to the Colonel.

"What is it?"

"I'm not sure."

They waited a moment more and then saw a figure dart from one shrub to another.

"Someone's definitely out there," said Simmons. "I just saw him peak out from behind that bush."

"Should we apprehend?" Rodriguez asked looking at the Colonel.

Barnes gave him a nod of approval.

Rodriguez turned to Simmons. "When I give you the signal, let's get him."

Rodriguez raised his hand, and as soon as he dropped it, the two men bolted in the direction of the interloper. When the trespasser saw the men coming towards him, he tried to run away, but Simmons—an athletic man with a strong build—was too fast and quickly brought him down with a fierce tackle. Within moments, the intruder was face down with his hands cuffed behind his back. Then, they pulled him up on his feet and escorted him into camp.

"Colonel Barnes, Sir, this is the man who was lurking around our camp."

"Is that so," said a perturbed Barnes looking the man over and determining he wasn't a threat. "You can take the cuffs off."

"Name?" Barnes barked out as soon as the man was seated.

"Covington, Ron Covington."

"My men tell me you've been spying on our camp. Suppose you tell me what you're up to," demanded Barnes.

"I'm here to get a story for the *National Reporter*."

Barnes had seen that tabloid in the supermarkets. He remembered some of the ridiculous headlines about things like alien invasions and immediately understood why Ron was trying to spy on them.

"He was carrying this when we caught him." Rodriguez held up Ron's briefcase and then cautiously opened it up, revealing the two hidden tape recorders for the Colonel to examine.

"A reporter?"

"Yes, sir."

"So that's why you travel with tape recorders?"

"Yes, sir."

Barnes pushed the briefcase back in the direction of Rodriguez and said, "You can give him back his briefcase. He couldn't have recorded anything from way out there."

As Ron took back his briefcase, there was a clicking noise that occurred as he closed the lid and faced the Colonel. "Sir."

"Yes?"

"The world wants to know what the Air Force has to say about these alien flyovers."

"I'm afraid you're going to be disappointed," said Barnes.

"Why is that?"

"Because there aren't any flyovers."

"That's not what I've heard, Colonel," said Ron.

"What have you heard?" asked Barnes.

"There's a rumor going around that this UFO is actually a top-secret Air Force mission. Would you like to confirm that?"

"No, Sir, I would not," answered the gruff Colonel. "I'm afraid there's no truth to that at all."

"You mean, no truth that it's a rumor?" asked the reporter.

"No, I mean no truth to the story."

"But if there truly is a rumor, then you would need to confirm that the rumor exists even though the rumor itself may be slightly off the mark, the fact that there is a rumor means that the statement should receive a positive confirmation. So, can I assume that you really meant to answer that with an affirmative?"

"No, you may not."

Ron tried another angle: "I understand that the Air Force captured the alien ship that was spotted last night, and you've been holding the entire alien crew as hostages."

"Absolutely absurd," Barnes blurted out.

"Which part of it?"

"All of it. If we captured the alien ship, it'd be big news by now…"

"Unless you were trying to cover it up," Ron added.

"If we were covering it up and the Air Force was lying to the American people, what would we possibly have to gain? Mr. Covington, this discussion is over, and this is not an interview. I'm afraid I can't help you."

Barnes stood up to leave. "In a few minutes, one of my men will escort you out of our camp. If we catch you lurking around here again, I'll have you arrested and thrown in jail."

"But Colonel, the people have a right to know,"

"Like I said, Mr. Covington, I'm afraid I can't help you."

A few minutes later, Barnes watched as Simmons shepherded Covington out of the area.

* * *

Back at the amusement park section of the Brotherhood Camp, the cameraman, David Melies, sat at a picnic table and watched and waited. It was early morning, and he was exhausted and disappointed after waiting all night in hopes that he might see another flyover. Amy had gone home for the night but had come back and was off to get something to eat at one of the booths. David was still occasionally looking up at the sky, but he was too tired to keep his eyes open for long.

A tall thin man came up and asked if he could share the table with David. Since the area was packed with people eating breakfast and there weren't any other places to sit, David had no problem with sharing the table.

"Sure, go ahead," David said as he motioned to the bench across from him.

"Thanks, buddy," said the man as he sat down. He carefully placed his briefcase on the table and opened it up. "The name's Ron."

"David."

"Nice to meet you, David."

Ron glanced around as if he were checking to see if anyone was watching him, then he started a process that David thought was a bit peculiar. Ron had a couple of tape recorders in his briefcase, and when he pressed the play button on one of the recorders, it caught David's attention. David listened but pretended to be half asleep and not paying attention.

If we captured the alien ship, it'd be big news by now...If we were covering it up and the Air Force was lying to the American people, what would we possibly have to gain? Mr. Covington, this interview is over. I'm afraid I can't help you.

David watched as Ron jotted down every word on a notepad, made a few cross outs and drew some arrows on his notes. Then, he turned on the second tape recorder. While he played segments of the interview on one recorder, he carefully recorded selected excerpts on the second recorder. He was able to slow the words down which made the cutting and pasting process easier. Ron played the first phrase a couple of times. Then, he mumbled to himself: "Hmmmm...let's see what would happen if we made a few changes. What if we cut a few words from this sentence," Ron mumbled "whoops" and giggled to himself as if the cut he so carefully engineered was an accident.

...we captured the alien ship...

David wasn't sure if Ron was aware, but Ron was saying all of his thoughts out loud as he worked through the process.

"And if we took a few words from this sentence," Ron said to himself, "and put them where he probably meant for them to be...." Ron pressed a button on the first recorder and then as he inserted those words on the second recorder he said, "Oh, my goodness" as if he had made yet another mistake.

...we were covering it up...

"That would be much more interesting," he said to himself all the while not noticing that David was watching him.

"Here I brought you some coffee and a couple of doughnuts," Amy said as she sat down and put the tray on the table. "I can't believe you stayed here all night."

David put his hand behind his ear to indicate that she should listen and then pointed to the man who had joined them at the table. Amy nodded without making a sound.

Ron looked at his notes again. "And if we take this phrase here and... ohhh, now how did that happen?" Ron asked dramatically and snickered to himself. Then he moved the phrase to its new location and acted like it was yet another accidental edit.

...the Air Force was lying to the American people...

When everything seemed complete, Ron whispered in a sneaky voice. "Let's see how this sounds now."

We captured the alien ship...we were covering it up...the Air Force was lying to the American people.

Ron smiled. "Sounds like you can help me, Colonel. I've got proof right here on my recorder." He closed up the briefcase, got up from the table, looked at David and said, "Thanks, buddy," and disappeared into the crowds.

"What was that all about?" asked Amy.

"I don't know. He must have been a reporter for the paper or something."

"What was he doing?"

"I think he was *making up* a story," said David who couldn't help laughing at whatever it was he just witnessed. "What a fraudster. Oh well, at least it brightened up my morning."

Chapter 29
The Intergalactic Special

The next evening, a few blocks from downtown Stonebridge, Scott, Brett, and their mother got out of their car and started to walk down the main street to the *Blue Moon Diner*. "I can't believe we had to park two blocks away from the restaurant," said Judy in disgust. "A few people think they see a UFO, and the whole town goes crazy."

It was apparent how the celestial sightings had changed the quiet little town. Several of the people passing on the street were wearing UFO glasses and shirts that read I saw an ET in SB. Judy seemed annoyed when she read one of the shirts: "What?!? I saw an ET in SB. Stonebridge is one word, not two. It should be an 'S' not 'SB.'"

"But then it wouldn't rhyme, Mom," argued Brett.

"No, Brett, I guess it wouldn't." She shook her head in disbelief as two more people passed by with the same shirts. "And who was the genius who came up with that idea anyway?"

"I heard that they sell 'em at the same place where you get the UFO glasses," answered Brett.

As they passed Joann's Antique shop, Abigail, who was in the front window soaking up the late afternoon sun, immediately stood up and began to sound what Scott had started to refer to as her *"there they are; the aliens from outer space"* warning.

"How come that cat got so worked up when it saw you two?" Judy asked the boys.

"We come by here and see her pretty often," said Scott. "She's probably just saying 'hi.'"

Further down the block, the Bijou theatre had dropped its current offering and was now showing the movie, *War of the Worlds*. The line for the movie stretched all the way around the block. Moviegoers, in the spirit of the times, were dressed in outfits that included everything from Martians to futuristic robots.

As the Harrison family passed by the local bookstore, books like *The Martian Chronicles*, *Fahrenheit 451* and *The Time Machine* filled the front window. The magazine racks out in front displayed the latest edition of the *National Reporter*. Brett grabbed Scott's arm and said, "Look Scott, there's a story in that newspaper about UFOs." Each copy had a headline that read: "Top Air Force Official Admits UFO Cover Up."

"Can we get one of those, Mom?" asked Brett.

"What? You guys don't read that trash. That's a waste of money."

There was a new sign in front of Earl's gas station that promised a free autograph with every fill up. Several interested customers were lined up and patiently waiting in their cars. There was another sign that read: *We close promptly at Eight p.m. for sky watching.*

When the Harrison family finally reached the door of the diner, the sign on the door said:

No Smoking
No Loitering.
No Credit.
No Aliens.

The fourth item had been added to the list recently with a black magic marker.

"I still can't believe we had to park two blocks away," Judy said as they entered the restaurant. "We should have just left the car at home and walked from there. It would have been faster."

After they were seated at their table, a waitress dressed in a tight green Martian costume approached the table. "Good evening. I'm Jenny. How are you all doing?"

An emotionless "good" was the response from Mrs. Harrison.

"Tonight, we're celebrating the arrival of alien beings with a meal that we call the Cosmic Special," said the waitress.

"What's in the cosmic special?" Brett asked.

The waitress leaned over and whispered: "I can't tell you that because it's a secret, but I guarantee you'll like it."

"Okay," said Scott, "I'll have one of those."

"Me too," chimed in Brett.

"But you don't even know what it is," said Judy.

"It's our hottest seller," said the waitress as she wrote down their orders. She turned to Judy. "And one for you, too?"

"No cosmic specials for me. I'm sick and tired of all this UFO stuff!!! Just give me a hamburger and fries."

The waitress seemed a little turned off by Judy's lack of festive spirit.

After she left, Judy turned to the boys. "What is happening to this town? Has everyone gone nuts?"

Scott and Brett just shrugged their shoulders, then looked at each other and smiled.

"And why'd they have to pick this town to visit anyway?" Judy asked.

The waitress brought their food, and the three plates were identical. When Judy saw this, she made a point of catching the waitress before she left. "Um...excuse me...Miss. I ordered the burger and fries, but they ordered the cosmic specials."

"Those are the cosmic specials," replied the waitress before she walked away.

"Oh...the cosmic special is a hamburger and fries? How origi-

nal," Judy said in a annoyed tone. "What's with this town?" she said
as she looked over at three people at the next table who were wearing
silver suits, with their faces painted and antennae attached to the top
of their heads.

For a moment it was silent until Judy spoke again, "Your dad
called this afternoon, and he wants to know what you guys want to do
tomorrow. He says he has the whole day free if you want to do something with him."

"I wanna go to the Brotherhood camp," Scott replied.

"You're kidding, right?" Judy said in disbelief.

"No, I really wanna go."

"Me, too," added Brett.

Judy shook her head. "Okay. That's what I'll tell him."

* * *

Later that night, Scott woke up sweating and shaking. In the
nightmare, he was trapped inside an enclosure made of glass, and
there were aliens looking in at him. His body was disintegrating. It
had turned into a cloud of dust and was floating in the air. It made
him wonder if he was dying, and this was his spirit leaving the body.
The dream was so real that when he opened his eyes, he was surprised
to see that his hands were still there and still attached to his arms. He
didn't know what it meant but was sure that it held clues about the
danger in his future.

Chapter 30
A Face in the Crowd

On the following day, late in the afternoon, Scott and Brett were at the Brotherhood camp with their father and thousands of other people from all over the country. Scott was a little surprised by the carnival atmosphere, the enormous food court, and an entire section of the camp devoted to amusement park rides. It was like the circus had come to town: there wasn't a serious sky watcher to be found. The song, "A Bicycle Built for Two," played each time the merry-go-round started up, but it was often interrupted by the screeches and screams coming from the riders on the Cosmic Coaster. The smells of cotton candy and caramel apples hung in the air, luring people in the area to stop in and taste the sweets.

As evening started to take hold, a row of cottonwood trees that served as a boundary along the creek were lit up with strings of small white lights. People could stroll under the trees if they wanted to get away from all the noise and frenetic energy of the booths and rides. It was a hot steamy evening and everyone—especially the numerous people dressed in costumes—looked forward to feeling some relief when the sun started to move lower in the sky. Despite the heat, for anyone who lived within 500 miles, this was *the* place to take your family and spend the day.

Scott and Brett's father, Rick, had custody of the boys on every other weekend. Scott was surprised that he agreed to take them to the Brotherhood camp as many of their weekends together were more about getting things done on Rick's 'to-do' list. It often felt like the visitations were an interruption in Rick's personal life, but everyone always pretended that they were having a good time together and everything was fine.

"You guys ready for dinner?"

Brett and Scott both said "yeah" at the same time.

They walked up to the Alien Burger stand and looked at the menu. Above the booth was a hand-painted sign of a burger with an extra-large patty of beef nestled inside a very small bun. The shape of the hamburger on the sign was purposely designed to recreate the shape of a flying saucer. The burger was depicted as if it truly was soaring through the universe and leaving behind a vapor trail in its tracks.

"What sounds good to you guys? Burger, fries and a lemonade?"

They both nodded.

Rick turned to the clerk and placed the order: "Okay, we'll have three flying saucer burgers, three orders of Jupiter fries and three large moon juices."

While one clerk put the food in bags, another one rang up the order. "That'll be $42.50."

"What?" said Rick with surprise. "Good grief!!! What a rip-off!" He looked through his wallet. "Do you take credit cards?"

While they were eating their dinners, Brett suddenly stopped eating and tugged on Scott's sleeve and whispered, "Scott, look. There's that sparkly lady."

Scott studied the crowd for a moment and then spotted Roselda. He carefully watched to see where Roselda went and then turned to his father, "Dad."

"What?"

"You know how you said you were gonna take Brett on the Ferris wheel after dinner?"

"Yeah."

"Can I um...look around on my own for a while and then meet you over there in a half hour or so?"

"Well, yeah, I guess so. Why?"

"Oh, I just wanna look around."

Rick looked at his watch, "All right. Why don't you meet us at the Ferris wheel at quarter to eight. That gives you about forty-five minutes."

"Thanks, Dad." Scott ran off through the crowd trying to retrace Roselda's steps. He passed by the alien fun house and stopped for a moment to look at himself in the wavy mirrors. Not only did the mirrors make Scott look tall and skinny or short and fat, but in each mirror, there was an image of an alien, so when you looked at yourself in the mirror, it appeared as if you were standing next to a creature from another world. Scott paused for a moment to figure out how they created the effect, but he knew he had to keep moving and could think about that later.

As he resumed his rush through the crowds, a loud booming female voice called out to him: "Hey you, come here."

Scott stopped abruptly and looked around to see where the voice was coming from.

"Over here," said the woman's voice.

Scott turned and saw an elderly lady with straggly white hair beckoning to him. With a large nose, mysterious blue eyes and a crackly voice, Scott's first thought to himself was *she's a witch*. It was almost like he felt her gaze as she looked at him.

"What is it?" he yelled back to her.

"Come here," called out the woman from the fortune teller booth, as she motioned for him to come and join her using her curled up arthritic finger. "I want to tell you your fortune."

"I—I can't. I'm in a hurry. I have to meet someone."

"But you have no idea what's in store for you," she argued. "There is much greatness in your future—and adventure—wild, fantastic adventure." She got more excited as she spoke, "out of this world adventure, half-breed. It's all there, in your energy field. I can see it. I've never seen a future quite like this before."

Scott's initial thought was that this woman was just another crazy carney after his money, but something about her was different. Something inside him wanted to step out of her gaze because it felt like she had the power to look right through him.

"I—I'm sorry. I can't right now," said Scott starting to walk away.

"But there is also danger coming, the potential for grave, grave danger, and I need to warn you," she cautioned.

"I have to go," he said shaking his head. "I'm sorry."

As Scott ran off, he could still hear her calling. "I know the truth about you. You can't keep these things hidden forever."

While part of Scott was glad to get away, another part of him wanted to find out what this woman had to say, but he knew he had to move on and refocus on finding Roselda.

At the far end of the carnival area, Scott spotted a gate that appeared to lead into the campground with the tents that they had spotted from above during their flyovers. Scott suspected that this was the camp where the people who were truly interested in contact with UFOs were staying. But the area was on the other side of the fence, and there was someone stationed at the gate, whose job, it appeared, was to keep people from the carnival out of the serious sky-watching area.

Scott figured he had nothing to lose by telling the truth, so he told the woman at the gate that he was here to see Roselda. He was surprised by her answer.

"She's been expecting you. Her tent is that way," the gate keeper said as she pointed to a row of tents, "the fifth one on the left. You can find her there."

Scott wondered how Roselda could have been expecting him. He shook off that concern and walked to the fifth tent and found Roselda standing outside with a group of Brotherhood members who were asking her questions. When she saw Scott, she said: "Ah, there you are."

She turned to the group and told them. "Please excuse me everyone, I have an appointment with someone who has come for a brief chat. I'll be back in a few minutes."

Roselda whispered to Scott, "Come on. Let's get away from all these people. We need to talk."

Chapter 31
Roselda Starchild

"**I**'m Roselda," she said extending a hand.

"I'm Scott," he said.

"Let me show you around."

They walked through the Brotherhood campground. In one area, there were several people sitting in a large circle carefully situated in such a way where they could view every part of the sky without missing any movement. As some watched the sky and looked through telescopes, others were looking at charts, jotting down notes and observing scientific instruments. Roselda explained: "This is where we watch everything that happens in the sky and then check to see if what has been spotted is an earth satellite or something out of the ordinary."

In another area there was an older man with maps of the stars, teaching the newer members the constellations and movements of the stars and planets. Scott overheard him mention a constellation and a star cluster: Cassiopeia and The Pleiades.

"And this is a very special place," Roselda said in a whisper as they passed by. "This is the meditation area. We believe that if we gather and send our collective love and thought patterns to the heavens, it is far more powerful than any messages we could send by a transmitter or satellite. Energy is more profound than words or radio signals."

They moved on through to the far end of the camp where Roselda hesitated for a moment and then pointed to the north. "You see that
field over there?"

"Yeah."

"One hundred and fifty of us spent two days out there making
twenty-foot letters, so we could send out a message if another UFO
should come. The letters are made of flammable materials. If the
aliens come at night, we'll light those letters with torches, and it will
instantly go up in flames. It'll be so big that they could read it from half
a mile away. That's how badly we want to reach them." She stopped
for a minute. "I don't want you to think that it's all carnival rides and
glow-in-the-dark glasses."

"No, I don't. I was really disappointed when I saw all of that."
Scott hesitated for a moment. "But then why do you let those people
in here? They're ruining the place. It's like a circus. I wanted to come
here so I could talk to people like you and find out what you know,
and..."

Roselda breathed a heavy sigh. "I know. I know. They seem to
show up everywhere we go. We don't have any control over that. We
can't stop them." She shook her head in disgust. "We're here because
it's something we believe in. They're only here to make money or turn
what is important to us..." she hesitated, "into a sensational news story. That's not what we're all about."

They continued walking to the far end of the camp where there
was a trail that led into the woods. As they entered the forest, there
was a rich, earthy smell from the trees, mosses, decaying leaves and
centuries of life that had existed there. "This is a good place to talk
where we won't be interrupted." Roselda sat down by a gentle stream,
under a gigantic maple tree and motioned for Scott to sit on a large
granite rock next to her. "This is where I come to meditate on my own.
I only discovered this amazing old maple tree a couple of days ago,
even though I'd taken many walks down this trail. I don't know how
I ever missed it when I came this way before, but I must have walked

right on past it until the last day or two."

An owl started to call out from one of the branches high above them.

Roselda paused for a moment as she listened to the owl and smiled. Scott could sense that she was very wise. There was something about her gaze that indicated she knew a lot more than she let on. He noticed that tonight she didn't have all the glitter and sparkles that she was wearing in the newspaper picture. Her outfit seemed much more ordinary: blue jeans and a plain purple T-shirt. "In every town we visit, every place we go, there's always someone who is fascinated by what we're doing and wants to know more. Sometimes they've already had encounters or contact with alien beings. Sometimes they just feel a connection that they can't explain. But in each and every case, they come because they're seeking out a person they can talk to who understands."

"That's it," said Scott. "That's me. You just described me, including the alien encounters, but I have so many questions, I don't even know where to begin."

"Just ask what's in your heart."

Scott thought for a moment. "I read an article about you, and when you talk about having those feelings about what's up there and knowing that there's some kind of connection between us...well... that's me too. I mean, I've felt that way for years. I don't know how else to say it, but I feel this incredible attraction towards outer space. I don't know why or where that comes from. It's just who I am."

"What's so wrong about being sensitive or knowing that you have a connection to the universe?" Roselda asked without expecting an answer. "It's okay to be who you are and honor what you feel inside."

"But except for my brother and my best friend, I don't feel like I fit in anywhere," countered Scott, "or with anyone. No one understands me, and there's no one I can talk to about this stuff."

"So, you're different," said Roselda. "We're all different," she said motioning to the people in the Brotherhood Camp. "In time, you'll start to attract others who share your feelings and beliefs. But in the meantime, be grateful that you are unique and not living the same life as everyone else. Your destiny is not going to allow you to be another face in the crowd. You are here for greater things."

As they sat together, Scott felt comfortable and safe talking to her.

"People make fun of all this," Roselda motioned to the Brotherhood Camp, "but this is important to me. Even after all of these years, a brief flash in the sky can turn me into an excited child again."

"I know what you mean," Scott said as he looked up to the sky. "Sometimes I can sit and stare up there for hours."

"Perhaps that's where we've come from or where we're destined to return," Roselda said with a smile. "There's some connection that we have to someone or something up there, and when the time comes, you'll know. That's all I can tell you. When you're ready, something will tell you where you're supposed to be. You don't have to worry about that. They won't forget you."

"But I don't want to wait."

Roselda smiled. "Your time hasn't come yet. Things will be revealed to you in their own time. As hard as it is to accept, you need to be patient."

"When I was about your age, maybe a little younger," said Roselda, "I lived on a farm in Minnesota, way out in the middle of nowhere. Sometimes, us kids, as we walked home from school would sneak off to this lake called Lake Marston. It was about a mile from the school, and the only way you could get there was by walking down this dusty old dirt road.

"One Friday afternoon, on the last day of school, I had to stay late after class and all the other kids went on ahead of me. It was right before summer vacation, so I didn't have any schoolbooks with me. All I had was a library book. I still remember the name of that book, it was called *From The Earth To The Moon* by Jules Verne. Anyway, I was walking fast, trying to catch up with the rest of the group who were already on their way to the lake, when I noticed that the sky and everything around me turned very dark and had an eerie green cast to

　　　　Star People: Mystery of the Hologram

it. I had been told that when the sky turns that color, it usually means there's a rotating cloud above you and you need to take cover."

"A rotating cloud?"

"A rotating cloud means there's a storm above that usually turns into a tornado," explained Roselda.

"But when I looked up, I didn't even notice the clouds because there was something far more amazing hovering directly over my head. It was a magnificent spaceship. I can say now—that it was magnificent—but I didn't feel that way at the time. It scared the hell out of me.

"We'd never even heard much about aliens or UFOs back then, especially living on a farm out in the middle of nowhere. I wasn't ready for something like that. In fact, I was so scared I just started running. I turned the other direction, away from the lake and ran towards home, as fast as I could."

"They wouldn't have hurt you," interrupted Scott realizing those words came out of his mouth even though he didn't mean to say them out loud.

Roselda smiled. "I know that now, but I didn't know that then. All I knew was that I was feeling shivers of fear moving through my body. In my panic, I dropped that library book and just ran. All I could think about was getting to the house and locking all the doors and windows behind me. Along the way, I could feel them following me."

"Who? The aliens?"

"Yes, I could feel their presence. As I ran, I would turn around from time to time and look back, and there was that ship, almost like they were stalking me. Finally, after I'd gone about a mile, in a flash, the ship darted off, and they were gone.

"When I got back to our farm, I could hear the storm sirens going off in the distance, sounding out their warning, all the way from town."

"So there really was a tornado?"

"There actually was a rotating cloud spinning above me, and it had turned into a twister. I could see it, out on the horizon, heading straight towards Lake Marston."

"So, they saved you," Scott said quietly to himself.

Roselda smiled. "I didn't know that then, but I do now. That twister went right over the lake. If I had kept on walking, who knows what would have happened."

"What about your friends?"

"That was the sad part," answered Roselda. "Most of them just had cuts and bruises because of all the flying debris, and one boy was knocked unconscious when something hit him in the head. But the strange thing was, there was this little girl who disappeared on that day, and they never found a trace of her again. Everyone naturally assumed that it was the storm that carried her away, but I wonder now if it really was the storm or if it was the aliens who took her," pondered Roselda. "They never found her body even though they searched for days.

"I wasn't ready to go with them, but maybe Angela—that was the girl's name who disappeared—was. I know that she wasn't happy. One time she told me about some of the things that were going on at home, and it was a pretty bad situation. So, maybe she wanted to leave the planet. I can't say for sure." Roselda hesitated and thought for a moment. "Of course, I didn't figure any of this out back then, but as an adult, I've thought about it a lot.

"A couple hours later, when the storm had passed, I left the house and went back to the lake to see what happened. The tornado had destroyed everything in its path. Big trees, old barns, the countryside was ripped apart. I looked for my library book, but it was gone too. My mom made me pay the library for it, earning money by doing extra chores around the farm, even though I didn't think losing it was my fault."

"What about your friends?"

"When I got back to the lake, no one was there. Apparently, two of them had gone to see the doctor, and the rest had all gone home. No one knew that Angela was missing until later that night. Turns out that, like me, she was separated from the others when the storm came.

"But the point is, they are watching out for us, all the time. They knew I needed help back then, so they came. And they'll know where to find you when the time comes. We are their children," continued Roselda. "I wasn't ready to go with them back then. But they've been back many times, and they'll be back many more times. They always know where to find me, and they'll know where to find you."

Roselda looked at her watch and stood up. "Oh my. I've lost track of the time. We have to head back now. I'm late for an interview. And you have to get back to your dad and little brother or else they'll start to wonder where you are."

"How'd you know that?"

"You're one of us. After all these years, I can spot one of my brothers a mile away. I saw you eating dinner earlier this evening. I knew you'd be coming to talk to me, and I'm glad you did."

They started walking back along the trail to Roselda's tent.

"I had an experience like yours, and I wish I had more time to tell you about that, but I have so many other things I want to ask you."

"Like what?"

Scott thought for a moment. "I wanted to ask you," he paused. "And I don't know how to say this."

"What?"

"Well...sometimes I feel things or know things...I mean...sometimes I know when things are going to happen, but if I say anything about it to anyone, they think I'm crazy."

Roselda smiled. "You're not crazy. There are other people out there who are just like you." She motioned over to her quiet camp and the other members of the Brotherhood. "That's why we're here. We understand each other. We accept one another and know that there is something unique about each one of us."

"But on the news, they say you're crazy."

"Oh, I hope so," answered Roselda with a laugh. "Much more interesting being crazy than normal you know." She hesitated and thought for a moment. "As long as you believe in yourself, that's all that matters."

As they drew closer to Roselda's tent, Scott spoke up again. "Roselda, there's something I want to tell you." Scott wanted so much to tell Roselda that it was his ship that was responsible for some of the Brotherhood Camp flyovers, but it felt like such a big betrayal, he couldn't get himself to say it. He hesitated for a moment. "Thank you for taking time to talk to me," was all he could say instead of the confession he had hoped to bring forth.

"My pleasure."

As they arrived at her tent, Roselda stopped and offered her hand to Scott, "Good luck, Scott."

Scott shook her hand. "You too, Roselda."

"I'm sure we'll meet again…in the future," she added.

"I hope so," Scott said and then headed back to the gate where the Brotherhood guard kept watch.

Scott retraced his steps, through the gate and into the area with the carnival rides. He found Brett in front of the Ferris wheel, but his dad was missing. Brett was wearing an "I saw an ET in SB" T-shirt.

"Nice shirt," observed Scott.

"I really like the picture on it," said Brett. "Do you think mom will get mad?"

"No. Just tell her you liked the little alien guys getting out of the spaceship," Scott suggested, describing the graphics on the shirt, "and she'll be okay." Scott looked around. "Where's Dad?"

"Over there. He's getting more tickets for the cosmic coaster." Brett hesitated. "How'd it go?" he asked referring to the meeting with Roselda.

"It was really good. I'm glad I got to talk to her."

Rick came back with the tickets.

"Come on. Let's go on the cosmic coaster again," Rick suggested and then turned to Brett, "It's one of the best rides we've been on. Don't you think so, Brett?"

"It's pretty good, but I've been on better rides."

"Really?" Rick seemed puzzled. "I thought this was your first time on a roller-coaster?"

Scott gave his brother a cautionary look to remind Brett not to say anything that might make their father suspicious of their nocturnal adventures.

Brett nodded to Scott, indicating he understood. "Well, yeah, maybe this is the best ride I've ever been on."

* * *

Later that night, Scott came into Brett's room just as Brett was starting to fall asleep. "Hey, Brett."

"Yeah."

"Thanks for keeping all of this a secret."

"I haven't told anyone."

"I know, and I know it's been really hard."

"Especially about the aliens," added Brett. "That's been the hardest. I wanted to tell everyone about that."

"That's been hard for me too, but we gotta keep it quiet. If they found out, they'd probably take our ship away."

"Do you really think so?"

"Yeah, they'd say it wasn't safe. And if you try to tell anyone about the aliens, they'll only make fun of you. Believe me, I know."

Brett thought about it for a minute. "Yeah, you're probably right."

"And thanks for finding Roselda for me," said Scott. "How'd you know I wanted to talk to her?"

"There's just something different about you. Just like there's something different about her. You guys are sort of alike."

"Yeah, I guess so."

"Are you gonna join that Brotherhood thing?"

"Maybe someday, in four or five years," Scott said as he got up to leave. "It won't be for a while though. You can't get rid of me that easy."

"I was ready to move all my stuff into your room," Brett joked.

"Go to sleep," Scott said as he threw a pillow at his brother.

Chapter 32
The Transformation

It was the night of the second full moon of summer. Scott and Brett were sitting on the porch of the work shed watching the sky for the return of the Antarians.

There was a warm steady breeze coming from the west and the crickets were singing. The sky had some faint shades of purple as the last light of day was turning into night.

"No sign of the Star People yet?" asked Christina as she came into the backyard and sat next to them.

"No, not yet. I don't think it's dark enough."

"Do you think they'll come to the field behind your house again?" asked Christina.

"Yeah, they'll have to come to us tonight. We can't take the ship out because my mom's home."

"What if she sees them? Aren't you worried about that?"

"No, I think they'll place that sleep wave over the whole area. That'll put her, and everyone else in the area, into a sleep state."

Christina noticed some deer out in the field grazing. "Do you think—"

"No, those are real deer. We've been watching them for a half an hour. We wondered about that too."

"I still don't quite get all this," said Brett.

"What do you mean?" asked Christina.

"I still don't understand how all this genetic stuff works," said Brett.

"It's where they take the genes of one thing and put it with the genes of another thing to create a creature that's half and half," answered Christina.

"Like our neighbor's dog where they combined a Collie and a Labrador Retriever?"

"Yeah, kinda," said Christina. "But the aliens were trying to put together things that don't go together."

"Like a dragon and a man?"

"Exactly,"

"So, what does this Zarco guy want with you?" he asked Scott.

"I don't know. Maybe we'll find out about that tonight."

Scott looked at the other two and he noticed that both Brett and Christina were struggling to keep their heads up and their eyes open.

"I think they're here," said Scott, but neither responded to him.

After the veil of sleep was cast over the area and all the lights in the neighborhood had gone dark, the ship came in for a soft landing. Scott looked around him and thought that the darkness was reminiscent of when they had experienced a blackout last summer. Only the soft green lights on the ship were illuminated.

Once it touched down, Scott jumped up. "Come on, you guys let's go," he said, but Brett and Christina didn't move. Both of them seemed to be in a trance.

The ship's entry ramp dropped down, and Scott could see Zula and Zocuul waiting in the doorway. Zocuul was holding the language board.

Scott walked over to the ship and tried to explain: "They're really dragging tonight. I think your sleeping spell must've got to them too."

The message board lit up.

They can't come with us tonight.

"Why not?"

It isn't safe for them.

Just then, Brett summoned all his energy and stood up. It took all his might to fight off the sleep and walk over to the ship. "I'm going with my brother."

Christina was fighting the grogginess as well. "We're in this together. He's my best friend, and we're going to protect him," she said as she struggled to stand up.

We admire your loyalty, but Scott will be safe. We will take care of him. The two of you would never survive this trip. Only he can come with us tonight. He can explain tomorrow.

"I wouldn't want anything to happen to them," Scott told the aliens. Then, he turned to Brett and Christina. "I'll be okay. I'll tell you all about it tomorrow."

Brett and Christina were fighting sleep and could barely stand up. Christina gave a nod of her head indicating it was okay. "Come on, Brett, we have to let them go."

The two of them turned back and shuffled towards their houses while Scott and the two aliens boarded the ship.

This time the aliens took him through the control room. The model of the solar system that floated in midair fascinated Scott. There were dozens of ships and satellites as well as planets and moons and even other stars.

This is where we are going.

Those words lit up on the language board as Zocuul stepped closer to the floating universes and pointed to what looked like a tube-shaped object.

"Is that?" Scott hesitated. Since he loved astronomy, the three-dimensional object wasn't a mystery to him. "Is that a wormhole?"

Yes.

Scott remembered what he had learned in his astronomy studies. He recited softly what he had learned: *Wormholes are a bridge between two points in time and space, and they may be a way to travel forwards or backwards in time because travel through a wormhole is faster than the speed of light.* Then Scott turned to the aliens. "The only reason, I can think of, that we would go through a wormhole is to go backwards or forwards in time."

Exactly.

"Where are we going?"

Back in time. But first we must prepare.

"What do you mean? What do we have to do?"

They escorted Scott through the control room. Many of the controls were holograms rather than traditional control panels. There were a couple of Antarians, he had never seen before, at the controls.

He was led into a room with several glass chambers in the form of long tubes that extended from the ceiling to the floor. Each of the chambers had a door where a person could enter and a handle inside the door so they could close the door behind them.

Zocuul was still holding the language board.

You will need to go into one of the chambers for this flight.

"What is it?" Scott remembered his dream. "Is it safe?"

We have been training you for this, for a long time. Take a moment and focus. You will remember how to do this. You have done it before. It is all recorded in your subconscious mind.

Scott looked over at them apprehensively. All of those dreams—at least what he had thought were dreams about being on this craft—may not have been dreams at all. Something about all of this did seem familiar, but as hard as he tried, Scott couldn't come up with a conscious memory of having done it before.

"What happens in the chamber?"

Your intact human body, the way it is now, could never withstand the high-speed travel it would have to endure for you to journey through a wormhole. You have learned how to change the form of your cells. For this flight, you must break your body down to its simplest form: pure atoms.

"Yeah, I guess that makes sense. It's just a little scary."

Watch as Zula demonstrates.

Zula started to break apart—as if she was crumbling right before his eyes—but then the pieces became smaller and smaller until her body looked like a fine golden mist.

By coloring the atoms in a golden color, we are still aware of her presence. Otherwise, she would disappear completely. Pure atoms can undergo the rigors of space travel whereas

our intact physical bodies could never survive the incredible speeds and intense pressures we will experience tonight.

That made sense to Scott. He often wondered how super high-speed travel would be physically possible. Still, the process made him feel uneasy.

It is your turn, Scott. We can't leave until you change form. Focus on transforming into golden atoms.

Scott didn't know what to do. What if something went wrong? What if he couldn't change back or something happened to the ship? On the other hand, Zarco was out to kill him, and he needed all the help he could get.

He tuned in. His hands started to feel warm, which was always an indication that what he was about to do would be positive. His intuition was telling him that he would be okay, and that he could trust the Star People. Scott entered the chamber and closed the door. He closed his eyes and began to concentrate. He tried to imagine his body transforming, breaking into simple atomic particles.

He was able to watch his hands dissolve into a sparkly powder. It was like they were turning into gold dust. Then, more of his body was able to dissipate into a golden cloud of atoms. He could still think and have an awareness about him, but soon, it was as if his body was gone, and he was floating. It felt like there was nothing more to him than his consciousness. There was an incredible lightness in his being.

Scott wanted to look down at his body, but he no longer had eyes. All he had was perception. In his mind's eye, he had an impression of his golden cloud of atoms, but he couldn't actually see the atoms swirling around.

At the same time, his sense of intuition and knowing became extremely acute. It was as if he knew everything that was going on around him even though he had no eyes or ears to record what was occurring.

Scott sensed that Zocuul gave a signal to the captain and then changed as well. He didn't know what was going on in the control room, but in his mind's eye ventured into that room and sensed that the captain and first mate had also undergone this transformation.

Unlike the other flights, this one seemed to take a bit longer, and it felt like the ship was under extreme pressure. With all the jerky motions and rattles and crashing sounds, Scott wondered if the ship would survive in one piece. Then, finally, all the shaking came to a stop and Scott felt the ship come to a gentle landing.

Scott. It is time to change back now. Scott became aware of those words. He concentrated and within moments, he turned back into his human form. Zula and Zocuul had already transformed into solid shapes again. *Please follow us.*

He followed the two aliens out of the ship. They weren't carrying the language board, so Scott assumed he would have to rely on listening to their voices in his head.

Even though he didn't know where they were headed, he expected it would be someplace new and different, perhaps some futuristic world, and that thought excited him.

Chapter 33
A Light In The Sky

When they opened the door of the ship, it was a total surprise. They had landed on a planet with trees and grasses that looked very much like earth. It was late at night, and it appeared that the ship had touched down in a mountain meadow. The forest around them was alive with evergreens and hardwood trees, and the air had a crisp pine scent. The stars above were glorious.

Zula and Zocuul motioned for Scott to follow them. It turned out to be a fairly long walk, but Scott didn't tire. He felt like he was a little out of his body, almost as if he was floating.

Finally, their journey took them into a small village. There was a sign up ahead on the road, and as they got closer, Scott was able to read it. The sign said, "Welcome to Lake Arrowhead."

The village was small with just a few shops and restaurants and a penny arcade. As they walked down the main street, a young couple came out of the Bluebird Café. They appeared to be young and in love and swaggered a little as they walked with their arms around one another. Since the two people were humans and the sign he had seen was in English, Scott suspected that they had actually come back to Earth, but it appeared to be some time other than present day.

As the couple approached, Scott started to worry about being seen. "Won't they see us," he whispered to the aliens. "Don't you need to make them sleep?"

He waited for their answer, and it came quickly. Scott heard their words clearly in his head: *We've gone back in time. No one can see us or knows that we are here.*

"Do you think you can walk back to the cabin?" the man asked the woman.

"Of course I can. I only had one glass of wine... or was it three," she answered with a giggle. "How far is it, anyway?"

"Maybe a quarter of a mile," he said. "Just up there by the sign that says *Vacancy*," referring to a neon sign with a red arrow that blinked off and on.

As the couple came closer, Scott got a better look and almost fell over with shock. Excitedly, he whispered to the aliens: "That's my mom and dad!" He took a closer look and was somewhat amused, "when they were really young."

You don't have to whisper. They can't see or hear us, was the answer Scott received back from the aliens.

"They look so happy," Scott said but then became overcome with emotions. He stopped for a moment and his expression changed dramatically. He couldn't stop the tears.

What is the matter?

"They look so happy. Sometimes I just wish they were still to-gether," said Scott sadly. When he was young, he wanted his parents to get back together more than anything in the world, but as he got older, he knew that they were a terrible match.

Zula and Zocuul started to glow in their pink color as they felt Scott's emotions.

"I guess I wasn't expecting this," mumbled Scott. "I guess I wasn't ready... not for all of these feelings." He looked at the glowing aliens. "I don't know whether I should be happy or sad. It is so amaz-ing to see them together, and to see them so happy. But I feel really sad that they're not together anymore."

The aliens waited for Scott until he was ready to move on. The young couple was moving slowly, so once Scott regained his composure, it didn't take long to catch up.

They all walked past the office for *Lake Arrowhead Cabin Rentals and Tackle Shop*. The office was dark now, and the sign said: "Please call the manager for after-hours check-ins." Next to the entrance was a pay phone.

The rustic motel was made up of about a dozen small cabins. Each had a view of the lake and its own wooden deck that looked out over the water. The moon was reflecting on the lake's perfectly smooth surface. Rick and Judy stopped at Cabin 12 where Scott's Dad fumbled in his pocket for the door key.

"It's such a beautiful night tonight," said Judy. "Let's sit out on the deck, under the stars."

"Yeah," said Rick looking up at the sky. "Let's do that." He opened the door, and they went inside.

Scott turned to the aliens. "What year is this?

1949.

"Before I was born," Scott said as more of a statement than a question.

Yes.

A few minutes later, Scott's mom and dad went out on the deck, unfolded a couple of lounge chairs and sat back so they could look up at the stars. Scott and the aliens walked around the outside of the cabin to where they could see the deck. There was a row of sticker bushes that kept them from getting too close, but they could easily see the young couple from their vantage point.

"Look at all the stars. Isn't it beautiful?" observed Judy.

"You can see the Milky Way," said Scott's dad, pointing to the thick band of stars in the sky.

Scott turned to the aliens. "I remember he used to always point out the Milky Way to me when I was little."

"What's that!?!" called out Scott's mom. "That bright light is coming right towards us."

That was the last thing Scott's mom said before the two of them immediately fell into a deep sleep.

A light from the sky illuminated the entire area. The light was coming from far off in space, but the intensity was a thousand times stronger than the light of the moon.

"What's going on?" asked Scott who was starting to get nervous about the brilliant light up above.

There was no answer.

Then, from out of the sky, a gigantic spotlight came down and completely illuminated just his mother.

Scott's mother's body gently started to float out of her chair and rise up slowly in the air as if the light was some sort of tractor beam pulling her up into the sky.

Scott started to panic. He wanted to run to her and help, but the aliens held out their arms to stop him.

Remember, this is the past. This has already happened. We can't change anything in the past.

Scott heard what they said and stopped and watched. An alien ship had moved in and was hovering above. It was a diamond-shaped ship with a soft green glow. Scott's mother's body—illuminated by the beam of light—floated up in the air and entered the ship through an open hatch.

"That's one of your ships?" Scott observed.

A ship of our people. The two of us were not there or on the ship at that time.

"Wait a minute," said Scott to the aliens. "When, exactly, did this happen? What month is this?"

June.

"Wait, wait, wait, wait," said Scott in a panicky voice. He started counting on his fingers. "July, August, September, October, November, December, January, February, March..."

Scott started pacing nervously. "No, no, no. It can't be," he said, backing up as if he wanted to run away. "I can't believe it."

Does this surprise you?

"No—I mean yes. I mean, I don't even know what to think."

Chapter 34
Hybrid

You know you're one of us.

"I didn't know that for sure. I'm not sure I ever really believed it. And then to actually see it all happening like this," argued Scott, "is too much of a shock. This is the night my mother got pregnant with me..." he said as his body started to shake with an uncomfortable feeling.

"So, I'm a...a Star Person?"

You're a hybrid, alien and human.

"That can't be true."

It is.

"So that legend of the Star People, the mythology of the American Indians, really happened?"

Not just Indians. There were others. But it is extremely rare that an abduction ever produces a child. One in a million at best.

"But I thought the alien father was supposed to come back for the child when he turned five."

Usually that happens. But we needed to keep you hidden or else you wouldn't be safe.

"I've seen enough. We need to go now," shouted Scott. "I don't want to see anymore."

He turned and stomped off in the direction of the ship. Not a word was spoken during the long walk back.

He felt betrayed, as if his whole life was a lie. No wonder he didn't fit in with other people: he *wasn't* a normal person. How could they have done that to his mother? And what would his life be like now that he knew he was half alien and half human? His head was screaming with thoughts.

When they boarded the ship, they went back into the room with the glass tubes. Scott felt angry and hurt. His world had just been turned upside down. Yes, there were clues. Maybe he should have figured this out. After all, he sometimes knew when things were going to happen. He was able to turn his body into atoms. How crazy was that? He should have known, but it was still a shock. Until now he was excited by these amazing things he could do. Now that he knew the truth, it was upsetting and scary.

The message board lit up.

We are very sorry. We want you to know that the two of us had nothing to do with any of this.

Scott sat quietly for a few moments. Finally, he spoke up. "How do I know this is real? How do you even know how to find a specific time in the past, like this scene, in a wormhole?"

It is a very complicated system, but wormholes have layers or rings just like rings in the trunk of a tree. The more pronounced layers represent years, lesser rings represent months and the lightest of rings or layers are the days. We can program our systems to go back to exactly where we need to go.

The two aliens moved towards their shapeshifting chambers for travel.

We're sorry. We know this is hard, but we have to keep moving. We need to show you something else.

"I need to vaporize again," Scott said, half as a statement and half as a question. He was still upset and had more questions. "I don't know if I can concentrate enough to do that."

Take your time.

Scott sat down for a couple of minutes, then he reluctantly stepped into his glass chamber. After a couple of minutes, his atoms began to separate from his body. He was surprised that with all his anger he was able to focus enough to shift into the atomic state.

Moments later, the ship was off again. When it came to a stop, Scott was apprehensive. He materialized back into a physical being, but he was worried about what he might discover at this next stop. His stomach knotted up with angst.

Chapter 35
The Gift

After the next leg of the journey and they had landed, everyone in the group became solid once again.

When Scott got out of the ship, he was surprised but a little relieved to see that he was back in the field behind his home.

"Oh good, were back home. I think I've had enough for one night. I need to go to bed and try to make some sense of all this. I just need some time. Maybe we can look at things tomorrow night, but I can't handle anymore tonight."

The door of the shed was partly open revealing a glow from the inside.

"Who left the light on and the door open?" Scott said in an annoyed tone. He marched towards the door to see what was going on when out stepped an old man. The man looked very frail and moved quite slowly. His back was curved to the point where he couldn't completely straighten up. He had thin white hair and wore a pair of thick glasses. It looked like the left side of his body didn't move much. Everything was done with his right hand.

"Grandpa!" yelled Scott with excitement.

No reaction came from the old man who was slowly walking out in the direction of the field.

"Grandpa, it's me, Scott," Scott called out.

The familiar voices of the aliens came back into Scott's head. *He can't hear you. This is the past.*

"Is that really him?" asked Scott.

It is.

"I miss him so much." A wave of emotion swept over him. First, he felt incredible joy as he was able to once again see the man who had meant more to him than anyone in the world. The feelings were so strong that Scott sat down on the ground and put his head onto his knees. He tried as hard as he could to hold his tears back. "I wish I could just talk to him one more time. I've got so much to tell him now."

The aliens shook their heads, but Scott's mind was made up. He headed straight towards his grandfather until he noticed a small space-ship parked out in the field, about fifty feet from where his grandfather was standing. This was a much smaller ship than what Scott was used to—perhaps a pod—about the size of a small bus.

Even though the ship was different, he recognized the aliens. The aliens were Star People. They came out with their arms full, unloading materials from their ship and carrying those items into the work shed.

"I cleared a place in the back of the shed where no one should find any of these things for several years," said Scott's grandfather as he led the aliens inside.

They unloaded some thin lightweight sheets of metal and a large board that appeared to be fiberglass.

"Wait, that's all the stuff we used to build the *Mercury One,*" said Scott. Two aliens carried a familiar object from their ship. "And that's the propeller. I always thought the propeller was from an old hovercraft or something."

Zula and Zocuul shook their heads.

When the materials were unloaded, Scott's Grandfather turned out the light and latched the door to the work shed. Again, everything was done with the right hand and the left arm just hung still by the side of his body.

"This must have been just before the end because he died a few months after his stroke," added Scott.

"It's time," the old man said to the aliens.

They nodded and followed him.

"Is that Zin?" asked Scott, recognizing the alien with the scar who, upon their first meeting, had transformed into the red-haired boy.

It is.

Scott noticed that Zula and Zocuul were glowing in a greyish color. They looked as if they were weeping. Right then he realized that they were having the same reaction to seeing Zin as he felt seeing his grandfather again.

As they approached the house, Scott noticed something else. "Hey," yelled Scott. "That's our old station wagon in the driveway. We must have been spending the night at our grandparents." Scott ran towards the house and then stopped in his tracks. He turned and looked back at Zocuul and Zula. "Wow. Am I going to actually see myself as a kid?"

You are.

Scott, Zula and Zocuul followed his grandfather and two other aliens inside the house.

"And there I am," Scott said excitedly. "We used to sleep in sleeping bags on the living room floor when we visited Grandpa and Grandma." He turned to Zula and Zocuul. "You have no idea how weird this is to actually be able to see yourself as a young kid again."

Scott's grandpa pulled up the covers on Brett who was only about three years old at the time. Then, he turned to Scott. He brushed back Scott's hair and gave him a kiss on the forehead. Then, the elderly man held his hands about three inches above Scott's body and from his hands came a flow of energy that spun like a tornado and glowed in a bright violet color. As the energy flowed out of his grandfather's hands, it appeared that his own life force greatly diminished. The transfer of energy lasted about a minute. It was clear that the violet energy moved from Scott's grandfather into the young Scott.

When he was done, the old man looked at the two aliens who had come in the small ship and had accompanied him to the house. They nodded at him to imply that he did the right thing.

Make sure you close the door. Scott heard that voice in his head. It wasn't an alien voice he recognized. It was the voice of one of the aliens who had come in with his grandfather.

"Yes, yes," his grandfather said. "I have to deactivate it, so it will be dormant. I have to close the door in his conscious mind, so he won't be aware of any of this. He isn't ready yet." With those words, Scott's grandfather gently put his hands to Scott's temples for a few more seconds.

"What just happened here?" asked Scott.

You just received one of Zarco's powers.

Scott was stunned. The impact of this revelation paralyzed him for a minute as he finally began to understand the implications of this in relation to Zarco's obsession to get him.

* * *

Scott felt like his head was still spinning when he returned to the ship with Zula and Zocuul. He sat down in front of the language board.

"So, I am a Star Person?"

Part Star Person, part human.

"And my grandfather was half human, half Star Person as well?"

Yes.

Scott was trying to make sense of all the events he had witnessed that evening. "So, my grandfather held one of those powers or gifts that you extracted from Zarco?"

Yes, we hid Zarco's gifts inside individuals who we thought would look like ordinary humans in hopes that Zarco would never find them.

"And before my grandfather died, he transferred that gift to me?"

Yes.

"Is that what we just saw?"

Yes.

"Why would my grandfather give me a gift that would make Zarco want to kill me?"

The gift is an incredible honor and gives you powers you aren't even fully aware of yet. Your grandfather never knew about Zarco. He was never told because, at that time, Zarco had no idea that his gifts were being hidden on Earth. We thought if we could hide the gifts here, and prevent him from getting them back, he would eventually die of old age. All your grandfather knew was that he was giving you an incredible power, and he was trying to help us. He felt more connected to the Star People than he did to humans.

"He always called himself 'an odd duck,'" added Scott, but his mind wouldn't stop from wanting more answers. "How much did he know about all of this?"

His mind wasn't unlocked until the end. All he knew was that he had a gift which he had been able to access during the last few years of his life.

"But now Zarco knows the gifts are here."

Yes.

"And he wants them back."

Yes.

"So, this is how the gifts transferred from one person to another?"

One can voluntarily pass the gift from themselves to another person of their choosing, just as your grandfather did. This is usually done when that person is older and knows they will die soon. Or a gift can be stolen.

"How does that happen?" asked Scott.

A gift can be stolen or pulled from someone who is taking their last breath.

"So, it can be taken from someone who is dying?"

Yes. And that is how Zarco plans to get his gifts back.

"Isn't there anything you can do to stop him?"

Only one of the gift-holders has the power to defeat him.

Zula motioned to the glass chamber.

We must get you back to present time. The sleeping spell—as you call it—which sits over Stonebridge, will wear off soon.

Chapter 36
The Possum Snack Café and Gift Shop

The next day, Christina and Scott were sitting on the steps of the work shed porch. Scott had already explained much of what happened on the previous night.

"So, the reason you and Brett couldn't go last night was because the travel occurs at such an incredible speed, our physical bodies would never be able to survive. That's why we had to change into atoms inside those glass chambers I was telling you about. I'm not sure I understand exactly how that works. The way I think of it is like this: if you were put into a blender in solid form, you'd be pulverized, but if you were in a gaseous form, your atoms might get jostled, but you wouldn't be turned into a milkshake."

"A milkshake? Do you know how crazy this all sounds?"

"Of course, it does, but you can't call me crazy anymore because you've experienced this too. You were there at the pyramids."

"Maybe it's all a dream?"

"No, I've thought about that possibility, but I have this," said Scott as he pulled the fire stone from his pocket. It was the one Zula had given him at the great pyramid.

"What's that supposed to do anyways?"

"I don't know. I keep forgetting to ask. Zula said something about using it against Zarco.”

“So, he breathes fire, has a genus brain, arms and shoulders like Mr. Universe, and you’re going to defend yourself with a rock?”

They both laughed.

“Sounds a little silly, doesn’t it.”

Then the tone turned more serious. “You could die. He could kill you.”

“I know. I’ve thought about that a lot.”

“Are you scared?”

Scott thought about it for a moment. “Yeah, I’m scared to death, but I don’t see any way I can get out of this. I can’t just run away.”

“He’d find you.”

“I know. So, I try not to get scared because I know I can’t win if I’m in a state of fear. That would make me weak and vulnerable.”

“Like an animal being stalked by a predator.”

“Exactly,” said Scott. “If I have any chance of defeating him, it’ll take all the courage I have.”

“Do you think they’ll let me and Brett go with you next time?”

“Not if we go through another wormhole. I’m not sure normal humans can do that atom transformation thing.”

“I’d just like to be there to help if anything happens,” said Christina as she put her arm around Scott and pulled him close to her for a brief moment.

Scott didn’t know what to say. He felt his heart begin to race. In a world where he always felt like an outsider, it was the first time he had experienced affection from someone outside of the family, and the first time ever from Christina. He felt happy that she was there for him and couldn’t imagine what it would have been like to have gone through all of this alone.

“Thanks. I really do appreciate that,” was all he could think of saying.

“Scott, your dad’s here,” called out Scott’s Mom from the house.

“Oh no,” said Scott with trepidation. “Tonight’s the night he’s taking me and Brett to the movies. I totally forgot all about it. We set that up weeks ago, and with all of this alien stuff going on, it completely slipped my mind. I haven't been able to think about anything else." Scott turned towards the house and called out, "Okay Mom, I'll be there in just a minute."

"It was so strange seeing what everyone looked like years ago. I can't even tell you. Especially my dad. Did you know he used to have muscles in his twenties?""

Christina looked like she couldn't picture that. "No, I can't even imagine."

Christina paused for a moment. "When are we going up again?" she asked.

Between the adventures with the Star People and the news report about the Air Force looking into the Brotherhood flyover, Scott had insisted they stay on the ground. It had been over a week since their last flight.

"I just feel like we need to hold off for a while, especially with Zarco out there."

"Scott," Judy's voice called out again.

"I gotta go," said Scott getting up. "We'll talk about it later."

* * *

The following day was one of those summer days where the steamy air never seemed to move. There was no wind, just waves of heat rising up from the streets and sidewalks. The hummingbirds were chattering and chasing one another from the feeder, but other than that, it was too hot for even most birds to be out. There was the non-stop buzz of bugs and insects in the fields who seemed to sing their loudest when the summer heat was most intense. It was too hot to go outside, so Christina, Scott and Brett sat in front of the TV watching *The Shirley Show* to see if there was any recent news about flying saucers.

"Interest in the UFO sightings in the Massachusetts area has really been on the decline due to the lack of UFO activity in that area lately," announced Shirley. "It's been seven days since the last sighting."

A collective sigh came across the audience.

"That's the bad news." Then, Shirley's face brightened up. "The good news, however, is that there have been recent sightings in the back country of Alabama. And we've got Elwood Burke here, who started the latest frenzy of interest with claims that he was abducted by aliens the night before last."

Elwood was a true hillbilly with a twisted smile that revealed big black gaps where his front teeth used to be.

"What? What are they talking about?" questioned Christina. "The aliens aren't in Alabama. We're not in Alabama. It's here. It's all still here in Stonebridge, *not* Alabama."

"So, tell us, Elwood, in your own words, what happened to you?"

"Well, I seen a spaceship out yonder in the hills, and I says to myself, 'I best check it out and protect the earth and whatnot.'"

Everything Elwood said in his dull, monotonous voice sounded like he had made it up and rehearsed it a dozen times.

"So, I pick up my shotgun and call my dog, Blitzen, but Blizten di'n't wanna come on accounta he was too scared. So, I lock up my restaurant..." Then, Elwood turned and looked directly into the camera. "...the Possum Snack Café and Gift Shop on Highway 36 at Range Line Road."

"What?!? He's making this up!" blurted out Christina. "This is a shameless plug for his stupid cafe. He's just trying to get more business because no one wants to go to his lousy restaurant and eat roadkill." Christina seemed outraged.

"And then the little green men got off the ship and said, 'We are from Mars. We have come to take you away.'"

"You've got to be kidding." Now Scott was getting upset. "There aren't little green men on Mars. Everyone knows that. He got that from watching some old movie."

"Then I says, 'No, I can't come with you. I got delicious meals to fix at the Possum Snack Restaurant at Highway…'"

"He's plugging his restaurant again," interrupted Christina. "What a fraud."

"Do you think people are actually buying this?" questioned Scott. "People don't believe everything they see on TV, do they?"

Elwood continued, "Since I wouldn't go with 'em, they says, 'Take us to your leader.'"

"Nobody uses that old cliché anymore," interrupted Scott. "Where did they find this guy?"

"This is really upsetting," said Christina as she leaned back and crossed her arms. "He's trying to steal all of the excitement away from Stonebridge."

"This isn't fair," added Brett. "Now everybody's gonna go to Alabama."

Christina complained. "This is pathetic. This Elwood guy is a fake. I miss Earl." Christina switched the channel to the news and turned down the sound of the TV.

"Me too," said Brett.

"At least Earl told the truth," added Christina. "We need to go up again and give them something good to talk about." She timidly looked over at Scott.

"No. It's too risky," argued Scott. "Do you know how much trouble we'd get in if we got caught?"

"How are they going to catch us? With a net?" Christina argued. "We didn't get in trouble last time when we buzzed the camp. Everyone loved it. All we have to do is fly over, give everyone a thrill and then fly away again."

"It just feels kind of risky right now," answered Scott. "Just wait a couple more days when everybody's gone to Alabama, and then we can go any time we want."

"But what about Earl?" Christina reasoned. "No one asks for his autograph anymore, and those long lines of cars that used to be at his gas station are all gone now."

Brett nodded his head in agreement.

"And what about the Brotherhood Camp," argued Christina. "They are starting to pack up and go home. These last few weeks have been a blast. The whole country is excited about our little town. It's like being famous without getting in trouble. One fly-over would make everyone so happy."

"Come on, Scott," Brett pleaded.

"For Earl," Christina suggested.

On the TV, the scene flickered and changed back to the familiar face of Amy Sanders.

"Hey, it's the Brotherhood Camp," observed Brett.

As soon as Christina saw what was on the television, she quickly turned the sound back up.

At the Brotherhood Camp, the number of people still camping had dwindled significantly. Amy, the TV news reporter, was recording a live update while, behind her, many of the campers were packing up their cars.

"It's been seven days now since people here at the Brotherhood Camp had the thrill of a lifetime when they had the chance to see a real UFO. But since that time," Amy paused and looked upwards, "the skies have been quiet. There hasn't been a single sighting. Most of the campers have already packed up and headed home. Only the most dedicated are still here, and the word is that the last of the campers—even the ones who haven't given up hope—will leave tomorrow morning."

Amy stopped a young boy to ask a question. "Are you going home?"

"Yeah. I don't wanna, but Daddy says we have to 'cause he has to go back to work."

"Did you see any UFOs?" Amy asked.

The little boy shook his head. "I didn't get to but...but I wish I could."

"See how sad that little boy is," said Christina. "Think of all those people who came halfway across the country to see a UFO. Look at how disappointed they are. It would mean so much to them if they got to see what they thought was a *real* flying saucer. I think we should go up one more time."

"Come on, Scott." Brett pleaded. "We've waited a long time."

"If the rest of Brotherhood people leave tomorrow, then tonight is their last chance to see a UFO," said Christina. "Think about it, if you had traveled all the way to Stonebridge to stay at the Brotherhood Camp and look for UFOs, wouldn't you rather see some kind of mysterious flying object than go home without seeing anything at all?"

"Yeah, I suppose," said Scott reluctantly.

Brett and Christina looked excitedly at one another.

"After all, the *Mercury One* is technically an unidentified flying object even though it is an earthly one," Christina pointed out.

Scott smiled and shook his head as he thought about Christina's argument. "All right, but when?"

"Mom's going out tonight."

"Well, I guess things have kinda settled down around here," said Scott. Then he looked outside at the still, steamy hot day. "And there aren't any storms out there to blow us around."

"All right!!!!" exclaimed Brett.

* * *

Later that night, Christina sat on the porch of the work shed and waited, but Scott and Brett didn't come at the appointed time. It was a warm night, so she sat in the shade, sheltered from the last rays of summer sunlight.

Soon, it became completely dark. Christina patiently passed the time by watching the swarm of moths and bugs circling around the light on the back porch.

Finally, Scott came out of the house.

"Where have you guys been?"

"My mom's not feeling well. She's got a headache, so she won't be going out tonight."

"So, we can't fly?"

"No, not tonight."

"But what about those dedicated Brotherhood Campers?" asked Christina. "Tonight's our last chance to give them the sighting they've been waiting for."

"I wish we could, but we can't go while my mom's home. It's too risky. She might see us take off."

Christina thought about the situation. "Those people are going to be so disappointed."

"Yeah, I know."

"And then they'll all go to Alabama because of that Elwood guy on TV. It's not fair."

Christina thought about it for a moment and then said, "What if I go?"

"What?"

"What if I go? I can fly the *Mercury One*. All you have to do is distract your mom for a few minutes while I take off. Then, I'll go buzz the camp and come right back. We'll synchronize our watches and I'll be back here at..." She paused to look at her watch, "at 10:00. At 10:00 you'll have to distract her again so I can land.

"It won't take long, and I know how to fly it," Christina assured Scott. "I can go solo."

"I guess that'd be all right," said Scott with a shrug, "but how am I going to distract her?"

"You guys can play a game or watch TV or something."

"Yeah, I guess we could do that." He looked over at the shed where the *Mercury One* was stored between flights. "Brett and I already checked the ship out this morning to make sure everything was working right, and the batteries were fully charged."

"So, the ship is ready to go?"

Star People: Mystery of the Hologram

"It's ready."

"I wanna do it!"

"Okay, I'll help you roll it out of the shed, and then I'll go in and keep my mom busy for a while. Then, at 10:00 I'll distract her again so you can land." Scott looked at his watch. "I've got 9:38 right now."

Christina looked at her watch and made a quick adjustment. "Okay. It's set. I'm really excited. A little nervous, but I can do it."

They pushed the *Mercury One* out of the shed.

"Give me about five minutes to get things set up with my mom," said Scott, and then he wished Christina luck and went back inside the house.

Chapter 37
The Plan

Scott and Brett got their mom involved in a game of cards, but Scott didn't pay much attention to the game. He kept watching out the window for any signs of the *Mercury One*. He had arranged it so that Judy's back was to the window that looked out into the backyard. He kept patiently waiting, but when Scott never saw the homemade craft pass outside the window, he kept wondering how he possibly could have missed Christina's take-off.

Finally, a few minutes after 10:00, there was a knock on the door, and it was Christina.

"Hi Chris," said Judy. "You're just in time to take my place at the card table. I've got a terrible headache, and I need to go to bed."

"What are you playing?"

"Hearts."

Judy turned to the boys. "My head is killing me. I'm going to take one of those sleeping pills that knock me out, and I'm going to bed. Can you guys turn out the lights and make sure everything is locked up?"

"Sure, Mom."

"Bedtime is 11:00," added Judy. "Chris, you can stay 'til then if it's okay with your mom."

"My curfew is at 11:00 since it's not a school night."

"Okay. I'll see you in the morning," Judy said as she kissed both Scott and Brett on the cheek, "but *it won't be early*. You know how groggy those pills make me. I'll be dead to the world until about nine."

"Okay, Mom."

"Night everybody," Judy said as she headed for her bedroom.

As soon as she was gone, Scott whispered, "What happened? I never saw you take off."

"That's 'cause I never did."

"What? Why not?"

"It didn't work. It wouldn't fly."

"What do you mean?"

"The motors turned on and the propellers spun just like they always do, but it wouldn't leave the ground," said a frustrated Christina. "Not even an inch up in the air."

"Why wouldn't it fly?" Scott said partly to himself. "Brett and I checked everything to make sure it was working. If anything, with less weight, it should have gone a little faster and... maybe a little higher."

"Well, I don't know what went wrong, but I tried everything, and it wouldn't budge."

"Now I'm curious. I'd like to go try it out and make sure everything's all right," Scott said and then looked at his watch, "but it's too late now."

"Or is it?" asked Christina with an excited look on her face.

"What do you mean?"

"Let's go now," said an enthusiastic Christina.

"Yeah!!" added Brett.

"But Mom's here," objected Scott.

"Yeah, but you heard her, she'll be dead to the world as soon as her sleeping pill kicks in," argued Christina.

Scott thought about the idea but wasn't sure.

"How long will it take to kick in?" asked Christina.

"I don't know," answered Scott. "Maybe a half hour or so."

Christina leaned in and whispered to the others. "Okay, here's the plan. I'll go home and say goodnight to my parents and pretend to go to bed. Then, after my parents are asleep, I'll sneak out my bedroom window and meet you by the shed. We'll make sure the *Mercury One* is working all right, buzz the camp, and then come right back."

"Yeah, I like it," said an excited Brett.

"I don't know. What if—"

Christina didn't let Scott finish. "Look, this is our last night to give the Brotherhood people a thrill, right? And, if there isn't another sighting around here, everyone's going to go to Alabama to see the roadkill guy and eat at his restaurant, and you don't want that to happen, do you?"

"No," said a reluctant Scott.

"And if everyone goes there, then the aliens might go there as well."

Scott really wanted to see the Star People again.

"Oh, all right."

"Then it's all set," said an elated Christina. "I'll be back over here in about an hour."

"That'll be close to midnight," said Scott, looking at his watch and concerned about how long that would delay their flight.

"I have to wait until my parents are asleep," explained Christina. "Come on. We built the *Mercury One* so we could have an adventure. Now we're really going to have one."

Chapter 38
Starlight Adventures

It was after midnight when they rolled the ship out of the old wooden shed. It was warm and muggy, and the air was still. There was the steady sound of crickets all around them, and the intermittent buzz of cicada bugs up in the trees. And, once again, in the distance, the call of the great horned owls traveled back and forth across the hills.

They climbed into the craft and turned on the main motor.

"I hope it works," said Christina sounding very doubtful that the *Mercury One* would take off.

But when Scott increased the speed of the propeller positioned underneath the ship, the craft gently lifted skyward.

"So why wouldn't it work for me?" she said aloud, but no one responded.

The craft seemed to hover on top of the still, humid summer air. This time Scott steered in a different direction than they were used to. Instead of following the road into Stonebridge, they made a long, slow turn and swept over the woods where they used to play when they were younger.

Brett leaned over the side: "Hey, that's where we used to play hide 'n' seek. And there's that little pond that freezes over every year. Remember that year when it froze all smooth and we would go sliding across it on inner tubes?"

The others nodded, but they were quiet.

"Where are you going?" asked Christina. "I thought we were just buzzing the camp, but we're coming into Forestville."

"I just want to try something," answered Scott.

Usually, they would glide at a higher elevation, but tonight Scott was flying only about twenty-five feet above the city streets.

"What are you doing?" asked Christina. "We never fly this close to the ground. Aren't you worried someone might see us?"

"Since it's so late, no one's out on the road. I always wondered what it would be like if cars could fly, and since it's so quiet down there, it's one of the few times we can do this without being seen," said Scott coasting above Park Avenue, the main street of Forestville. The *Mercury One* floated above the traffic signals and road signs.

"You just ran a red light," Brett said with a laugh.

"It gets pretty narrow up ahead by the park," warned Christina.

Winding its way through the park was Park Avenue, the most scenic street in the city of Forestville. It was lined with giant deciduous trees, which, in the fall would turn into vivid shades of reds and gold.

"No problem. I can get through there."

The *Mercury One* made it through the trees with about five feet of clearance on either side. It was like flying through a forest.

Then Scott pulled the craft to a higher altitude, and it seemed like the ship had become a part of the night sky. It was higher than the *Mercury One* had ever flown on its own. There were a million stars around them, with only a crescent moon as the guardian of the sky. It felt as if they were light years away from earth, soaring through the heavens on their way to another galaxy, gently rising higher and higher.

It was silent except for the muffled sound of the motor, and they were above what little noise there was from the city streets below. It was as if the three of them had quietly become entranced by the majestic beauty of the celestial skies.

"You know, it's really awesome up here," observed Christina as she leaned back and looked up at the stars.

"I've always dreamed about doing this. Just being a part of the sky...part of the stars...part of the heavens. It's so peaceful." Scott motioned out the window in the direction of the moon. "I wish we could keep going and going—soaring under the starlight—and fly all the way to the moon."

The ship gracefully floated higher and higher as Scott, who was at the controls, went into a dreamlike trance focusing on the magnificence of the night skies and imagining what it really would be like to fly to the moon.

Finally, after a few minutes, Brett broke the hypnotic silence. "Hey, you guys, we're getting really high up in the air."

"What do you mean?" asked Christina, sounding like she was in a bit of a daze. Christina blinked a few times, then looked out the window with surprise. "Oh my gosh, Scott, we're like a mile high off the ground."

Those comments startled Scott out of his dreamy state of mind. He, too, was amazed at how high they had risen.

"That must mean the aliens are back," he said excitedly as he started to bring the ship back down in elevation.

Christina looked out each of the windows and out of the moon roof. "No. No, I don't see any alien ships."

"Me neither," added Brett also looking for visitors from outer space.

"They had to be here because it is impossible for us to fly that high in the *Mercury One*. It defies the laws of physics."

"What do you mean?" asked Brett.

"The *Mercury One* is like a hovercraft," explained Scott. "The air from the bottom propeller pushes us up from the ground. That is why we can only reach an elevation of about fifty feet. The aliens had to have been lifting us up because our ship can't go that high on its own."

Puzzled, Christina and Brett were still looking around.

"I don't know. I don't see signs of any alien ships," she said.

Without a word, Scott brought the ship back down to the elevation they were more accustomed to and then steered back in the direction of the Brotherhood Camp.

* * *

Only the most devoted Brotherhood members still remained in camp, numbering about fifty to sixty people. Those who weren't watching the skies had joined together for a final meeting and their last group meditation.

The gathering had gone well beyond midnight, and many of the members were staying up, visiting with old friends, and hoping for one final sighting on their last night in Stonebridge.

Finally, Roselda got up to say goodnight. "I'm afraid it's time for me to turn in. Goodnight, all. I'll be heading out early in the morning, and if I don't see you then, I wanted to tell you how great it was to see all of you again. Have pleasant dreams, everyone."

After the group said their goodbyes, Earl saw Roselda heading to her tent and caught up with her. "Roselda, you're not really leaving, are you?"

"I'm afraid so, Earl. It's time to move on. I'm leaving tomorrow morning."

"But you can't give up," Earl insisted.

"Who said anything about giving up?"

"Where'll you go?" asked Earl. Without giving her a chance to answer, he continued, "Are you goin' to Alabama? I hear there've been more sightings 'round there."

"I don't think so." It was clear by her voice that Roselda was discouraged. "I hear that the source of that Alabama information is pretty questionable. Turns out he owns a restaurant or trading post or something nearby, and they're saying that he might just be trying to generate some extra business for himself."

"So, where'll you go?" asked Earl sensing that Roselda was disappointed and trying to be understanding. When Earl thought about her leaving, he felt sad inside. He wondered if he would ever see her again.

"I think I'll just head home for a while," said Roselda.

* * *

"Do you think it's too late for the campers to see us?" asked Christina as the encampment started to become visible in the distance. "It's almost one in the morning."

"No, they still have a few people watching the skies all night long."

"What about the ones who are asleep?"

Scott thought about it for a moment. "We'll fly over twice," said Scott. "There'll be such a ruckus from our first flyover that it will wake everybody up. Then, we'll turn around and come right back so the ones who were asleep will have a chance to see us as well."

As they approached the camp, Scott turned to the others. "Okay, after we buzz the camp a couple of times, then we're going straight back home."

Scott steered the craft in a good position for a flyover.

Brett looked out the window. "There aren't very many of 'em left."

There were only a few scattered campfires and a handful of tents still standing in the field that was once covered with campers, RV's and excited sky watchers.

"That's all right," answered Christina. "We'll do it for the dedicated ones." She looked over at Scott. "You still wanna do this?"

Scott nodded. "For some odd reason, it feels like we need to," was all that Scott could say. Then, he turned to Brett. "Okay, Brett, get the lights."

The lights went out and Scott made a wide turn in preparation for the flyover.

* * *

As the *Mercury One* came closer to the camp, the spotters with binoculars and telescopes were the first to call out. Earl was on the way to his pick-up truck when he heard all of the commotion and ran back into the camp to be with the others.

A signal—the ringing of bells—rang through the camp and alerted the members to a possible sighting. Everyone on the ground immediately stopped what they were doing and looked up at the sky. They couldn't see much more than a dark, obscure mysterious flying object, but as the ship passed over them, a loud cheer rose up from the crowd.

By the time the *Mercury One* had turned around in preparation for its second pass, the remaining Brotherhood members were scurrying around at a frantic pace. From the tents emerged campers wearing pajamas and fuzzy slippers, some dressed only in underwear and others with curlers in their hair and night cream covering their faces. One camper hopped through the camp trying to get his shoes on while another was jumping around in a sleeping bag with a broken zipper. No one was going to miss this moment.

They quickly gathered torches and ran out to where they had so carefully laid out the message in the field. Flashes of light from lighters and matches ignited the torches and then those torches were, in turn, used to light up the letters arranged in such a way that they could only be read by alien crafts passing overhead. Earl was excited to be part of the crew assigned to the lighting of the letters. In his heart, he felt gratitude and elation that he was part of the effort to connect to the aliens in a peaceful way.

* * *

Brett was the first one to spot the glowing message. "Hey, you guys, look back at the camp. There's some writing down there in the field."

It was the message that Roselda had described to Scott when they had their meeting, and she gave him a tour of the camp. It took a few moments for the letters to ignite. From the air, the letters looked to be large, at least twenty feet across. At first only the letter 'W' lit up, but the fire quickly spread to the adjacent letters spelling out the word "Welcome."

Scott and Christina looked out the back window.

"Wait, there's more."

Finally, the entire message lit up in a bright yellowish-white color. It wasn't like a wood fire: it was some sort of material that glowed like white-hot embers. When all of the words were illuminated, it said: "Welcome to Planet Earth."

For a few moments, all they could do was silently stare out the back window of the *Mercury One* at the glowing letters.

Christina turned to Scott, "Thanks, Scott. I know we took a risk, but we made a lot of people really happy."

"I feel like we tricked them a little bit," confessed Scott.

"Maybe," said Christina. "But we are a UFO, and we gave them the thrill of a lifetime."

"Yeah, I guess so." Scott shrugged. "All right, let's go home now."

* * *

Earl came running back with a torch in his hand, searching for Roselda. A few minutes earlier, she had looked despondent, but now Roselda was radiant. Her eyes were beaming with joy. After the craft disappeared, she raised her arms towards the sky, and closed her eyes. Earl assumed that she was somehow communicating or sending out a message.

"I'm mighty glad they came back so you could see 'em one more time," said Earl as he extinguished his torch.

"Me too, Earl. Me too."

* * *

Scott, Christina, and Brett hated to leave the glowing letters that continued to smolder in the distance behind them. Gradually, the letters started to get smaller and slowly started to burn out, but it seemed to mesmerize them just the same.

So far, everything about that night had been calm and peaceful until they turned back away from the camp and headed for home. As they did so, emerging from the darkness heading straight towards them was a six-ton, combat-ready helicopter.

Chapter 39
The Chase

"Scott, look out!!!" Christina screamed.

"Hold on!!!" Scott yelled as he quickly decreased the power to the motor for a few seconds, causing the *Mercury One* to abruptly drop about thirty feet in elevation in order to avoid a collision. After the rapid descent, he gave *Mercury One* a quick burst of acceleration to get the engine back up to speed so the ship wouldn't continue to drop and crash into the earth.

"That was close!"

"Too close," Scott agreed as they rose again. "What is that guy trying to do, kill us?"

"I don't know," Christina said as she glanced out the window, "but he's not going away. He's coming back again. He's after us."

* * *

Colonel Barnes watched in wonderment as the little craft vanished from view, causing him to overshoot it. *It was a maneuver worthy of a dogfight*, he told himself as he looked around trying to relocate his target.

Then Barnes scanned the sky for a second Air Force helicopter, but it wasn't within sight. He got back on the radio to get some answers: "Rodriguez, where are you? You're supposed to be up here providing back-up."

"Sorry, Colonel," Rodriguez answered quickly. "I was lining up communications with our base camp and the local police force. We're all set up now to use the same frequency. If the alien ship goes down, the police on the ground will know immediately, and they'll be there in minutes."

"Right," answered Barnes, "but your job is to be here for support. Air Force protocol always requires a back-up in these situations, so get your chopper here on the double."

"I'm on my way, Colonel."

Barnes looked around, and as soon as he was able to spot the mysterious craft, he pushed the throttle forward and thundered over the Brotherhood Camp in pursuit.

* * *

"Oh, no! What are they doing?" questioned Roselda as the helicopter passed overhead.

"It's one of them military choppers from the Air Force camp," observed Earl.

"They're chasing them. The aliens come to our planet in peace, and we go after them with our war machines." She looked over at Earl. "We've got to do something."

Earl thought for a moment. "Well, I don't know that we can do anything to stop 'em in the air, but I gotta truck over there, an' I'm willin' to drive as fast as I can to see if there's anything we can do on the ground to help out."

"Let's go, Earl."

As they ran over to the field which had been used as a parking lot, Roselda asked: "Is it that tow truck over there?"

"Yeah, my regular truck ain't workin' so good right now, ever since I chased after that alien ship a couple of weeks ago, so I've been usin' the tow truck from the gas station."

They quickly jumped into the truck. Earl backed up, spun it around and then took off, building up his speed by pressing the accelerator all the way to the floor and maxing out the potential of the powerful engine. As he drove, he started fiddling around with the knobs and buttons on the radio and accidentally drifted onto the bumpy shoulder of the road causing the truck to bounce up in the air and then crash back to the ground.

"Earl, what are you doing? Forget the radio and watch where you're going."

"This ain't no regular radio. It's a police scanner, and I know what frequency the cops in town normally use. We'll know exactly what they know the second they do. Don't know if that'll do us much good, but it's something, and it'll help us know where to go."

Earl played with the dial until the sound of static was suddenly replaced by the chatter of the police dispatchers and the voice of what they presumed might be an Air Force officer, shouting orders and directing the police cruisers.

"Sounds like they got every unit they have out there," Earl said, working the radio with one hand while keeping the truck on the road with the other. "Canazera's probably leading the whole pack of 'em."

"Canazera?"

"He's the guy in charge at the Forestville Police station. Smart guy, but he's got a bit of a mean streak."

"You've had run-ins with him before?"

Earl smiled. "You could say that," he answered as he downshifted, sending a fresh surge of power through the truck, "nothin' too serious."

Earl listened as Barnes directed the police to head west of town in the direction they believed the mysterious craft was headed. "I know exactly where that is," Earl said as he made a high-speed, impromptu

U-turn slamming Roselda into the passenger door. He began racing back down the road, drawing a yelp from Roselda.

"Sorry 'bout that. It's not far, but we can't get there from this road. Don't worry, though. I know these roads like the back of my hand. I can get us wherever we need to go."

* * *

That night, when cameraman David Melies got the phone call, he was sound asleep, but the excitement of another UFO sighting quickly took over, and he was dressed and gathering his camera equipment in minutes.

On his way to the television studio, the news of the flyover and Air Force pursuit was on all of the car radio stations. There were interviews from eyewitnesses as well as reports about the helicopters that were chasing the unidentified flying object.

People were starting to come out of their houses to look up at the sky. David figured that if the helicopters didn't wake them, then they had probably received calls from friends or neighbors.

As he drove into the studio parking lot, the News Eight helicopter was waiting. He had never ridden in a chopper before and was feeling the adrenaline start to flow as he thought about being able to follow a real UFO in the air.

Amy, the news reporter, was talking to an older man who David assumed to be the pilot. But there was another man with them. The other man looked familiar, but he couldn't place him.

"Is this your cameraman?" asked the older man as David approached.

"It is," answered Amy. "David, this is our pilot, Mitchell. Mitchell, this is David."

Mitchell, the News Eight pilot, was a friendly old guy who looked to be a few years from retirement and seemed to have the calmness and confidence of someone who'd been flying for years.

After that introduction, David turned to the other man, so he could introduce himself and then stopped abruptly, "Ron?"

"That's right, Ron Covington. And you are—"

"David. We met at the Brotherhood Camp."

"Oh, yeah. I remember now."

David wasn't sure why Ron was there. "Are you a reporter?"

"Sure am. Work for *The National Reporter*."

"And you're coming with us?"

"That's right. The same company that owns Channel Eight also owns the *National Reporter*," said Ron. "Everything's run by big conglomerates these days."

"Hey, we need to get going," interrupted Mitchell as he directed the two men to get into the back and Amy to get into the passenger seat next to him.

As Mitchell started working the controls, he said, "This must be big. They don't send out the news copter unless it's a major story."

After he fired up the engine, Mitchell tuned his scanner to the same frequency that was being used by the police and the Air Force. "Good, everyone's on the same frequency. That way we can be in position to get the best coverage."

The helicopter lifted off with its tail slightly higher than the cabin. Amy quickly grabbed her stomach, and David grabbed hold of the seat in order to brace himself.

As they were gaining altitude, a report with an updated position came in on the radio. "They aren't far from here," Mitchell said after hearing the location of the Air Force choppers, "only a couple of miles away."

"Good, let's go." David kept his camera ready. He felt like this was the most exciting thing he'd ever done in his life. He couldn't help imagining what it would be like to be the first news cameraman to capture live footage of a real UFO.

A helicopter circled around and approached the *Mercury One* at full speed. Scott frantically steered out of the way, avoiding a collision.

"Wow, he came right at us again!" exclaimed Christina.

Initially, Scott didn't know who the helicopter belonged to, but this time it came so close he could see the Air Force emblem and lettering on the side of the ship.

"It is the Air Force," said Scott confirming what he had suspected.

"Do you think we can get away from them?" asked Christina.

"They're so much faster than we are. They can fly circles around us. I'm doing everything I can, but we have to think of an escape plan."

"Where's the helicopter now?" asked Scott.

"Right behind us. I can see him through the back window," answered Brett.

"But then—" Scott stopped in mid-sentence. "What's that coming up on our right?"

"It's another one," confirmed Christina. "There's two."

"And it's got the Air Force emblem as well."

Seeing a second Air Force helicopter made Scott feel like a spike had just been driven into his stomach. Both helicopters had searchlights attached to the sides of their crafts which blinded Scott when they illuminated the *Mercury One* with their powerful beams. Scott tried to stay away from the searchlights, but the two military pilots were persistent and kept flying at them.

* * *

As Colonel Barnes continued his pursuit of the *Mercury One,* another message came in on the radio: "Colonel Barnes, this is Air Force ground control reporting from base camp. We are picking up another flying object on the radar." At first, Barnes's body tensed up with fear. *What if it was another alien ship—perhaps a heavily-armed warship—coming to the defense of the first craft?*

But the message continued: "It looks like it could be a third helicopter, perhaps a civilian chopper. It is heading your direction, coming from the east, over."

"What!?!" barked Barnes with annoyance. Whatever it was, he had to check it out, and that meant it took his attention away from the chase of the UFO.

Barnes pulled back from the action for a moment so he could get a better look. "It *is* another helicopter," he radioed back to base camp. Then Barnes got on the radio and spoke directly to the intruding chopper: "Air Force 619 to unidentified helicopter, this is Colonel Gregory Barnes of the United States Air Force, identify yourself immediately."

There was a long pause before the pilot's timid voice came on the radio: "This is Sky Chopper News Eight."

"This is Colonel Barnes of the U.S. Air Force, and I am ordering you to vacate this area immediately. This is a military mission. Keep all civilian personnel out of this area. I command you to land at once."

* * *

Mitchell quickly gave in. "I guess we'd better turn back."

"We can't land now," protested Amy. "This is the biggest story of our lives."

"I agree," shouted David from the back seat. "The people have a right to know what happens, and we are the only news crew around here to cover it."

"He can't order you to land, can he?" asked Amy.

"If it's a military emergency he can. I could lose my pilot's license, possibly go to jail."

"But this might become another government cover-up," protested David. "If we don't watch their every move, it might become another Roswell. We have to get this story. What if you tell them that we'll keep back at a safe distance?"

"I don't think they'll go for that," Mitchell answered.

"But it won't hurt to ask, would it?" asked Amy.

The pilot fingered his mike button and told Barnes he would move back to a safe distance, but the reply was an abrupt demand that he land immediately. "I tried," Mitchell said as he shrugged and looked as if he was about to turn the chopper around.

"Here, give me that communications device," Ron said from the back seat. "Let me talk to the Colonel, we're buddies," said Ron with a wink. Mitchell handed him his headset.

Covington put on the headset and immediately started making static noises with his mouth. There was hissing and clicking sounds coming from his teeth, tongue and pursed lips. "Sorry Colonel, we're having a hard time hearing you. You're breaking up. All we heard was that the Air Force has a confirmed sighting of a UFO and is mounting an attack. Is that correct, sir?"

* * *

Colonel Barnes cocked his head as if he couldn't believe what he was hearing: "What?!? That is not correct! I said nothing of the kind."

The same voice came through on Barnes' radio. "Just want to make sure I heard you right. There's a lot of static on this end. Please confirm, you said, 'That is correct.'"

"Negative," answered Barnes forcefully. "I said NOT correct. NOT Correct. I am not confirming that statement. I repeat, you are interfering with a military operation and are hereby ordered to return to your point of departure immediately. Understand?"

"Sorry, didn't get all that," came the voice from Copter Eight. "All I heard was something about the Air Force planning a cover up. Please confirm."

                    Star People: Mystery of the Hologram

"No, I will not confirm. I said nothing of the sort," yelled Barnes. "Get your ship out of military air space. Repeat: Get your ship out of military air space."

"Trouble with transmission, Colonel," was the reply accompanied by a barrage of hissing, clicking and guttural sounds. "We *did* receive your last message, and I quote: Air Force has taken an alien hostage. Repeat, Air Force has taken alien hostage. We will disseminate that information to local media."

"What!?! Who is this?" shouted Barnes into the radio. "Is this that goofball, Ron Covington?"

Barnes' earlier confusion was quickly replaced by rage now as he realized what the guy in the news chopper was up to. "I'm warning you, Covington. I'm about to shoot down a news helicopter if you clowns don't get outta here in about three seconds."

* * *

Mitchell took the headset back. "That's enough games for tonight folks," he said forcefully. "I doubt if they'd ever do that, but I'm not in the mood to find out," he said as he spun the chopper around.

"So, you're giving up?" Amy asked as the chopper headed back towards Boston.

"That's right," Mitchell replied. "I'm two years from retirement; I don't need to be a hero."

"C'mon, he wouldn't shoot. We're setting up a live feed to the station," said David. "If he tried anything like that, he'd be tried for murder. He's bluffing!"

"Good bluff," Mitchell replied as he pushed the throttle forward in an attempt to put more distance between himself and the Air Force chopper.

"Look, Mitchell." Amy spoke in a voice David could barely hear from the backseat. "This story may not mean anything to you, but it means a lot to us. I owe my cameraman back there a second chance," she said motioning to David. "I think I may have lost him his big break. We were at the Brotherhood Camp, covering the story of a lifetime, and he missed it because I talked him into going to a disco. I want to give him another opportunity—and this is it."

Mitchell didn't answer.

"Look, I'll take the heat for whatever happens. All we have to do is keep an eye on things from a safe distance just in case anything big happens. Surely, they wouldn't care as long as we stayed out of the way."

"I get what you're saying, but I don't wanna go to jail or lose my retirement."

Amy looked exasperated. Then, she tried another approach. "Look, how long have you been in the news business?" she asked.

Mitchell took a look at her. "Probably since before you were born."

"And didn't you ever take any risks to cover a story?"

"Every damn day when I was a war correspondent in World War II."

"And now you're going to put your tail between your legs and run away?"

Mitchell hesitated and thought about it for a minute. "In my forty-three years in the news business, I never turned and ran from a story before," he said with pride. He stopped and gave the situation some thought. "And I ain't gonna start today."

Mitchell made a sharp one-hundred-and-eighty-degree turn.

"Thank you, Mitchell. You're a good man."

Mitchell started to soften. "Well, it does seem like a big story, and I kinda want to see for myself what happens."

* * *

Scott kept the *Mercury One* low and close to the treetops, flying with a skill he didn't even know he possessed. He was especially adept at zigzagging between the trees, giving the craft cover from the Air Force choppers who were hovering in the distance, illuminating the forest with their searchlights.

"How are you doing this?" Christina asked with a tone of awe in her voice. "I can barely see anything and you're swerving right through the woods like it's broad daylight."

Scott nodded. "See those?"

"See what?" Christina asked as she tried to see what Scott was talking about.

"Those little blue orbs just ahead of us."

It took Christina a minute to see them, but soon she was able to clearly make out a rotating circle of blue orbs several yards ahead of their vessel, moving through the trees.

"What are they?" she asked.

"I don't know, but I spotted them the second we came down over the trees. I've been following them as best I can. They seem to be leading me."

"Scott, look behind you," Brett warned.

A helicopter suddenly came right up to the window behind them.

"Hang on," said Scott as he directed the craft towards the orbs. While he took them slightly down in elevation, this time it was a much more gradual drop.

"See, that time the orbs told me not to go as low, and the helicopter guessed wrong and ended up going underneath us."

"He's turning around and coming back," warned Brett. "He's coming up on your tail."

"Hold on," Scott yelled as he piloted the ship into almost a straight vertical drop while steering directly at the orbs.

It worked. The *Mercury One* moved far too slowly to outrun the Air Force, but Scott avoided a collision by following the orbs and rapidly changing direction and altitude.

* * *

Barnes kept trying to corner the small ship, but the vessel was too crafty. He was both frustrated and in awe of the skills of whomever was behind those controls.

"Damn...we lost 'em again," exclaimed Barnes. *How did they do that? For a ship that's so slow and clumsy, that was an incredible maneuver.*

"I can't believe they got away from us. We had them..." Barnes radioed to Rodriguez.

"They were cornered with no escape," answered Rodriguez, "but somehow they pulled it off."

"Don't worry, Rodriguez, they haven't gotten away yet. We can still bring them down."

Colonel Barnes was watching the radar screen while he talked on the radio. "Attention all ground support, apparent course of UFO has changed, and the unidentified craft is heading northeast towards the city of Forestville."

* * *

Aboard News Chopper Eight, David finally got the signal that the station was ready to go live. "Put your headset on, Amy. We're going live in thirty seconds."

"Let me turn on the monitor, so you can watch what's going on at the station," said Mitchell as he turned on a small screen that was mounted on the dashboard and was directly connected to a feed from the Channel Eight studio.

At that moment, a blurry-eyed Bill Danville was straightening up his tie and smoothing down his disheveled hair. He appeared to have bolted out of bed and just arrived to cover the story.

As soon as Danville got his cue, he quickly snapped into position. "We are interrupting your regularly scheduled programming at this time to bring you this special late-night story as it unfolds in the skies over Forestville. We have word that there has been another UFO sighting in the Jefferson County area and two Air Force military helicopters are in pursuit of the unidentified craft. In a moment we will be providing live coverage from Weather Chopper Eight and reporter Amy Sanders, who is there at the scene. Amy, can you hear me?"

Amy was beginning to look a little pale from the ride. She took a moment to compose herself.

"Yes, I can hear you, Bill."

"What's happening?" Bill asked.

"We're about five miles northeast of the city of Forestville watching two Air Force helicopters pursue what appears to be an unidentified flying object."

"A *UFO?*" Bill confirmed, in what sounded like an effort to grab the attention of the audience. "Have you had the opportunity to get any footage of the object at this point?"

"No, unfortunately, we haven't been able to get close enough for that yet. We do have our cameras running, though, and hope to be able to get some footage to you soon. Naturally, we don't want to interfere with Air Force operations, but we're following every minute of this pursuit so we can keep our viewers up to date."

"Where are the helicopters now?" Bill asked from the studio.

Amy signaled for David to turn the camera toward the horizon. A second later the lights from a pair of helicopters could be seen in the distance. "It's hard to make out exactly what's happening," she explained, "but you can see the lights of the two helicopters in the distance. It appears as if they have been aggressively pursuing what we believe is some sort of alien craft.

"Our outstanding cameraman, David Melies, is here with us," Amy added, "and he is dedicated to capturing every second of the mid-air chase."

"Can you tell what the helicopters are doing now?" Bill asked.

"It's hard to say, but—"

Amy jumped as a flash of light suddenly lit up the horizon, illuminating the surrounding area for miles in every direction.

Chapter 40
On The Run

"Something's happening!" Amy shouted, responding to the blinding flash of light. "I don't know if they've attacked the UFO or what! I can't tell."

"I think it's a flare," Mitchell said off camera, trying to calm Amy.

"A flare? Is that what you think it is? How do you know?"

"I'm pretty sure," whispered Mitchell. "I've seen the military light 'em off before."

"Bill, we think that the helicopters might have ignited a flare," Amy reported back to the studio.

"So, you think they're firing flares at the object?" Bill asked, trying to regain control of the interview.

Amy nodded. "It looks like it! I don't know why they would do that—perhaps to see better—but that's what appears to be happening. And now the helicopters are moving more aggressively, as if they've spotted something. We're going to go in closer now to get a better look," she said, nodding at Mitchell, who reluctantly pushed the throttle forward and headed towards the light show on the horizon.

"I am so going to lose my license over this," Mitchell mumbled under his breath as they closed in on the action.

* * *

When the flare ignited, Scott, Christina and Brett were temporarily blinded by the brightness. Scott thought his heart was going to explode.

"What was that? Are they shooting at us?"

After the initial shock had passed and Scott had a moment to assess the situation, he said, "I think it's a flare."

"A flare? Why are they doing that?" asked Christina.

"It's probably so they can see us better. It lights up everything." Scott turned the ship to get away from the illuminated area. "Let's get out of here."

Christina's face was looking tired and worried. "What're we gonna do?"

"I don't know," answered Scott who was surprisingly calm and composed. "We can't go home or else they'll follow us. If they know where we live, they'll find out who we are. Then we'll really be in trouble."

"But they won't leave us alone," said an exasperated Christina.

"Scott, look behind you," Brett warned.

A helicopter suddenly became visible in the rear window right behind them.

Scott dropped the *Mercury One* lower over the city of Forestville and then spotted his destination.

"Where are you going now?" asked Christina.

"The park in Forestville," answered Scott as he carefully swooped down and flew the craft between the rows of trees on Park Boulevard, the same route they had taken earlier that evening.

"We can fly just above the boulevard. They're too large to follow us in there," Scott said as he navigated the ship through the tight space between the trees, "it's too narrow."

The helicopter that was following so closely behind them had to pull up as it approached the tree-lined passageway. Instead, it hovered at the far end of the boulevard and appeared to be waiting for the

Mercury One to reemerge so it could continue the chase. But when Scott reached the end of the street, he wove between some of the trees in the park and then turned and flew back down the boulevard in the direction from which he had come.

"It worked," said Christina. "Now he's got to turn around. He's facing the wrong way."

"I have another idea," said Scott.

"What's that?"

"I was thinking about the barn at Miller's Pond. It's about ten miles from here. Maybe we can land in there and from above it'll look like we just disappeared. Maybe we can lose them that way."

"It's worth a try," said Christina.

Scott stayed low over the city so the helicopters couldn't get too close. The *Mercury One* could easily dip under or fly around tall trees. The helicopters still followed them but were too large to match their tight maneuvers.

* * *

As Barnes continued his quest, another message came in from the Air Force base camp: "Colonel Barnes, this is Air Force ground control communications from the base camp. Sir, we thought you should know that the News Chopper, which is still up in the air at this time, is providing a live feed to the television station in Boston. Every move you make is being seen on live TV across the country, over."

Barnes shook his head and mumbled a few angry words to himself, then got back on the radio and tried to regain his composure, "Thank you for the heads up. I'll pass the word on to Rodriguez."

"And sir, they're asking for an update on the situation. Do you want to give them a statement? Over."

"That'll have to wait," said Barnes. "I'll talk to them when this is all over."

* * *

Two police cars passed Earl's truck. A third police car crossed in front of them at the intersection.

"They got police cars goin' everywhere," observed Earl. "Our only hope is if we can get there first," he said as he stepped on the accelerator.

Earl was doing what he called "country drivin'," bouncing over ditch banks and occasionally cutting through fields when he needed to get from one road to another. The tow truck had been keeping up thanks to the information from the police scanner and thanks to Roselda's sharp eyes as she kept her attention on the action in the sky.

As Roselda watched the helicopters chasing the craft, she became more and more upset. "Why are they doing this? The aliens haven't hurt anyone. Why can't they leave them alone? They've come in peace, and we're chasing them away. No wonder they're afraid to visit."

The police scanner blurted out an updated report of the location of the unidentified flying object as being over the shopping mall in Forestville. When Earl heard the position, he pulled the truck over and pounded his hands down on the steering wheel in frustration.

"What's the matter?"

"They just flew over the shopping center," said a dejected Earl. "That's way off in the other direction. We're miles from there. Every time we go one way, they go the other."

"We can't give up."

"No, I ain't givin' up, jus' frustrated, that's all."

He turned the truck around and raced back, in the other direction, towards the town of Forestville.

* * *

"Scott, look down there. There are police cars everywhere," said Brett.

Numerous police cars, with their red lights flashing and sirens blaring, were speeding through the city streets.

"Actually, there are a bunch of regular cars down there, too," said Christina as she looked out the window. "It looks like all kinds of people are watching us."

Scott looked down at the shopping center. He could see the multitude of flashing lights. "Once we head back out into the country towards Miller's Pond there aren't many roads. At least that way, the cars can't follow us."

"Let's do it."

"But I still don't know what to do about the helicopters."

Christina looked up through the moon roof. "Scott, there's a chopper right above us!!!"

"Get ready, I'm gonna do a hard right...now!!!" As Scott finished his sentence, he jerked the steering lever to one side, cut back on the power, and the ship took a sharp turn. He discovered that by cutting the power to the propeller under the ship, he could use the force of gravity to get the *Mercury One* to turn much faster.

Christina watched out the window. "You lost them for a minute, but they're coming back. Isn't there anything else you can do?"

"No," said Scott shaking his head. "Those helicopters can go about 100 miles per hour. They can move a lot faster than we can."

"Maybe we should give ourselves up," suggested Brett.

A firm "NO!!!" came from Scott and Christina at the same time.

"Scott, there's another helicopter hovering over the mall," said Christina. "But it's not from the Air Force. It says News Chopper Eight. I think it's the weather chopper for the TV station."

"Good. At least that helicopter won't attack us. I'm going to go underneath the news chopper so I can get these Air Force guys off our tail."

With that, Scott darted under the weather chopper and the two Air Force helicopters had to pull away from their pursuit in order to avoid a collision.

* * *

After being forced to turn away from the chase, an angry Colonel Barnes got back on his radio: "News chopper, I thought I ordered you to land! You just interfered with a military operation. That is a Class A violation. I want to talk to the pilot."

"What's a Class A violation?" asked Amy.

Mitchell shrugged. "I don't know. Probably some military rule."

"Don't worry, I can handle him," said Ron taking back the headset.

"Sorry, Colonel, the pilot is busy right now. He is flying the ship, but I can talk to you. Would this be a good time for an interview?"

"No, it isn't! I want to talk to the pilot."

"Sorry, Colonel, you're breaking up again," said Ron with another barrage of crackling and shushing sounds coming from his mouth. "I think you said you've been talking to the pilot of the alien ship. Does that mean the aliens can speak English? Or is it that you can speak their language because you too are an alien perhaps in a clever disguise? Please confirm that you are an alien, over."

The news crew could hear Barnes mumbling, "I don't have time for this idiot," and then a loud click indicating that Barnes had turned off his communication to the news chopper.

* * *

A booming voice came over the radio in Earl's truck. "This is Air Force Sky Two," said the voice over the police scanner. "Unidentified craft is now heading south southwest. Please provide approximate location for ground support."

Earl pulled the truck over on the shoulder and waited for a reply.

There was a short delay before a response came: "It looks like they are heading out towards Highway 95 and Eagle River Road, over."

When Earl heard the latest message on the radio, he let out a scream of joy. "They're headed right for us, Roselda. They should be passin' overhead any moment now."

Another voice emerged from the scanner. "Colonel, I have instructed our squad cars to take different roads out of town in all directions."

"That's the police chief, Canazera, again," added Earl. "Sounds like he's talkin' directly to the Air Force pilot."

The voice on the radio continued. "That way we cover the most territory. We might not be able to stay right with them, but one of us should be in the area if they land. Current direction of UFO is moving towards Highway 95 and Eagle River Road. I've instructed four cars to get on Highway 95. Can you confirm? Over."

A few moments later, just as Earl predicted, the unidentified craft, followed by the Air Force helicopters, flew directly overhead.

* * *

Suddenly, a message for Barnes came in—on a private channel—from Rodriguez: "Colonel Barnes, this slow-moving vessel would be an easy target. Now that they are over the open countryside away from civilians, I could easily take them down with one shot."

"Negative, Rodriguez, do you hear me!?! Absolutely not!!! Even if we are out in the country, we cannot risk civilian casualties. And now our every move is on live TV. We've got a news chopper on our tail and probably half of the country watching in their living rooms. If we shoot them down, it would be a public relations nightmare for the Air Force. Do you read me?"

"Yes, sir. I read you."

"But, Rodriguez, I think we can force them to have a little mishap, if you know what I mean. And we could say they just accidentally crashed on their own. Do you understand what I am suggesting?"

"Loud and clear, Colonel."

"Good, bring your chopper up on my right side. I have a plan."

Scott turned to Brett and Christina. "If we don't lose them at Miller's Pond, when I land in the barn, I can let you two out, so you'll be safe. If you go home on that trail through the woods, it's only a few miles and no one will see you. No one will ever know that you were on the ship because when I take off again, they'll follow me. That way I'll be the only one who gets caught."

"I'm not getting out there," said Christina. "I'm not leaving you."

"Me neither," added Brett.

"We're in this together," said Christina. "But maybe once we land in the barn we can come up with another plan if we need one."

"Okay, but we've got another problem."

"What's that?"

"The battery for the engine only holds enough charge for about an hour and a half of flight time, and we're getting close to that now," he said pointing to his watch. "If we run out of power while we're in the air, we'll have to land right away or else we'll crash. It's not like a glider where you go down slowly. We'll drop like a rock."

* * *

Barnes could see the other Air Force helicopter outside his window as they flew parallel to one another. "Okay, Rodriguez, you're with me now, so I want to try something. Stay in current position. We'll take a long turn at 35 degrees, so they'll think we've given up, and then we're gonna come back around and force them down by approaching the alien craft head on. If the ship goes up or to the right, she's yours. If she goes down or to the left, I've got her. I expect she'll drop altitude again because that's been her pattern, but this time I'm going to go so low that she'll have no room to duck beneath me."

"Affirmative, Colonel." answered Rodriguez. "Where do you approximate position of confrontation?”

“I expect the confrontation to be right over that group of trees about a mile to the west. We can use the trees to our advantage. I want to force the ship to crash by cutting them off just above the tree line.”

Colonel Barnes was determined. *You're not getting away this time. We got you now.*

* * *

“How come it got quiet all of a sudden?” asked Scott. “What happened to the helicopters?”

“It looks like they're flying off in the other direction. Maybe they gave up,” suggested Brett.

“I don't think so,” said Christina. “Why would they give up now?”

Scott was cautious. “Something's up. I don't like this.”

“But the orbs are back,” pointed out Christina. “They formed a target over there.”

“Yeah. I'm still following ‘em.”

Suddenly the glare of searchlights filled the cockpit again as the lead chopper skewered them with its beam, temporarily blinding Scott.

“Scott, look out!!!” yelled Christina.

Scott spotted a second helicopter hovering just above the tree line, a few yards away, and realized he was on a collision course.

All three of them screamed as Scott forced the ship down to avoid a collision with the helicopters, but as the ship dropped, it was impossible to avoid crashing into the treetops.

“Hold on!” Scott shouted as he saw a massive branch come into view and knew there wasn't a thing he could do about it. “We're going down!”

Instantly, the air was filled with a loud explosion followed by the sickening sound of snapping branches. There were scraping and scratching noises as the tree limbs dug into the sides of the craft. The front windows went dark from the dense foliage, and the screams from inside got louder and louder as the *Mercury One* sunk deeper into the thick tree limbs, until suddenly, everything went silent.

Chapter 41
Marooned

"We got 'em!" Barnes shouted as he watched the craft disappear into the top of a massive maple tree, followed by the sight of leaves and small branches tumbling to the ground. "Where'd they go? Do you see them? Are they on the ground?"

Barnes turned his searchlight on and began scanning the ground, but other than some broken branches, there was no sign of the vessel. "I'm not seeing them, Rodriguez. Are you sure they went down?"

"Affirmative. I saw them go into that big maple tree."

Barnes spun the light around and began moving the beam across the top of the tree. Finally, he spotted a dark object perched precariously within its upper limbs.

"I see them now, Rodriguez. They're stuck in the upper branches of the tree. They don't appear badly damaged, but they're not going anywhere."

Rodriguez' voice immediately came on the scanner, "Command Center, the ship is down. Repeat, alien ship is down. Provide position for ground support immediately, over."

The response came within seconds: "Ground support, this is Air Force Command Center. Alien ship is down, and we need immediate ground support from all units available. Approximate location is about one-half mile west of 95. Take the Eagle River Road turnoff from Highway 95 and head south."

* * *

"They've crashed!" Amy shouted over her headset, startling everyone in earshot. "Those helicopters just forced the UFO into the trees! It's down!"

"The helicopters forced it down?" Bill Danville asked. His expression on the monitor screen was one of astonishment.

"It looks like it," Amy said breathlessly. "I can't believe it! It looks like they forced it to crash!"

"What does the craft look like?" Bill asked.

"We're too far away to get a good look from here," answered Amy as she squinted in the direction of the collision. "Mitchell, can't you get us closer?" she said to the pilot.

"I don't know," said Mitchell. "Not sure how the choppers would react."

"They're concentrating on the UFO," David said from the back seat. "They won't do anything, especially if we're filming them."

"He's right," Amy added. "We've got to get closer."

With a sigh of defeat, Mitchell pushed the throttle slowly forward, moving the media chopper towards the crash site.

* * *

"Oh my God, they forced them to crash. They tried to kill them," said Roselda when she heard the details of the crash over the police scanner.

"Now, why would they go and do that?" asked Earl, feeling both angry and sad.

Since they were already in the area, Earl and Roselda reached the turn off to Eagle River Road ahead of everyone else. Eagle River Road was a narrow dirt road that led back into the woods to a popular fishing spot Earl knew well. Earl pulled off the road and started to strategize.

Earl could see the red lights of a pair of police cruisers approaching from behind him, in the distance. "Looks like we got company."

"We've got to get there first. We don't know what they might do to the aliens if we aren't there to stop them."

"Okay, Roselda, I got a plan. There's only one road into them woods, and this is the turn-off to get there."

The entrance to Eagle River Road from Highway 95 cut narrowly between two enormous outcroppings of rock. Earl wedged his vehicle between the two rock formations so that it blocked the access to the road. The truck was positioned so that no one could get in or out of the area.

"I may not be able to do anything about them helicopters, but the police cars ain't gonna be able to get onto Eagle River Road as long as it's blocked. I'll probably spend the night in jail for this, but I can't think of anything else to do."

Roselda looked at Earl with a look of gratitude.

"Now, Roselda, can you see that group of trees where the helicopters are shining their lights?"

"Yes."

"That looks like where the ship went down. You'll have to get there on foot, but if you set out as fast as you can, maybe you can help somehow. I'll stall the cops as long as I can, an' then I'll catch up with you."

"I'm on my way," said Roselda as she jumped out of the truck and started running across the field, towards the crash site.

Earl turned off the motor, opened the hood, disconnected a couple of wires, closed the hood back down, sat on his back bumper and waited.

* * *

Star People: Mystery of the Hologram

Barnes was growing increasingly angry at the news chopper as it moved closer to the scene. He wanted to run them off, but he was also aware that his every move was being filmed. He had to handle this delicately.

"News chopper on my starboard beam, this is Colonel Barnes of the U.S. Air Force. We are conducting a dangerous military recovery operation here and demand you stay back for your own safety."

* * *

"Oh boy," said Mitchell. "I know they can't be too aggressive, especially while we've got the camera running, but messing with a military operation is pretty serious."

"But what if they cover all this up and pretend it never happened?" protested David.

"And what will they do to the aliens if no one is there to stop them?" said Amy.

"Mitchell, this might be the biggest story of your life," added Ron. "Are you going to let them scare you away?"

Mitchell was silent for a moment and then shook his head. "It might be the end of my career. Hell, we'll all probably lose our jobs over this, but it might turn out to be the story of the century in these parts, and I'm not going to let them chase us away."

He picked up the mike. "Sorry, Colonel, but the public has a right to know what's going on in the skies over their own heads. I'll keep a safe distance but I'm not going anywhere until we figure out what we've got here."

Amy looked over at the suddenly courageous Mitchell and patted his shoulder. "Thanks, Mitchell. I owe you one," she said with a smile.

Even Ron managed a smile but said nothing from his perch at the back of the chopper, scratching down a few words on his notepad.

* * *

Inside the *Mercury One*, Scott, Christina and Brett were shaken up and terrified. The *Mercury One* was suspended in the limbs of a giant maple tree, almost as if the tree had caught the ship and prevented it from crashing to the ground. The ship was tilted at a forty-five degree angle, and the three passengers had fallen out of their seats and were all leaning against the side of the craft. The branches of the leafy maple tree were so thick that the view out of the front windows and moon roof was completely obstructed.

"Is everybody all right?" Scott asked.

"I'm okay," answered Christina rubbing her head. "I hit my head, but I'm all right."

"Brett? Are you okay?"

"My arm hurts a little from where I landed on it. But I can move it, so it's not broken."

"What happened to the orbs?" asked Christina.

"I was following them when we crashed, just like all the other times. I was headed right for the circle of orbs. Maybe I went too low, but—"

"If you were any higher, we would have hit the helicopter and we'd all be dead now," said Christina.

"I know. I couldn't have gone any higher," answered Scott in a discouraged tone.

"So, what do we do now?"

"I don't know yet. We're too high up off the ground to jump out and run. Can either of you see what's going on out there? This window's completely blocked. I can't see anything."

"I can't see much from here either," added Christina. "What about you Brett?"

"I can see a little. I'm lyin' right next to the rear window."

"Okay. You'll have to tell us everything you see," advised Scott, "even if it doesn't seem like it's important."

"We're at the very edge of the woods. There is a huge open field that we were flying over before we crashed. Right now, the field is dark, but those two Air Force helicopters are just hovering around out there, like they're keeping an eye on us."

"What about the police cars?"

"I don't see any of those."

* * *

Two police cars, coming from opposite directions, arrived at the intersection of Highway 95 and Eagle River Road at the same time. Both cars had to slam on their brakes to avoid crashing into the side of Earl's truck.

"What's going on here?" one of the officers yelled from his car. "Get that tow truck out of the way."

A man jumped out of a second car with an air of authority. "This is Police Captain Tony Canazera, and I am ordering you to move that vehicle at once. We have a police emergency, and you're blocking access."

Earl tried to stall as best he could and spoke very slowly. "Officer, I was turnin' my truck aroun', an' it jus' up an' quit on me. The thing jus' died. I know it ain't outta gas. I got half a tank. Maybe you can help me get it started." Earl fumbled around for a minute or two as if he couldn't figure out how to open the hood. Finally, as he popped it open, two more police cars arrived at the scene.

"Look mister, there's no time for that now. We've got an emergency situation."

"An emergency situation," repeated Earl. "What kinda 'mergency is it?"

"That's none of your concern," Canazera answered abruptly.

"I'm mighty sorry to be causin' such a problem, officer. Maybe you all could give me a push," responded Earl in a helpless manner.

"All right, get in," ordered Canazera. He motioned to the other officers to come over and help push. "Men, get over here and push this truck out of the way."

The other officers ran over to help, but as Earl was getting into the truck, he dropped the keys, kicked them under the tow truck and fumbled around on the ground for several minutes trying to find them.

"What's the hold-up?" yelled one of the officers lined up behind the truck.

"Do any of you all have a flashlight?" Earl said from his hands and knees. "I dropped my keys an' it's kinda dark out here."

One of the officers pulled a flashlight from his belt and quickly located the keys and handed them to Earl. With an "ooops," Earl dropped them again and got down on his knees for a second time. Earl found his keys much faster this time, but he moved very slowly as he climbed into the truck with a groan saying: "This ol' back seems to be givin' me trouble again."

A loud, angry call came in on the radios in the police cars. "Where the hell's the ground support? The aliens could be calling for help or mounting an attack or planning an escape and we're waiting out here like sitting ducks. Where are you guys? Over."

Since Canazera was out of his car and trying to get Earl's truck out of the way, a different voice came on the radio: "The entrance to Eagle River Road is blocked, and no squad cars can get through, sir. We hope to remove blockade and gain access shortly. Over."

* * *

An impatient Colonel Barnes radioed over to Rodriguez: "Rodriguez, we've been hovering out here for fifteen minutes. I don't know what happened to ground support, but I'm gonna have a few words with Captain Canazera's commanding officer when this is all over. In the meantime, it's up to you and me. We'll have to land the choppers in the field, and then you and I will go in."

"Roger, Colonel. From what I can see, I don't think the alien craft is operational, sir. I don't think they can go anywhere."

"I roger that," said Barnes. "Probably best if you and I handle this anyway. Those cops aren't trained for these types of emergency situations."

"Roger, Colonel. I'm landing as we speak."

"And Rodriguez, treat this like a high-risk operation: wear full gear and follow all armament procedures."

"Roger Colonel, over."

* * *

Earl took forever to get situated in his truck and finally yelled out: "Okay, push."

Four officers scrambled to get lined up behind the truck and pushed with all of their strength. Their muscles were straining, and they moaned and groaned as they gave it every ounce of energy they had, but the heavy tow truck wouldn't budge.

Finally, after a minute or two, Earl leaned out the window and said: "Oops, I guess the parking brake was still on. Let's try again."

Earl released the parking brake, and the tow truck was quickly pushed away. Once the entrance to Eagle River Road was cleared, the police got back into their cars and sped off towards the crash site. Two ladder trucks from the fire department arrived and followed the cops to the scene.

Earl quickly got under the hood of his truck, reconnected the wires he had disconnected earlier, and followed them down Eagle River Road, keeping an eye out for Roselda.

* * *

"The helicopters are landing directly behind us," said Brett.

"North of us?" asked Scott.

"I'm pretty sure that's north. It's the opposite direction from the nose of our ship."

"Yeah, that's north."

"One helicopter is on the ground, and the other is landing right now."

"Keep watching them, Brett, and let me know when the pilots are out and starting to come this way," said Scott.

"Why?"

"I've got a plan. Once they're far enough away from the helicopters, I'm going to try to start the motors again, and maybe we can make a run for it. By the time the pilots get back in their helicopters and take off again, we could be halfway home."

"Do you think the ship will still work after the crash?"

"I don't know, but it's our only chance."

"Okay, both helicopters are now on the ground," observed Brett. "The propellers are slowing down and coming to a stop. The pilots have gotten out, and it looks like they are putting on some kind of protective suits," said Brett. "Uh-oh."

"What's going on now, Brett?"

"There are police cars—lots of 'em—coming this way. And a couple of fire trucks."

"They probably called the fire department so they'd have ladders to get up to us," deduced Scott.

* * *

Earl drove up just in time to see Roselda trying to stop the Air Force officers who were dressed in protective suits and directing the operation.

"Leave them alone," Roselda screamed. "They didn't hurt anyone."

She tried to block their path and hold them back, but Roselda wasn't strong enough to stop them as they pushed her aside and warned her not to interfere with military operations. The police quickly grabbed her and escorted her out of the area where she then joined Earl.

"Are you okay?" Earl asked her.

"I'm okay. I'm just upset about what's going on here."

"They're setting up a barrier to keep us all out," said Earl. "An' it looks like them firetrucks are raising their ladders right up to where the ship crashed."

More police cars pulled up to the scene with their red lights flashing. One of the firemen had a high-beam flashlight and kept the light directed towards the top of the tree.

Within minutes, the open fields quickly filled up with police cars, news vans, and curious people who had watched the air chase unfold and wanted to investigate. Earl watched as some people even arrived in their pajamas and bathrobes. Some set up lawn chairs where they could sit and watch the action unfold. Others were carrying around kids who were too tired to keep their eyes open. One man pulled out a camp stove and was popping popcorn. Another couple was sipping drinks from martini glasses while they lounged back in reclining patio chairs. There were frequent flashes from the cameras of spectators who were trying to take pictures. Earl could see that the ship was too far up and hidden too deeply in the tree for those pictures to show much of anything, but it wasn't stopping people from trying. Even the news photographers with telephoto lenses were complaining about how they couldn't get a decent shot.

The police formed a line and continued to push everyone back, urging them to go home. Once that barrier was formed, the two Air Force pilots, wearing protective suits, drew their weapons and started heading towards the ladders.

"Come on, Roselda, I can't just sit back and watch this anymore," Earl said as he tried to break through the line of officers. Two of the cops grabbed Earl and pushed him back. Earl tried again, this time with a running start, but he was quickly tackled to the ground.

"Back off, mister," one of the cops said as he pulled a gun from its holster.

"C'mon, Tommy. You ain't gonna shoot me?" Earl asked the cop he recognized from his days back in high school.

"Who's that?" the cop replied, shining his flashlight in Earl's face. "That you, Earl? Whatcha doin' out here? Was that your truck that blocked us out?"

"You know this guy?" the other cop asked.

"Yeah. He's okay. He's a local," Tommy said and then turned to Earl. "You know you're not supposed to be out here."

"We came to make sure you don't hurt them," Roselda said stepping forward.

"Ma'am, we're not here to hurt anybody," the cop stated. "We're just here for crowd control."

Just then a pair of military trucks pulled up and a dozen armed Air Force personnel with MP printed on arm bands jumped out of the back of the trucks and began surrounding the area. Even Tommy appeared to be a little intimidated by the overwhelming and sudden show of force.

"It's all right, officer," a burly sergeant, wearing an MP arm band, said as he walked up to them. "We'll take it from here. You and your partner should head back to the highway and keep this side road blocked off. Authorized personnel only. Got it?"

Tommy appeared uncertain but nodded. "Okay. Travis, I guess we need to move out," he said to his partner.

"Hey, I think I see it up there," said Travis who hadn't really been paying attention to the discussions on the ground. He pointed his flashlight into the tree's branches. "Up there on those highest branches."

"That's fine, officer," one of the MP's said pushing the two cops back towards their squad car. "We'll take it from here."

"What is it?" Travis asked.

"Nothing you need to be concerned about," the MP replied.

"And nothing you need to remember seeing either," he added darkly. Both cops got the drift and nodded.

"Who are these civilians?" asked the captain of the MP's who was watching the exchange and wanted to know more about Earl and Roselda.

"Just a couple of locals," Tommy answered. "They saw all the commotion and just came to see what was going on. I'll escort them out."

The captain looked uncertain. "They saw all the commotion. I dunno. I think I'd like to keep them here until I get word on what to do with them." He turned to Earl and Roselda. "I want you two to wait with my sergeant here."

Gradually, the headlights from the cars started to dim and then go dark as did the flashlight held by the fireman. The sound of the sirens had begun to fade and then went completely silent.

"What happened to all the lights?" asked Tommy switching his flashlight off and on trying to get it to work.

"I don't know," answered his partner tapping on an electrical device in his hand. "My radio went dead too. I'll have to use the one in the squad car." They walked over to the police car and sat down inside.

"This radio's not working either," said Travis trying to get response from the scanner. "I guess we lost the signal somehow. I wonder what's causing this outage?"

* * *

Inside the news chopper, Mitchell started frantically flipping switches and turning knobs, trying to adjust the controls as he circled above the activity on the ground.

"What's going on?" asked a nervous Amy who felt uncomfortable with the pilot's behavior.

"I've never had anything like this happen before," observed Mitchell.

"Like what," asked David?

"We're losin' power," warned Mitchell. "I didn't want to land with those military choppers down there because they're going to bust my butt, but we don't have a choice."

"Are you going to be able to land all right?" asked Amy who was starting to hold on tightly and brace for a crash landing.

"We'll be all right," answered Mitchell calmly. "We're not going to crash. We're at a low altitude, and I can land just north of those military helicopters. Everything's okay. Nothing to worry about."

As soon as the chopper touched down, all of the power and lights on the dashboard began to fade and then go dark. The propeller continued to spin a few more times and then gradually came to a stop.

Amy, David and Ron quickly jumped out of the craft. David estimated that they were about a quarter of a mile from the crash site, so he handed a couple pieces of camera equipment to Ron and Amy and said, "Let's go."

He looked back and saw Mitchell lagging behind but trying to keep up.

When they arrived at the scene, they were stopped dead by the police barricades.

"Let's get set up over here," said David as he motioned to a place that wasn't as crowded but appeared to still be a good vantage point. "I want to make sure we don't miss anything."

* * *

"Okay, Scott, the guys in the protective suits are starting to climb the ladders so they can get up to us," said Brett.

Christina had managed to shift the position of her body enough to get a partial view out the window. "Let's see if it'll work. We need to get out of here."

Scott took a deep breath and then tried to start the motor. It sputtered as if the battery was dead.

"Come on, *Mercury One*, don't let us down now," Christina begged.

Scott tried again. It sounded like the motor wanted to start but the propeller made a chopping sound as if it were cutting up the tree branches underneath the ship.

"It almost started."

"Come on, the third time's a charm."

Scott tried again and this time there was a ringing sound. "That doesn't sound right, but maybe something got damaged in the crash," observed Scott.

"As long as it gets us home, I don't care what it sounds like," said a nervous Christina. "Just get us out of here."

The *Mercury One* started to slowly shake as it moved upwards. It tipped and rocked back and forth trying to dislodge from the tree branches. The movement was gradual at first as the ship struggled to get free. It took a moment for Scott, Christina, and Brett to get back in their seats and reestablish balance. As soon as they were back in place, the craft became level again, parallel with the ground. Then, the *Mercury One* gently rose up over the trees and began to float in mid-air.

From the windows, Scott could see the tops of the trees moving away, farther and farther below them. People on the ground became smaller as the craft went higher in the sky.

"You got it to work," said an excited Christina. "Now let's make a run for it."

"Those guys are running back to their helicopters," reported Brett.

"Can we get home before they get the choppers back up in the air and come after us?"

"They're almost there." Brett added another update as he watched from the window.

"But it's not working," said Scott ignoring what the others had said.

"What do you mean?"

Scott leaned over and put his ear next to the motor so he could hear, and then he shook his head. "Our motor isn't working any more. It's not even turned on."

The ringing got louder. It seemed to be coming from above and moving closer to them.

"Then where's that sound coming from, and how are we able to fly?" asked Christina.

Then the craft started to gently vibrate, and a bright green light engulfed the craft, growing in intensity.

The emerald light was so bright that everything outside of their ship took on an eerie green color. It wasn't long before Scott realized that what they were experiencing was strangely familiar.

"It's the aliens. They came to rescue us!!!" screamed Brett looking up through the moon roof.

"They're back! They've come back for us," said Scott.

"We're saved!"

Chapter 42
Outfoxed By A Fox

A gathering of police officers and the news crew from *Chopper Eight* stared up in the sky in amazement at the fading streak of green light that had been left behind, almost like a trail of stardust from a falling star.

David was mesmerized by the experience but also thrilled to have been able to record everything on camera. He turned to Mitchell with jubilation: "I got it. I got it all on tape. That was amazing!!!"

One of the Air Force officers heard David's burst of excitement and quickly ran over to see what he had recorded.

"But isn't that little red light supposed to be on when your camera is running," asked Amy?

David looked at his camera and found that the red light was, indeed, off. He turned the recording device around to look through the viewfinder and pressed 'rewind.' A crowd of people, including the Air Force pilots, had gathered to see the replay.

After running it back and forth a few times, David shook his head and announced, "It's gone. There's nothing there." Just then, he started to wonder whether the force field the aliens used to shut down the helicopters also froze up and stopped all forms of electrical gadgets and machinery from working. When he rewound the tape, there was no footage of the alien rescue. "It's gone," was all he could say over and over again.

"All of it?" asked Amy.

"No, all of the chase scenes when we were up in the helicopter are there, but all the stuff that happened when the big ship came down is gone. I can't believe it. How could I have missed it again," complained David as he rubbed his eyes and then shook his head.

The Air Force Colonel had a big smile on his face when he heard that there was no evidence of the alien ships on tape.

"It wasn't your fault," said one of the police officers who overheard the conversation. "That big alien ship shut everything down. All of our electronic equipment stopped working. Must've been some sort of force field the aliens use to make sure no one can attack 'em. That's why your camera was off."

"That's brilliant," said another police officer who was part of the group. "They shut everything down in the area in case anyone should try to use weapons against them. Our military would love to have that technology."

* * *

Barnes pulled Rodriguez aside from the crowd and said to him, "We need to talk for a minute."

They walked away from the group because Barnes wanted to strategize before they conducted any interviews with the media.

"Let me handle the press," Barnes instructed Rodriguez. "I'll do all the talking. I've got lots of experience with these sorts of things."

He could tell that Rodriguez wasn't really listening. Rodriguez was still looking up at the sky in disbelief.

"What just happened, sir?" asked a bewildered Rodriguez after pulling off his protective helmet. "In my fourteen years in the military, I've never witnessed anything like that."

                    Star People: Mystery of the Hologram

Barnes just smiled. He leaned over towards Rodriguez implying that what he was about to say was to always be a secret between them. "Now I know you just joined our department a couple of months ago, but between you and me, Rodriguez, you'll get used to this. I've seen lots of UFOs. Hundreds of 'em. You'll be seeing them all the time now. But I will say...that was one of the more impressive sightings I've ever seen." He patted Rodriguez on the back and laughed. "Welcome to the Alien Investigations Task Force. Welcome to our world."

"Would this be a good time for an interview, Colonel?" asked Ron Covington from *The National Reporter* who had snuck up from behind and had apparently been eavesdropping on what Barnes had thought was a private conversation.

When Barnes saw Covington standing behind him, his demeanor immediately changed from light-hearted to serious. "Covington, you're under arrest," snapped Barnes.

"Officers," Barnes called out, and motioned for a couple of military police to come over to him. "Come with me please." The MP's followed his instructions and joined Barnes. The Colonel grabbed Ron's arm and escorted him over to where the News Eight crew and Mitchell were standing.

"I am arresting every one of you," Barnes informed the news team. "And you," he pointed towards Mitchell, "Are you the pilot of that helicopter?"

"Yes, sir," replied Mitchell.

"I'm taking away your license for good." Barnes turned to the policemen: "Officers, I want these four people arrested for interfering with a military operation."

"Colonel," Amy said as she stepped forward. "I am taking full responsibility for everything that happened with the news helicopter. I ordered the pilot to stay in the air, so everyone else on board, including the pilot, is innocent. If you want to arrest someone, then arrest me. Let the rest of them go." She stepped forward and put out her wrists expecting to be cuffed.

"Cuff her first, and then cuff the rest of 'em," ordered Barnes.

"Now hold on just a second, Colonel," objected Ron.

"You're not going to talk your way out of this one, Covington, so don't even try," snapped Barnes.

"No, Colonel, I probably can't, but I thought you might want to hear this before you haul us away. Here, listen." Ron opened his briefcase and took out one of the tape recorders. He held up the tape recorder and played back the audio of what Barnes had thought he had said privately to Rodriguez.

Now I know you just joined our department a couple of months ago, but between you and me, Rodriguez, you'll get used to this. I've seen lots of UFOs. Hundreds of 'em. You'll be seeing them all the time now. But I will say... that was one of the more impressive sightings I've ever seen. Welcome to the Alien Investigations Task Force. Welcome to our world.

Ron turned and addressed the group that had gathered. "This is historic. An Air Force Officer admitting for the first time that UFOs really *do* exist. *You* are going to be famous, Colonel.

"And what will happen when that recording goes public," Ron continued, putting his hand on his chin as if he were contemplating the possibilities. "Tomorrow morning, your face and your words will be on every newscast around the world, as you will be the first high-ranking Air Force official to go on record saying that there really are such things as UFOs."

Barnes was fuming inside but trying not to let his anger show. He knew Ron could cause a tremendous amount of trouble for him with that admission.

Ron wasn't finished: "Well, I for one think it is refreshing for the Air Force to finally come out and tell the truth about UFOs, don't you guys?" Ron asked the others in the group, and they all agreed that they would like to hear that.

"And you'll be famous, Colonel. Well, except for the fact that your reputation might be *just* slightly tarnished." Ron held up his thumb and forefinger to indicate a very small amount.

"So, Colonel, if you arrest us, and take away this fine gentleman's pilot's license," Ron said as he put his arm around Mitchell, "your voice will be heard around the world. And the Air Force can either support you or discredit you. I... I wonder which one it would be."

Barnes was quiet as he thought about how the Air Force would feel about his admission.

"I can confiscate that recorder," argued Barnes.

"But you've still got about a dozen witnesses who heard your voice says those words," refuted Covington.

"So, Colonel, I can push one of two buttons on this recorder. This button here," Ron held up the recorder for everyone to see, "would erase the admission by a top Air Force official clearly stating that UFOs do exist, and he just saw one with his own eyes. Or this button here," Ron pointed out a different button on the recorder, "when I play that recording to my editor, who, in turn, will transmit it to news stations all over the world."

The Colonel was seething inside.

"So, it's your call. I could press this little button that says erase on it, and we could all walk away as friends. What do you say, Colonel?" asked Ron.

Barnes thought about it for a moment. "All right, all right, Covington, you've got me, but I want that tape."

"Do I have your word that there won't be any charges filed against me or any of these fine people?" asked Ron.

"Yes," barked Barnes. He looked at the others. "And not a word about this from any of you, or I *will* get you locked up, you hear. And I'll deny any of this ever happened, and Rodriguez is my witness."

Everyone in the group nodded their heads in agreement.

"And Mitchell keeps his pilot's license?"

"Yes, yes, you have my word," muttered the angry Colonel. "Now give me that tape."

Ron held up his tape recorder for all to see, ejected the cassette and handed the tape over to the Colonel. "There, none of us heard a thing," said Ron.

Barnes snatched the tape out of Ron's hand and stormed away with Rodriguez.

* * *

After everyone thanked Ron for getting them off the hook, David pulled Ron aside and said, "I can't believe you gave up that tape. That would have been a huge story for you."

A big smile came across Ron's face. "Now, David you should know by now that I'm a man of my word. Of course, I gave him that tape. You all saw me do that, but…" Ron opened his briefcase only enough so David could see what was inside. "I always carry two tape recorders just in case one isn't working. And I always keep them both recording to make sure I never miss a word."

"David," interrupted Amy as a message came in on her headset. "I can hear a signal from the station again. They want us back on the air. Is your camera working yet?"

David turned on his camera and saw the red light glowing. "It's okay now. It's working again." David put his headphones back on and listened for a moment. "Okay we're on in three… two… one…."

David could tell that Amy didn't know what to say to the television audience or how to describe what she had just witnessed.

"It's hard to explain to our viewers at home what just happened during the last few minutes when we were off the air. I've truly never seen anything like it. Two Air Force helicopters forced an alien ship to crash in that cluster of trees behind me." She turned around and gestured in the direction of where the ship had been lodged in the branches of the maple tree.

"After that," Amy hesitated for a moment, "a much larger vessel, perhaps some sort of mother ship, came out of nowhere and rescued the smaller ship."

For a moment, Amy looked skywards as she recalled the event. "It was the most remarkable thing. The large ship made a soft whirring sound and had very intense green lights that were so bright that it was difficult for us to look up into the sky. The ship was silver and shaped like a diamond. Somehow, it pulled the smaller craft out of the trees, and while the smaller craft was suspended in mid-air, it latched onto it with four mechanical arms. Then, when both ships were docked together, they disappeared in a streak of light."

Chapter 43
Defying Gravity

The Antarians gently set *Mercury One* down and then landed their own ship in the field behind the Harrison's house.

Scott, Brett, and Christina couldn't wait to get out of their ship and enjoy the feeling of freedom again. After being cramped in a small craft for hours and feeling exhausted from the grueling experience, it was an incredible relief to have their feet on the ground and know that they had escaped what could have been an epic disaster.

Once again, Scott noticed how everything grew dark and still around them. The wind completely vanished and even persistent chirping and singing of the insects was absent.

When the door of the alien ship opened and the ramp dropped into place, the first aliens to emerge were the four shapeshifters which, once again, transformed into four deer and bounded off in each of the four different directions.

Then Zula and Zocuul emerged from the doorway of the craft.

Scott, Christina, and Brett were so thankful after being rescued that they immediately ran over to meet the Antarians.

Scott was the first to reach them. "I know you can't speak, but thank you, thank you, thank you...thank you for saving us."

"You guys saved our lives!" added Brett.

Zocuul came out of the ship holding the message board. After glowing for a few moments, he gently let go and it floated in the air.

"How did you know we were in trouble?" asked Scott, and just like before, when Scott spoke, his words appeared on the large screen.

How did you know we were in trouble?

The message board flickered for a moment and then the broadcast of the Channel Eight news, from earlier in the evening, appeared on the screen.

Everyone watched as Amy gave updates and the camera followed the flight of the two helicopters.

"Those are the helicopters that were chasing us," observed Brett.

"Wow. That was on TV?" asked Christina.

The thoughts of the aliens appeared on the language board.

All over the country.

Scott and Christina looked at each other in disbelief. They had no idea that their chase and escape had attracted so much attention.

Zula stepped forward. She didn't speak, but Scott had observed that when one of the aliens came forward, it indicated whose thought was appearing on the language board.

It sounded like you needed help. It took us some time to reach you. In the meantime, it was Earl who delayed the police and saved you.

"Earl?" asked Scott.

Earl and Roselda blocked the road so the police couldn't get through. That gave us the time we needed to fly to your planet.

"Wow. Earl's all right," said Scott.

Tonight, Earl was a hero.

"How do you know Earl?" Scott asked the Star People.

The big screen replayed a recording from Earl's first interview that took place on *The Shirley Show:*

> *Shirley: So, you were out in the field when you saw a strange object in the sky?*
> *Earl: Well, first I heard a whirring sound coming from up above, and then I felt this eerie breeze all around me. Then I looked up and there was this spaceship goin' overhead.*
> *Shirley: What did it look like?*
> *Earl: Well, it was hard to see because it was pretty dark that night, but I could tell it was some kinda UFO.*

"Wow, we never saw that interview before. When did that happen?" asked Christina.

June 4th

Scott thought for a moment. "That was about the time we took our first flight."

Another message came up on the screen.

The television and radio signals from Earth are broadcast to satellites out in space. They are easy for us to receive and monitor.

Scott nervously started searching the sky. "I forgot about the helicopters. Will they be able to follow us here?"

That would be impossible. Our ship can move a thousand times faster than your fastest airplane. When we took off, all the earthlings saw was a flash of light that was gone in a millisecond. It would be impossible for them to follow that.

"Thank goodness," said a relieved Christina.

We don't understand why they would try to hurt you.

"What do you mean... the Air Force?" questioned Scott.

Yes, the Air Force.

Scott looked at the others for ideas because he couldn't think of an answer. "Um...I don't know. I guess they're afraid of anything that they think is a threat."

"Maybe they thought we were aliens from another planet," added Christina.

But then why wouldn't they welcome you?

The Antarians looked at each other with what appeared to be a lack of understanding. Scott didn't have an answer.

Their conversation was interrupted by a voice calling in the distance: "Christina. Christina."

"That's my dad." Christina looked a little embarrassed. "He has the loudest voice in the neighborhood: you can hear him from a mile away. He must have been awakened by all of the noise from the helicopters. I'm going to be in soooo much trouble. I gotta go." She turned to the aliens. "Zula, Zocuul, you guys really saved us. Thank you."

Christina ran off.

"Why didn't the wave of sleep affect him?" asked Scott.

Sometimes when people are very worried or distraught they can resist the desire to sleep.

Zocuul started to glow in a blue color. Scott remembered that blue was the color that indicated the aliens were going into a telepathic state where they could read the thoughts of others, like when they were able to get the name of Scott's grandfather by reading his mind.

The phone in your house is going to ring in about a minute, and it will be Christina's mother.

Scott became very interested in what he had just witnessed. "You guys can see into the future?"

We use a lot more of our brains than earthlings do. Although there are a few earthlings who have learned how to do that and they, too, can predict the future.

Scott turned to Brett. "Hurry, go in and turn the ringer on the phone down so it doesn't wake Mom. And tell Christina's mom that she's fine and she's been with us all night."

"Okay," Brett said reluctantly because he didn't want to leave. "Bye Star People guys. You guys are really neat," For a brief moment, the aliens started glowing in a soft pink color.

"Hurry, Brett," said Scott.

When Brett was gone, Scott still had questions. "If you guys can predict the future, then will there ever be a time when humans and aliens connect with each other?"

Some things in the future are uncertain.

"And why does everyone want to come to our planet anyway?" asked Scott. "Why do we have all these UFO sightings? They happen all the time now. There are lots of other planets to visit."

Zula stepped forward as if this was her question to answer.

There are. But your planet is the most beautiful. You have mountains and oceans and waterfalls and tall trees and amazing animals and birds. That is why so many alien ships come to earth: there is so much beauty here. They just want to see it. There is no other planet like it... anywhere.

"None of the other planets have that?" asked Scott.

There are some, but yours is exceptional. Most of the other planets are made up of rock formations and craters and great ice fields, but planet Earth is magnificent. It is a living planet. Earthlings are very fortunate to live in such an amazing place.

"Last time, when you were here, you said I'd been on board your ship many times. That you'd been training me. What have I been learning?"

Zocuul reached up and took hold of the language board and walked towards Scott. He handed the large screen to Scott.

Make it float, were the words that appeared on the screen.

"I... I... I don't know how to do that," protested Scott.

Close your eyes, go into a place of deep, deep focus and envision what you want to create.

Scott closed his eyes. They gave him a few minutes to go into a trance-like state. He let go of any doubts in his mind and concentrated on seeing the message board leave his hands and float above him.

Then, Scott could hear a voice inside his head. It helped him intensify his focus. *Release all other thoughts. Go deep within your mind. Visualize what you want to manifest. Use the power of your mind and make it happen. Imagine the screen rising up out of your hands and hovering in the air.*

After a few moments of concentrated focus, Scott heard their voices.

Scott, can you hear us?

"Yes," answered Scott.

Open your eyes.

Scott opened his eyes and saw the message board suspended in the air. He was in a state of heightened focus and noticed something unusual: his whole body was lightly illuminated in a violet cast.

The voice continued: *Why do you think you can hear us? Or that you can make the language board float in the air? Why do you think the ship you built is able to fly?*

At first, Scott didn't answer. He was still intensely focused on keeping the message board suspended in mid-air. Then, he thought about their last question and started to answer using his critical mind: "Our ship was able to fly because we designed it so that the lift from the propeller..."

No!

Scott clearly heard that single word in unison from the aliens because it interrupted his thoughts. *It flew because you have a special power to make it fly; otherwise, it never would have left the ground.*

"So I have to be on board?"

You make it fly with your mind.

Zocuul came forward and took the message board back from Scott.

You are one of the gifted ones.

Scott objected to what he was being told. "You say I am gifted, but I am doing the same things that you can do. You can make things float, and you can hear the thoughts of others," Scott said aloud.

But it has taken five hundred years of training for us to develop those gifts. You can do these things, and you are only fifteen.

Scott had no answer for that. It was hard for him to accept that he actually had these gifts or that he had the ability to make things fly.

Just then Zula made her high-pitched call. The four deer came back to the ship and transformed back into their alien shapes as they climbed the ramp.

It is time for us to go, but we will return in seven earth nights.

Zula called out again but this time with softer cooing sounds. She gestured as if she were beckoning something to come to her. From several different directions, seven glowing orbs came out of the sky—moving swiftly and swirling together in formation—responding to her call. They slowed down and hovered as if they were patiently waiting for her. Zula opened a beautiful golden box lined with purple silk. Each of the seven illuminated spheres landed in the box as if it was the place where they would sleep after a long night of work.

Then, Zula called out again. Scott wondered who else might come forward.

A few moments of silence passed while they waited. Finally, a magnificent great horned owl came forth out of the night sky. As it flew towards the ship, his appearance changed in mid-air as he shapeshifted from a great-horned owl back into a young Antarian and gently landed on the ramp. The language board hanging on the wall behind Zula lit up with her thoughts to them.

Thank you for watching the skies and keeping us informed. And thank you for keeping an eye on our children.

The shapeshifting Antarian glowed in a soft pink color and gently bowed to Zula as he passed by her and entered the ship.

At that moment, Scott realized that on many of the nights when they were out in the *Mercury One,* they had heard owls, but it seemed like there were always a couple of them calling back and forth to each other. Where was the other one, he wondered?

His thoughts were interrupted when Zula called out again, this time in a low guttural tone. For a moment, nothing happened, but then, in the distance, the earth trembled much like when an earthquake rocks the countryside. As the sound came closer, it became a forceful thunderous pounding noise with each thud louder than the previous one. Scott deduced that the sound must have been approaching them since the eruptions were growing in intensity, and the ground was shaking a little more violently with each thunderous crash. It sounded like a giant was walking the earth and slowly coming towards them.

The methodical pounding came closer and closer until a gigantic maple tree emerged from the forest and came walking towards the ship. As it approached, it began to shapeshift. The large tree wavered, almost as if its atoms were transforming. From the shape of the mammoth tree, a tall, thin Antarian materialized. The alien had wounded arms which slowly oozed green sap-like blood.

When Zula saw the injury, she held her hands over the wounds, and she began to glow in a dark purple color. The bleeding stopped and the wounds started to heal. It wasn't instantaneous, but in a few moments, the process of healing had begun, and the lacerations were undergoing a transformation.

Star People: Mystery of the Hologram

Zula's words showed up on the screen as the shapeshifter boarded the ship.

Zetree, you were magnificent! You saved our children. We couldn't have done it without you.

Zocuul and Zula turned to leave. It took Scott a moment to come out of his state of deep concentration. As he regained his presence, he called out: "Thank you, again, for tonight, and for how much you've helped me."

Again, the aliens had a pink glow, perhaps feeling moved, as they walked back up the ramp to their spaceship.

Before they left, Scott turned around to tell them one more thing. "You know, since Earl and Roselda helped us tonight, when the helicopters had us trapped, it'd be nice to do something to thank them." Scott paused for a moment, and then an idea came into his head. "You know what would make them happy?"

The aliens started glowing in their telepathic blue color. He could still see the message board, behind them, which lit up one last time.

Okay, Scott, we'll take care of it.

"Thank you. And thank you for rescuing us," Scott called to them.

The Antarians slowly climbed up the ramp, and the ringing sound from the engine started to increase in volume.

The alien ship, with all of its lights turned off, slowly lifted off the ground and hovered for a while. Then, it was gone in a flash, leaving nothing behind it but a trail of glittering vapor.

Chapter 44
Conflicting Reports

Scott went inside and turned on the TV to catch the early morning news. It took a few moments for the power to come back after the aliens had shut things down. When the picture on the screen finally lit up, reporter Amy Sanders was still at the site of the confrontation and rescue, conducting one of her field interviews. On the bottom of the screen, it said "Special Report."

"I'm here with Colonel Timothy Barnes of the U.S. Air Force. He oversees a special task force that has come to Stonebridge to investigate this rash of UFO sightings. Thank you for joining us, Colonel."

"My pleasure."

Amy was beaming with excitement. The Channel Eight reporter seemed to be almost too enthusiastic to keep steady enough to do the interview. Scott noticed that the hand Amy was using to hold the microphone was trembling.

"Sir, once again, the skies over Massachusetts were lit up with UFOs, in front of our cameras and witnessed by several thousand citizens in the Forestville area. Can you explain to us, in your own words, what happened?"

"Yes, Ma'am, I'd be happy to. After an initial investigation conducted by the U.S. Air Force, we have come to the conclusion that there never were any unidentified flying objects in the skies over Forestville or Stonebridge."

"But—"

"It was all the result of a weather balloon and a few people with overactive imaginations."

Amy's eyes widened in shock. "But what about the chase that took place in the sky earlier this evening?"

"What the viewers witnessed tonight was merely a stray weather balloon. We've been releasing weather balloons in the Stonebridge area over the last couple of weeks, which explains what the local people have been seeing in the sky recently. The weather balloon we released tonight, unfortunately, got blown off course. The Air Force was concerned that it might crash down and possibly damage property or injure innocent civilians. So, we followed the balloon in our helicopters until it got caught in the top of a tree. Eventually it worked its way free and headed up in space where it was supposed to be going in the first place. No damage done, and no one got hurt."

Amy seemed outraged by the denial. "But, Colonel, what about the large alien ship that came down from the sky?"

Colonel Barnes looked at Amy as if she had made everything up. "I heard those rumors too, but if that had happened, certainly someone on the ground would have taken a picture or your camera crew would have gotten some footage. Did your cameraman get any tape of what you refer to as the alien ship?"

"No, but—"

"No, because that was simply a low flying plane," Barnes interjected. "Probably some kooky UFO chasers who heard the news reports on their radio and then dropped by to check it out. It was a low-flying plane that came in to get a better look, that's all. When they saw it was simply a weather balloon, they got bored and continued on their way."

Amy fired back: "And how do you explain the streak of light across the sky?"

"Well, there was something very interesting that did happen tonight," Barnes mused.

Finally, Amy looked like she was going to get something compelling for the viewers. "What can you tell us about that, Colonel?

"There was one of the most fantastic shooting stars I have ever seen. I never get tired of seeing a shooting star. The people on the ground were mesmerized by the streak of light across the sky, and so was I. It was spectacular."

"But, Colonel, I was there for the chase scene and also on site during the rescue. What I saw was a small alien craft that you chased for miles in your Air Force helicopters. Then, after the alien ship crashed into the top of a group of trees, another much-larger mother ship came in and rescued the smaller ship. They docked together and then blasted off in a flash of light. How can you explain to the people who were there, that what they saw wasn't real?"

Colonel Barnes started to chuckle and then his tone became belittling. "I can see how it might have looked that way to the untrained eye, but we professionals handle these situations every day. I can assure the public it was an off-course weather balloon that got stuck in the trees, a low-flying plane and a shooting star. Nothing more, and certainly nothing to get alarmed about. Once again, I'd just like to reiterate that the Air Force can reassure everyone that there was no UFO activity in the area."

* * *

During all of the commotion of the alien rescue, Earl and Roselda quietly slipped away from the MP's and hopped in Earl's truck. He drove to a secluded area where he knew no one would find them. It was right by the edge of a river where they could share their thoughts while they listened to the gentle flow of the moving water.

Earl felt like this was the best night of his life. Not just the excitement of the sighting and rescue, but he loved talking and laughing with Roselda. He had started to feel a kinship with several members of the Brotherhood, and it felt like his life had a renewed purpose.

Finally, after much discussion of the night's events, Roselda said, "It's been quite a night, Earl, but I'm getting tired. Are you ready to head back to the camp?"

"I think all the MP's and the police are packed up and gone, so I think it's safe."

They got into the tow truck, and Earl turned the key, but the engine wouldn't start. "Hmmm. That's odd."

"What's wrong?"

"The engine won't start. I don't know what's wrong. I hooked them distributor wires back up from before. Let me get out and take a look under the hood."

But before Earl could open his door, the wind started to blow up swirls of dust, and the tree branches nearby started to shiver.

"Feels like a storm is blowing in," said Earl. "Can't imagine where that came from. It was still as could be just a few minutes ago."

"It does seem strange. There isn't a cloud in the sky. Just stars."

"Let me see why the truck won't start. It'll just take a minute."

Earl tried to open his door. When that didn't work, he tried to jiggle the handle but still had no luck. "My door won't open."

"What do you mean?"

"It's like my door is locked shut," said Earl, feeling a bit confused.

"Does your door open?" Earl asked Roselda.

She tried to unlatch her door. "It seems to be locked too."

"That's odd—"

"Shhh," whispered Roselda as she put her finger to her lips indicating they needed to be silent.

Earl sat still, trying to listen. "What? What did you hear?"

"That sound." Roselda cocked her head and listened more closely. "First, it was the sound of the wind, but now it's like a high-pitched hum."

"Yeah. I hear it too."

"And look out the window," said Roselda. "Everything out there has an eerie look to it."

"Wow. It's like the sky turned green."

A ringing sound came down from above and then Earl's pick-up truck started to slowly lift off the ground.

"What's happening, Earl?" Roselda asked, with a shaky voice, as the truck started to gently rise up in the air. "We're moving."

"I don't know," answered a stunned Earl. "We're not on the ground anymore. We seem to be—to be floating."

Roselda grabbed hold of the handle on the passenger door. All she could say was: "How can we be floating, Earl?"

"I don't know. I don't have control no more," he said and proved it by turning the steering wheel back and forth showing that the truck wasn't responding. "The truck's engine ain't even running."

Roselda stuck her head out the window and looked upwards. Her mouth dropped open and her eyes became large. "The aliens have come for us, Earl. They're hovering right over us," she said pointing up in the air. "I've waited my whole life for this."

Earl stuck his head out the window and watched as the alien ship lifted his truck straight up in the air and then latched onto it with robotic arms. Then, the truck started to move slowly over the countryside, about fifty feet above the ground.

Earl felt his body tighten up. His fingers clamped so tightly to the steering wheel he felt like they were merging with the plastic and would never come off. He looked at himself in the rear-view mirror and noticed that there was a green tint to his skin.

"Earl? Are you all right?" asked Roselda. "You don't look so good. The aliens turned off their green lights, but you still look a little—"

"Green?" said Earl. "I know. I can see it in the mirror."

"It'll be okay, Earl. They won't hurt us."

"I'm kinda embarrassed to admit it, Roselda, but I'm deathly afraid of heights, and bein' up in the air scares me real, real bad. Maybe if I close my eyes," he said and shut his eyes as tightly as he could.

The flying motion stopped momentarily, and it felt like the truck was hovering in a stationary position in the air. "Why are we stopping?" asked Earl, keeping his eyes shut. "It feels like we're just staying in one place."

"Maybe they want to show us something," said Roselda looking all around outside her window. Suddenly, her face lit up.

"Earl, if you can open your eyes for just a moment, the aliens want you to see something."

Earl slowly opened one eye and then the other.

"Look down below," she told him.

In the field below there were some words that had been cut into the grass, surrounded by fancy swirls, intricate stars and decorative embroidery-like designs. It appeared to be a glowing crop circle but with a message in the center.

When he read the message, Earl's face broke into a huge smile. He pulled out his handkerchief and wiped his eyes. The message read:

Thank you, Earl.
You were a hero tonight.

"I'm sure that means they are our friends, and we are safe," said Roselda trying to reassure him.

At that moment, the spaceship above them—with the tow truck secured below—took off at full thrust. Roselda was thrilled and her face lit up with delight. Earl, however, was still struggling. As the ship jumped into hyper speed and disappeared into the night sky, Roselda let out a squeal of joy and Earl let out a scream of terror, the combination of which resonated for miles across the countryside.

Chapter 45
The Gift

It was almost dawn when Earl and Roselda were "dropped off" a few miles from the Brotherhood Camp. The aliens gently set Earl's truck down in a deserted field and then were gone without any attempts at communication. Earl's truck fired right up and the two of them arrived at the Brotherhood camp in mere minutes.

As Earl was walking Roselda back to her tent, he said, "You know, the most interesting thing about that ride, Roselda—"

"Wow, there were so many interesting things. I don't know how you could pick just one. I feel like we saw the entire planet in just a couple hours, but what was it that stood out for you?"

"Well, I been 'fraid of heights my whole life, but after a few minutes, that fear was completely gone. It's like the aliens cured me from that fear. You don't think they coulda done that, do you?"

"I do. I really do. There's no telling what kind of healing powers they might have, and what we could learn from them."

They walked in silence for a minute or two until Roselda spoke up. "This is my tent right over here on the left."

"Ouch," she said as she tripped over what appeared to be a package left just outside of the entrance to her tent.

"Are you okay?"

"Oh yeah. Just stubbed my toe when I kicked that package."

"It looks like a book," said Earl, noticing that a hardback book had come partially out of the wrapper that was holding it.

"One of the other campers must have found a book they liked and wanted to pass it on to me," said Roselda as she picked it up. "We do that a lot in the Brotherhood community."

"Well, open it up. Let's see what it is."

"Looks like an old book," she said as she quickly unwrapped it.

"Oh my," she exclaimed. "*From The Earth To The Moon* by Jules Verne."

Roselda looked touched. "Now isn't that the sweetest gift."

"What do you mean?"

"Well, I met with a young man named Scott a couple of nights ago and told him how I had lost a copy of this book many years ago. He must have gone out and found a copy and left it as a gift. That was so thoughtful of him. I'm just sorry that I wasn't here when he brought it by, but this was a crazy night."

"Did he write anything in it or leave a note with it?"

"Oh, I doubt it," she said, and then as she opened the book, Roselda quickly started to sit down as if she were about to faint. She grabbed hold of a tent pole to steady herself so she wouldn't fall.

"Are you all right, Roselda?"

"I'm all right," she said sitting herself down in a chair next to the entrance of her tent. "Just stunned."

"Why? What's it say?"

"This isn't from Scott after all."

"It's not?"

"No, it's from the Mission Hills Library. Mission Hills," she said softly, "that's where I grew up. This is the book," she said, gently touching its cover. "This is the book I lost many years ago when I was a young girl, and a tornado almost swept me away."

She showed the book to Earl. "See, it has my name and the date I checked it out written in the inner sleeve."

<hr>

"Looks like there's an inscription as well. Someone wrote in it," said Earl as he handed the book back to her.

Then, she looked at the words that had been written inside and read it out loud to Earl.

We will come back to see you again, but it is too soon. You are still needed on this planet for a while longer. It is not your time yet, but your time will come.

Roselda's mouth gaped open, and she put her hand over her heart. Earl wasn't sure if she was feeling love or if her heart was truly aching. "There's more."

"What else?"

"It's signed."

"By Who?"

"By Angela."

"Who's Angela?"

"One of my friends who disappeared from my life a long time ago. I'll tell you all about it later, but I just need some time to think it all through first."

"I understand," said Earl. "Now Roselda, as we talked about earlier, I gotta get back and open up the station, but I can't leave you unless I know you're all right."

"I'm more than all right, Earl. You can go. I know you're already late for work. We'll talk later," said Roselda. "And thank you for being so valiant tonight."

When he heard that compliment, Earl took a deep breath and tried to hold in the tears that were starting to build up inside him.

* * *

On the night following the dramatic chase and rescue, the skies over Massachusetts were calm and peaceful once again.

As soon as the clock struck eight p.m., Earl closed up his gas station and took a moment to scan the sky just to make sure he wasn't missing anything. He was exhausted after losing a whole night's sleep the night before. He turned out the lights and was ready to head home when he noticed a mysterious package, with his name on it, on the steps just outside the back door of his business. As near as Earl could tell, this gift looked like an earthly one, not one that came from another planet or beings from another world, and it didn't look like a book.

The package contained some homemade chocolate chip cookies and a hand-written anonymous thank you note. The note echoed something the aliens had said in their message: that Earl was a hero. That brought a smile to his face. The last few days made him feel more important than he had ever felt in his entire lifetime. He carefully slipped the note into his front shirt pocket and savored every bite of those cookies on the way home.

Chapter 46
Journey Through Time

Scott felt a lot of anxiety about what might be revealed on his next journey with the Star People, but he had to be patient. Christina had been grounded for a week, for sneaking out of the house on the night of the rescue, so it was up to Scott and Brett to make repairs to the *Mercury One*. That didn't stop Christina from calling a couple times a day to check in on their progress. But even after the ship was ready to fly, Scott was very hesitant about taking another flight in the homemade craft.

Finally, the night of the full moon came. As Scott waited on the steps of the work shed, he thought he could actually *feel* the presence of the Star People. But despite his intuition telling him they were nearby, by 10:00 pm nothing had happened, and he knew his mom would be expecting him back inside. So, he reluctantly returned to the house.

As Scott got ready for bed, he kept looking out his bedroom window in the direction of the field, but there was no sign of the Star People. He thought about calling Christina, but it was late, and he figured if she didn't turn the ringer down on the phone, he'd wake up her parents.

He went to bed and fell fast asleep, but around 2:00 a.m. he awoke to that familiar ringing sound he had heard before. He quickly jumped up and looked out the window. There was a green light emanating from the field behind his house.

He dressed quickly and pushed open his bedroom window. As he started to disconnect the screen so he could sneak out, he was hit by a momentary thought: *What in the world am I doing? I don't know what they want to show me. It feels like things are about to get very dangerous.* But something inside kept him going. He had had plenty of positive encounters with the Antarians. They seemed to be safe, and from what he could tell, he needed their help if he had any hopes of surviving Zarco.

Scott gently released the window screen, lowered it to the ground and climbed out, wondering what they could possibly want to show him tonight.

As he walked through his yard and unlatched the gate, he noticed another figure approaching the ship. It was too dark to see who it was. Scott was apprehensive about who else might have been summoned to be there with him.

When he got closer to the ship, Scott could see the other person was Christina.

"Christina," he called out to her, "I thought you were still on restriction."

She appeared to be fighting to stay awake as she whispered, "I am."

"So, did the aliens call you too?" he asked.

"No," said Christina groggily. "I think they're trying to put me to sleep. I don't think they want anyone else here for this, but I promised... wait for them..." She started to ramble as if she were mumbling in her sleep. "I don't sleep... everything wakes me up... now I feel really, really tired. But here to help."

Scott and Christina approached the ramp of the ship where Zula and Zocuul were waiting for them. The language board was hanging on the wall behind them.

"I'm here to help him," Christina said but she was starting to stagger.

Scott, you have a very loyal friend. You are very fortunate.

Scott, afraid that she might collapse in her groggy state, put his arm around Christina to keep her from falling.

We tried to come earlier, but Zarco's ship has been following us all night. We had to lose him and make sure all of you were safe.

"Can she come with us tonight?"

No. She wouldn't be able to survive the intense speeds.

Christina looked disappointed that she couldn't go, but she also looked spellbound and needed to sleep.

He will be safe, we promise.

Scott turned to Christina. "Do you think you can make it back home okay?"

"Yes."

"I'll tell you all about it in the morning."

Christina looked worried.

"I promise," said Scott, and he gave her a quick kiss on the cheek without realizing what he had done.

He felt a rush of embarrassment and wondered if she might be upset, but Christina flashed a little smile, turned around, and headed for home.

Scott waited for a moment before boarding the ship. He wanted to make sure she would be able to walk home all right. When he saw that she was getting there safely, he turned and said, "Okay I'm ready."

The aliens led Scott back to the room that held the glass chambers.

"Time travel again, huh?" said Scott. "Where are we going tonight?"

There was no answer. They just led him to his chamber. He watched as the aliens turned to atomic vapor.

Here we go again. He entered the chamber and closed the door behind him. It took a minute to build up his concentration enough to turn his body into particles. Once the process started, the ability to see was quickly replaced by an acute sense of knowing or imagining what was occurring. It started with a tingling sensation in his fingers and toes, followed by those digits dissolving into flecks of golden glitter. Then, he could feel the transformation move through his feet, legs and arms as the conversion moved closer to the core of his body. Once the process started, it was mere seconds before the use of his physical senses was replaced with a sense of pure consciousness. On a deeper level, while in the glass chamber, he was acutely aware of everything everywhere around him.

* * *

When the ship had come to rest, Scott sensed that there was a knocking on his chamber and knew it was time to solidify his body. All it took was a quick visualization of what he wanted to achieve, and then, in mere seconds, his body changed back into human form.

When that was done, Scott and Zula walked down the ramp that led them off the ship back to solid ground. Scott immediately knew where he was. He was surprised to see that he was in a field not far from his house. His first thought was that they had returned to the past and he would be able to see his grandfather again. That possibility brought up an incredible burst of excitement. Even to see himself again—at a younger age—would be amazing.

But suddenly, the sky cracked with thunder. Scott jumped, and his heart started to pound because it felt like the thunderous crash was extremely close. A moment later, a bolt of lightning lit up the sky and struck a tree about forty feet away. Scott flinched at the incredible blast that quickly followed the fiery explosion.

"We should take cover," he said to Zula. "It isn't safe out in the open during an electrical storm."

Remember, we are not in the present. As you know, nothing can hurt you when you are observing another time. Those thoughts, from Zula, only reassured him a little. After his ride on the night of the electrical storm, the fear of lightning and thunder had been imprinted deeply inside his brain.

But Scott's attention was quickly diverted to something else that was happening: a small spaceship was emerging from within the Antarian mothership. The pod wasn't much larger than the delivery vans that brought milk to his neighborhood, and as it approached, Scott could see that Zocuul was the driver. Zocuul motioned for Scott and Zula to board, so each of them climbed in and took a seat. The pod rose up in the air and floated slowly over the countryside.

In the field down below them, Scott was surprised by what he saw: it was another version of himself. It looked like this Scott was his same age, not a younger Scott from the past. He appeared to be running as fast as he could, running for his life. The Scott, on the Earth below, seemed to be unaware that the Star People and another version of himself were watching from above in the space pod. The running was erratic, zigzagging back and forth in a chaotic fashion.

It soon became clear why the behavior was so irregular as a bolt of lightning struck the ground, nearly hitting the running Scott below.

"That's me," Scott said to the aliens followed by "wow, look out!"

Zocuul flew the pod over the fields, keeping up with the Scott scurrying around below.

Another spike of lightning hammered into the ground right near running Scott's feet.

"Can't we help him?" yelled Scott to the aliens.

They both shook their heads. *We can't. Remember, we are in another time.*

A bright flash of light sizzled and crashed just a few feet away.

Scott turned to Zula and Zocuul. "And where is this coming from?" he said looking up at the sky. "It's not even raining."

The aliens motioned for Scott to look up higher.

He hadn't noticed that the sky above them was lit up with a crimson ship, and there was the figure he knew well from his drawing: a muscular man with dragon wings, leaning out of an alien ship, conjuring up lightning bolts and hurling them down at the Scott who was running for his life. He had never seen him in person, but Scott knew right away that it was Zarco.

Between Zarco and the Scott on the ground, a full-sized Antarian ship was trying to provide a shield so the running Scott wouldn't be hit, but many of the bolts still managed to make it past the shields to the ground.

As Zula, Zocuul and Scott watched the scene unfold, they could see a shelter in the distance.

"That's the old barn at Miller's Pond," Scott observed. Then he hesitated. "But that's not going to protect him for long. Zarco can destroy that barn in a minute."

Yes. He can.

On the way to the shelter, the running Scott dodged several more deadly airstrikes fired by Zarco.

Then, the running Scott took shelter in the barn. For a few moments, the sky was quiet as if Zarco might have been waiting for a better opportunity.

What time is it, Scott wondered?

He looked at his watch and saw that it was a few minutes before ten.

Suddenly the meaning became clear to Scott. He turned to the aliens. "This isn't the past, is it? This is the future."

It is.

"And Zarco is trying to kill me."

Yes.

"Why doesn't he... why don't *I* just vaporize? Zarco wouldn't be able to see me then."

You can't vaporize out in the open like that. The wind would scatter your atoms in all directions, and you'd never be able to regain solid form. That is why we use the glass chambers.

"Can't your ships stop him?"

Again, the answer came from the telepathic voices of the aliens. *Our ships are trying to use defensive force fields to protect you. While we're in our ships, we are safe. But outside of the ships, whether it's you, or us, or Zarco, everyone is vulnerable. Look up above Zarco's ship and you can see one of our ships firing at him and one below trying to protect you with shields, but it does no good. His defenses are too strong, and his ship is too elusive.*

Scott craned his neck to a point where he could see the Antarian ship trying to provide a protective barrier between Zarco's vessel and Scott on the ground. Above that, he could see another Antarian ship firing down at Zarco, but it looked like the firepower coming from their weapons was easily deflected by Zarco's force field.

Scott came up with another thought. "What if I just stay in my house on that night that this happens? What if I don't leave?"

Then he'll destroy your house and everyone in it including your brother and your mother.

"So, I *have* to leave the house."

Yes.

"And what happens if he kills me?"

If you die, he will suck the gift out of your life force.

"You mean he'll pull the gift out of my body?"

Exactly.

"And then he becomes more powerful."

Yes.

"I'm not sure I want to watch this anymore," objected Scott, but as soon as those words left his mouth, he saw the other version of himself sprint from the barn at top speed. "What's he doing now?" yelled Scott.

Zarco fired more bolts of lightning which the running Scott tried to evade as best he could.

Finally, down below, the running Scott headed for the cover of a solitary oak tree, but before he got there, one of the blasts hit its target and he collapsed to the ground. Within moments, a shadow slowly passed over them, momentarily obscuring the crimson light. It was the dragon–winged figure floating down to the spot where injured Scott was lying on the ground. The dragon hovered over Scott with his wings slowly moving up and down to keep him airborne. Above him, his ship, a couple hundred feet off the ground, shielded Zarco from Antarian weapons.

"And this is where Zarco extracts the gift?" said a disturbed Scott, motioning over to the dragon figure who had landed and was shrouded over the future Scott's body.

Much like a vampire bat, he will suck out the energy.

"I don't want to see anymore!" Scott screamed at the aliens.

Zocuul looked at him and seemed to understand Scott's distress. He quickly turned the pod in the other direction, and they headed back to the mother ship.

You don't need to see anymore, but we wanted to warn you.

On the ride back, Scott thought about what he had just seen. His mind was scrambling with possible ways to escape this horrific outcome. Finally, a thought occurred to him. "But wait. This is the future," argued Scott. "Can't we change this?"

Sometimes. Sometimes not. It is almost impossible to change the future. That is why we wanted to show you. Maybe we can somehow prevent this from happening.

"But how?"

The aliens shook their heads.

"But he knows where I live. I saw the hologram on my window that night a few months ago. Wasn't part of that hologram a map to my house?"

Yes.

"So, he knows where to find me," Scott said as more of a statement than a question.

"And when is this supposed to happen? How far in the future are we?"

Tomorrow night.

"Tomorrow night?"

At ten o'clock.

"There must be *something* we can do," suggested Scott.

There was no response, only silence.

Chapter 47
Contemplation

When Scott got home, he crawled back into bed but never slept. The scenes of Zarco hurling lightning bolts at him kept replaying in his head all night long. The possibility that tomorrow could be his last day on earth was very scary. He found himself going over a million different thoughts in his mind, hoping that somewhere in his analysis would be a solution. *I don't want to die, but I don't know if I could fight Zarco or kill another being.* He knew of other boys who would go hunting with their dads, but he never wanted to do that. He was a peaceful soul. *But if it's him or me, I have to fight. I can't just let him kill me.* There has to be something I can do, Scott kept telling himself. *If I had a gun maybe I could shoot back at Zarco while I dodged the lightning bolts, but where would I get a gun? I don't even know how to use a gun. And what would my chances be of hitting a moving target while I'm running for my life?*

Scott kept trying to think of solutions, but nothing came to him. All he came up with was that he wasn't going down without a fight.

* * *

The next morning, Scott told Christina everything about his journey into the future but didn't tell Brett much except that Zarco would be mounting an attack that night and he might need his help.

That afternoon, the three of them sat in front of the TV watching the midday news to see what the latest was on the UFO front, but Scott wasn't able to concentrate with continuous thoughts of Zarco running through his head.

At the end of the program, Amy Sanders came on the screen with an update from the Brotherhood Camp. "I'm coming to you from the Brotherhood Camp where things have been relatively quiet for the last week or so. Some of the members have observed a couple of streaks of light in the direction of Stonebridge over the last few nights, but nothing too unusual."

The camera zoomed out far enough to show that Amy was prepared to conduct an interview. "I'm here with Roselda Starchild, the leader of the Brotherhood, and she has agreed to answer a few questions for us."

Amy turned towards Roselda. "It seems that the UFO activity has dwindled over the past week or so. Many of your members left for Alabama, then came back after that amazing night about ten days ago, but not much has happened since. Is your group losing interest?"

Roselda looked a little weary. She smiled but it felt like it took a great deal of energy to be enthusiastic. "Not at all. Like you said, there have been some sightings in the Stonebridge area." Roselda hesitated as if she wasn't sure she wanted to continue her next thought. "And there is another factor we consider to be just as important as actual alien sightings."

"And what is that?" asked an interested Amy.

"Sometimes we sense the presence of aliens in the area."

"You *sense* them?"

"Yes, sometimes we do."

Amy was careful to be respectful and not show any disbelief. "And have you been feeling that recently?"

"Very much so. We can tell they've been in the area over the past few nights." Roselda held her arms up in the air and closed her eyes for a moment. "I've been sensing their energy. They have been very active lately, but the feeling has been a bit ominous."

"I have to say, that Roselda woman is pretty tuned in," observed Christina.

"She is," added Scott. "They always make it look like she's crazy, but she's not. She's probably more together than any of those people."

"Do you think she could help us?"

Scott thought about it for a moment. "I don't know." With Brett there, he carefully chose his words. "I know she'd help us if she could. I'm just not sure there's anything she can do."

"Got any other ideas?" asked Christina in a worried voice.

"I've thought about a dozen different things to try, but I don't know if any of 'em would work."

Brett interrupted. "Hey, there's that Air Force guy on the TV now."

"Turn it up," ordered Scott.

The network cut away from the scene at the Brotherhood area, and Amy was now reporting from the Air Force camp. "I'm here with Colonel Barnes from the U. S. Air Force. Thank you for joining us today, Colonel."

"My pleasure."

"We talked to some of the people at the Brotherhood Camp earlier this morning, and they say they've had a few minor sightings over in the Stonebridge area. Can you comment on that?

"We've seen a few streaks of light in that direction as well." Barnes dropped his eyes and started to look down and to the side.

"Look at his eyes," pointed out Christina. "This Colonel Barnes guy is lying. He won't look at her. He knows more than he's willing to tell. I wonder if the Air Force is picking up on the visits over the last few nights, and he doesn't want to admit it."

"Yeah, you're right," said Scott watching Barnes's expressions. "He knows a lot more than he's letting on."

The Colonel continued with his explanation. "We've seen a few fabulous shooting stars, but we haven't seen a single thing on the radar, and if something is out there, our equipment would pick it up."

"And if something does show up on your radar, will you investigate?"

"Yes, Ma'am, we will. See those two helicopters over there?" He motioned to where the two helicopters were waiting. "They're ready to go. If something shows up, we can be up in the air and in pursuit within three minutes tops."

"Turn it off, Brett," said Scott. "I think I've got an idea. We need to make a plan."

Chapter 48
The Plan

By eight o'clock that evening, the plan was in motion. Scott's mom was going to be at her book club meeting, so there was adequate time to get everything in place.

"Okay, Brett, you are a key part of the plan. You know exactly what to say on the phone," confirmed Scott as they climbed into the *Mercury One.*

"Yes," said an exasperated Brett. "We've rehearsed it about a thousand times."

"And remember, don't make the call until you see the first flash of lightning."

"And don't forget the waterworks," added Christina. "You have to sound like a child who is crying because he's absolutely scared to death."

"Right, I got it, but can't I just make the call from here, so I don't have to walk home."

"No, they might trace the call, so it has to be made from the pay-phone down at Earl's gas station."

"All right," Scott looked at the others. "Everybody ready?"

"Are *you* ready?" asked Christina.

"If I truly have a power from Zarco, I'm going to use it the best

I can to defeat him."

"Then, let's go."

Scott started up the *Mercury One*. The first stop was on the top of a hillside just outside Stonebridge, a short distance from Earl's gas station, where they let off Brett with a pocket full of coins.

"From here, you'll be able to see the lightning. Remember, on the first flash, run into town as fast as you can and make the call," said Scott.

"I won't let you down. I'll see you guys back at home."

Scott hesitated. He wasn't certain that he *would* see Brett at home, or ever again. Then, as he thought about his plan, he tried to stay positive. "Yeah, we'll see you in a couple hours."

After Brett got out of the ship, Christina asked Scott, "You think it'll work?" motioning towards Brett and his phone call.

"I do. Those guys won't want to fly their helicopters as long as there is lightning and thunder, but if an eight-year-old kid says he's in danger, they'll go up. They'll risk everything to save him."

Scott turned over the controls to Christina. "Okay, you're the pilot tonight." They changed places and Christina took the ship to a deserted field to wait a few minutes.

"You get to do one of your favorite things, tonight," said Scott. "Buzz the camp."

"Two camps," added Christina, trying to smile.

"You ready?" he asked her.

She nodded.

Scott looked at his watch. "It's time. Let's go."

On this flight—potentially their last together—Christina stayed as far away as possible from any houses or people to make sure they wouldn't be seen. They were both quiet. Scott could feel a tingling sensation rising up his back as if there were electric sparks going from the base of his spine up to his brain. He kept looking at his watch. Every minute was going to count if the plan was to be successful.

They hovered a short distance away from the Air Force camp, floating just above the treetops, waiting silently. "It's time," said Scott.

Christina carefully circled around so that she would be facing the right direction.

"Okay, let's buzz the Air Force camp," said Scott. "Now."

Christina pushed the *Mercury One* to full speed and dove down to about fifty feet above the heads of the Air Force personnel. Scott could see the men on the ground dive for cover fearing that they were under attack. As the *Mercury One* pulled away, they quickly ran towards their helicopters.

"That shook 'em up," she said.

"Great job. Now we've only got three minutes to buzz the Brotherhood Camp and disappear before those choppers are up in the air and on our tail."

Christina flew quickly and within a minute was sailing over the Brotherhood Camp. Then she accelerated as fast as she could in order to make a fast getaway.

"Now, Miller's Pond," she said calmly.

A few minutes later Christina quietly landed the ship beside the dilapidated barn at Miller's Pond.

The two of them quickly pushed the ship into the old wooden structure. Once the *Mercury One* was inside, Scott hesitated, "This is the part of the plan where I have to go home and wait for Zarco."

Without thinking, Scott put his arms around her. He just wanted to hold someone who made him feel safe. Christina tried to force a smile. Scott wanted to stay there and just keep holding her, but he knew he had to go. "Now, when I get back here, Zarco will be chasing me, so I'll have to take off fast."

"We can do it," Christina assured him.

"So, remember, I'll run into the barn, get in the ship and take off. Brett will make his phone call. The Air Force will immediately rush to Stonebridge to help that poor little boy on the phone. I'll fly the *Mercury One* as fast as I can to Stonebridge, trying to dodge Zarco's lightning bolts on the way, and that will lead him head on into the Air Force helicopters. I'll disappear into the woods, and we have to hope that the Air Force will engage in a fight with Zarco. If nothing else, since I'm not going to be on foot when I leave the barn, maybe we can change the future."

"I think I should do the flying," said Christina. "You'll be out of breath and all worked up. I'll have a calm head and be able to fly better."

"No, that's too dangerous for you. There's no use in risking your life as well. He only wants me. If he shoots down the ship, he might kill us both."

Scott looked at his watch. "Okay, I've got about fifteen minutes to get home before Zarco starts his attack. Wish me luck."

This time, she gave him a hug. He held her for a moment. If that was going to be the last hug he ever got, he wanted it to be meaningful.

He looked at his watch again, took a last look at Christina and took off running.

As Scott jogged through the woods towards his house, he could hear the Air Force helicopters and police sirens in the distance. He tried to be calm and assure himself that everything would be all right, but his heart kept pounding and the scene from the night before—the one the aliens had shone him—kept replaying in his mind. He kept thinking about those images. *What if it plays out exactly the way he watched it unfold last night? I saw myself go down when the lightning bolt struck. Could I have survived the strike? And even if I survived the lightning, what would it be like to have Zarco hovering over me and sucking the life force from my body. And would I still be alive after Zarco was done with me?*

Never was Scott less excited to be home. He looked at his watch, and he only had about two minutes before Zarco would arrive, based on his estimate from what he had seen in the future. Scott pulled out three letters he had written that day; one to Christina, one to Brett, and one to his mom. He put those letters under his pillow just in case he didn't make it. *I hope they never see these,* he thought to himself.

He looked outside. The sky was starting to light up in a crimson hue. It was time.

  Star People: Mystery of the Hologram

Chapter 49
Running For His Life

Scott dashed out his back door of his house as fast as he could. By the time he got down to the end of the street, the bolts of lightning began to fire from the sky above. Even though he was fairly sure he wasn't going to be struck by lightning between his house and Miller's Pond, he still kept changing direction to make it as difficult as possible for Zarco. For a brief moment, he looked up and caught a glimpse of an Antarian ship trying to run interference and block Zarco's offensive. But Zarco was evasive and many of the electrical charges still landed dangerously close. While the bolts weren't actually striking him, Scott could feel the scorching heat when each of the explosive spikes blasted into the ground.

* * *

Just moments after the flyover, Barnes and Rodriguez were on board their helicopters and up in the air. Rodriguez' voice came over the radio. "Colonel Barnes, sir, so far I've seen no signs of that alien ship that just flew over us."

Barnes was frustrated, "They seemed to have just disappeared."

Then, he switched channels and talked to Police Chief Canazera. "Canazera, have you got any leads from ground support?"

"Negative, Colonel. We received several calls saying that a ship was spotted in the area of the Brotherhood Camp, but our officers on the ground have not witnessed any unusual activity since the initial sighting."

Then Colonel Barnes saw a flash of light out of the corner of his eye. Moments later, another blaze of lightning caught his attention. He quickly radioed Rodriguez and the base camp. "Men, we've got an electrical storm brewing up here. We need to land these ships and wait for the storm to clear. It looks like the activity is all over for the night anyway."

"Colonel Barnes, this is base camp," a voice on the radio interrupted the Colonel. "We are picking up a couple of very large objects on radar hovering about two miles south of your present location. Would you like coordinates?"

"Negative," answered Barnes as his ship was rocked by the explosion of another bolt of lightning. "Conditions are unsafe. I'm ordering both choppers to land. I'll check it out as soon as I return to base camp."

Another voice came over the radio: "Colonel Barnes, Canazera here. We just got a distress call I think you need to hear. The dispatcher was able to get a recording and can play it for you when you're ready."

"Go ahead," answered Barnes.

The recording was full of static, but Barnes was able to hear it just the same. "Hey mister, I'm really, really scared. There's a spaceship in the sky right over me and I think they're trying to get me. You gotta help me. Can't you get those Air Force guys to come and save me? I'm really scared. I'm here all by myself. Can you help me?"

"What's your name, son?"

"It's Jonathon. Jonathon Harper."

"And how old are you?"

"I'm eight, and I don't wanna die. Please help me. Please."

"Don't worry Jonathon, we'll get somebody there right away. Where are you?"

"I'm in Stonebridge. Right near the Blue Moon Diner. Please Mister, you gotta hurry. There's a spaceship getting closer and closer. They're coming straight down in my direction, and I'm afraid they're going to get me." The call cut off at that moment, leaving the sound of a dial tone.

The Colonel was silent for a moment as he thought about what to do.

"Barnes, are you there?" came a voice over the radio.

Barnes knew he had to help the boy. Storm or no storm, he couldn't ignore the plea of a young child. "Rodriguez, we're turning around and heading back to Stonebridge."

"Sir?"

"We just got a distress call from a young boy who needs our help. Says the UFOs are right over Stonebridge, and he's afraid they're going to get him. Must be that small pod that buzzed our camp," Barnes hesitated. "Storm or no storm, I'm not going to leave that boy out there on his own."

"I'm with you Colonel. I'm turning around and heading for Stonebridge. Do we have any details?"

"That's about all I know. Canazera says they are sending ground support as well."

"Keep this channel open and give us updates as they come in. Over," instructed Barnes.

* * *

Scott's sprint to the barn was exactly as he had witnessed it the night before, complete with lightning strikes and thunder so loud it felt like it shook the flesh off his bones. There were a few fire bolts that exploded so close to him that it seemed like the heat singed his skin and his clothes. He kept rubbing the hot spots to make sure his clothing was not on fire.

He didn't want to look up at Zarco, but he could feel his ominous presence. He was careful to continually zigzag and change directions in order to dodge the bolts and be a more difficult target. Just because he made it safely to the barn in last night's preview, he wasn't completely convinced that he would be safe getting there this time. After all, the aliens indicated that sometimes the future can be changed. He didn't want that to happen on this part of his journey, so he decided to take every precaution.

When he saw the helicopters flying back in the direction of Stonebridge, Scott assumed Brett's phone call must have worked and that part of the plan was in motion. Now he had to hope that Zarco and the military would come face to face, and the encounter would divert Zarco's attention from him to the Air Force helicopters. Then, he had to hope that the Air Force would have the firepower to destroy Zarco's ship. *Come on Barnes, let 'em have it,* Scott thought to himself.

* * *

"Canazera, we're over Stonebridge now in a holding pattern. Anything to update?" asked Barnes.

"My men have arrived at the address the boy gave us and are talking to the owners."

That information was interrupted by a more urgent message. "Warning! Warning! Colonel Barnes, this is base camp. A large unidentified object on our radar has just moved in and is hovering about two hundred feet above you. Please be aware."

Barnes looked up and saw the crimson ship. "Oh my God," he said to himself. It was enormous, and he felt all of the muscles in his neck and back seize up. He had seen many UFOs before but always from a distance, never this close. His job was to make sure everyone stayed out of the way of any alien ships and then cover up any evidence afterwards. He was never supposed to engage, but with this young boy in danger, what was he supposed to do? He'd have to fire on them to save the boy. He had no choice. If he didn't take action and something happened to the boy, he would never be able to live with himself. But he also knew that if he fired at the crimson ship, it was almost a certainty that it would destroy him. A ship that advanced must have powerful weaponry. He just knew that intuitively.

"Rodriguez, I've spotted the alien ship," Barnes took a moment and tried to calm himself, "and I am preparing to attack."

"Sir?" Rodriguez answered with trepidation in his voice. "The alien vessel is in my visual field. It is enormous. Are you sure, sir? Are you sure we should attack?"

Barnes looked down at his radar screen. He was confused by what he saw. Instead of objects showing up on the grid, there were words.

Do not attack the alien ship.

"What the hell?" Barnes tapped the screen, but the words wouldn't go away. "Rodriguez, what do you see on your radar screen?"

"I've got your helicopter and the alien vessel, sir."

"Anything else? Any words?"

"Words? Sir, no sir. No words, sir."

Barnes tapped the screen again. The words wouldn't go away.

Do not attack the alien ship.

Why were those words showing up there? How was that possible? In all of his years in the military, he'd never seen words come up on a radar screen.

Another message, from the radio, interrupted his thoughts. "Colonel Barnes, we just got word that there is no eight-year-old living at the address that was given, but officers have had numerous sightings of an unidentified flying object hovering in the area," reported Canazera. "We traced the call to a pay phone in Stonebridge. I have multiple officers in town searching for the child."

"Update received," answered Barnes. "We will remain in the air, above the Stonebridge area, in case the boy is discovered and needs possible assistance. Over."

* * *

Scott could see the barn in the distance. The adrenalin kept his body moving at full speed. Slowing down, even slightly, could mean death, and he wasn't about to take that chance.

He truly wished it would all be over when he reached the barn, but that was really only the beginning of the plan. That is where he hoped his plan might change the images from last night. He figured that by flying out of the barn in the *Mercury One*—rather than running—meant that the outcome would have a chance of being different.

When Scott reached the barn, the first thing he saw was Christina with a distressed look on her face. She looked heartbroken. She motioned for Scott to look over at what was making her feel so uncomfortable.

In the dim light of the barn, Scott could see that Christina was not alone. Zula was there, standing next to a young boy. Scott's first thought was that it was Brett, and something had happened to him. Scott's heart jumped as that thought went through his brain. He walked towards them expecting to see Brett and then stopped suddenly when he realized it was someone else.

"It's Zocuul," announced Christina.

Scott stooped over to get a better look since the barn was dark. Christina turned on a flashlight and lit up the figure.

"Oh no," was all that Scott could say.

The young child was starting to get older. Right away Scott recognized who it was.

"It's me. Zocuul has become me," said Scott looking at a slightly younger version of himself.

"He's turned human. He shapeshifted into you, and is sacrificing himself, but that means he's going to die," blurted out Christina.

Scott's memory went back to the night they first met the Star People. Zin had become human and then perished right in front of them.

Scott heard Zula's voice in his mind. *It was the only way we knew to save you.*

"No, Zocuul, you can't do this," argued Scott. "We don't want you to die. We had a plan."

Zocuul looked at Scott. He was about Scott's age now and wearing an identical outfit to what Scott was wearing that night.

"Please help our people. All our hope is with you." Those were the last words of Zocuul who, now, looking exactly like Scott, burst out of the barn and ran as fast as he could. Within seconds, Zarco was firing lightning bolts trying to strike him down.

"We've got to stop him!" As soon as Scott said those words, it was too late. Zocuul was heading straight for the fateful area Scott remembered from the night before. He knew that as soon as Zocuul got about a hundred yards from the barn, in the vicinity of the oak tree, it was all over.

And just as it had happened the night before, Zocuul approached that very same area and a flash of lightning crashed down on top of him. Zocuul collapsed to the ground.

The crimson ship dipped down just above where Zocuul was writhing in pain. Zarco emerged from the crimson ship and slowly floated down towards the wounded figure who appeared to be Scott. He hovered above his prey triumphantly for a moment, letting his great white wings beat against the still, warm air. It appeared that he was hesitating in order to revel in the victory.

"Christina, get in the ship!" screamed Scott.

Christina rushed over and started to climb inside.

"You drive!" he ordered.

She quickly scooted into the driver's seat, turned on the motor, and the *Mercury One* was almost immediately airborne and speeding out of the barn.

"Go after him."

Christina did what she was told.

Zarco paused in mid-air, looking up at the Antarian ships with a look of defiance and satisfaction. Then he descended on his victim.

"Come up behind him. Make sure he is on my right side," instructed Scott as they flew towards the dragon.

"Come in low—like ten feet above him—and keep the ship completely steady."

As Christina brought the ship in, right behind Zarco, Scott reached into his pocket and clamped his fingers around the fire stone which Zula had given him at the Great Pyramid. It felt hot to the touch.

Scott stood up with his entire upper body out of the moon roof. "A little closer, a little closer," he instructed her. "Now down a little so we're right beside him."

The *Mercury One* snuck in behind Zarco who was preoccupied with his prey. Scott pulled back his arm and launched the fire stone with all his might. As the stone left his hand it started to glow like a red-hot coal and then morphed into a molten rock. It was as if Scott had thrown his hardest fastball, except this one wasn't heading for the strike zone, it was aimed directly at the batter.

"That is for Zocuul!" yelled Scott.

It wasn't until the last second that Zarco turned and saw the *Mercury One* and the fire stone coming directly at him, but it was too late. He tried to move, to get out of the way, but there wasn't enough time.

At the moment of impact, the fire stone burst into a bright explosion of flames. Zarco's wings lit up in the fiery blast and the dragon let out a scream of agony. Moments later, Zarco was rolling on the ground, emitting terrible shrieks and cries, trying to put out the flames.

Christina quickly steered the *Mercury One* into the woods in an effort to hide from Zarco's ship, but the red craft appeared to be more interested in its master than chasing down the *Mercury One*. Zarco's ship landed on the ground next to the flaming body which was clearly in agony. The greys swarmed around Zarco, trying to extinguish the fire.

The green ship of the Star People quickly tried to swoop in. It appeared that the Antarians wanted to inflict more damage on the dragon figure now that he was vulnerable, but Zarco's ship immediately fired at the Star People and wouldn't let them get close enough to get to the wounded dragon.

* * *

At that moment, the two Air Force helicopters came onto the scene.

"What the hell is going on down there?" said Barnes to himself.

The craft of the Star People quickly fled and disappeared, but the red ship stayed in place. Barnes saw a group of dark figures carrying a charred body back on board their ship.

Rodriguez' nervous voice came in on the radio. "Colonel Barnes, do you still want to open fire?"

"Negative, Rodriguez. That isn't some defenseless pod we can force into the trees. It's a sophisticated warship. We don't know what kind of weaponry it's got, but we wouldn't stand a chance. They'd probably blow us to pieces. Just stand by."

The Air Force choppers backed off and anxiously watched as the crimson ship loaded the body of its master on board and then roared off into space.

Chapter 50
Safe at Home

Christina piloted the ship back to the field behind the Harrison's house. As soon as they were on the ground, Scott and Christina pushed the *Mercury One* into the shed as fast as they could.

Brett was waiting there for them. Scott was relieved to see that Brett was safe. He gave his brother a big hug.

A few minutes later, Zula arrived in an Antarian pod. She had brought the language board with her so she could communicate with everyone. Her body had that ashen color that occurred when it was filled with sadness. It seemed like it took all her energy to express what she needed to share after losing her companion, Zocuul.

Thank you, Scott Harrison.

Zula turned to the others.

Brett, Christina, Scott, you saved us. Our people owe you much gratitude.

"But is he dead?" asked Scott.

We don't know for sure. Only time will tell. But he is seriously injured. I don't think he will ever fly again. And now that he no longer has his immortal powers, it would be difficult for him to survive such extensive trauma.

"But what about Zocuul?"
Zula shook her head.

He didn't survive.

"Zocuul is dead?" asked Brett, suddenly turning very sad.
"I'm so sorry, Zula," said Christina.

We willingly give our lives to help our race survive. I would do the same. He had no choice.

"What happened?" asked Brett.
"We'll tell you later," Christina whispered to Brett.
"I was so upset about Zocuul that something inside of me just snapped." Scott tried to justify his actions of throwing the fire stone. "I just reacted. I felt so terrible about Zocuul's sacrifice for me. I didn't want him to die, and I didn't want anyone to get hurt. I didn't know what else to do."

Every one of us has moments in life where we have to act in ways we wished we hadn't. By defending us and defending yourself, you did what you had to do. Through that one act, you may have saved a whole race of people. There will always be forgiveness for you, Scott Harrison. We hope that you can forgive yourself.

Chapter 51
The Alien Summer of 1964

Over the course of the next few nights, nothing happened. There was no sign of Zarco or the Star People, so Scott took that to mean that Zarco was dead, and his otherworldly adventure was over. Now, he just wanted his life to get back to normal.

For the town of Stonebridge, things never really did settle down. No one was about to forget the alien summer of 1964. Scott seemed to find reminders everywhere, but those little reminders were somewhat purposeful because it made the town of Stonebridge a very popular tourist destination, and the city council wasn't about to discourage the influx of revenue.

A stroll down Main Street was different now. The art gallery prominently featured a new painting in the front window of the shop: it was a picture of an alien ship—looking like the green Antarian ship--soaring over the Brotherhood Camp. Below the ship, on the ground, the campers were waving and celebrating and lighting their *Welcome* message for all to see. Scott loved the picture but felt that the depiction of the spaceship was entirely wrong.

On dance night at the retirement home, songs like "Fly Me to the Moon," could be heard emanating from that normally-quiet establishment.

A couple nights after the final encounter, Scott and Christina stopped in at the *Mystic Delights* coffee shop for hot chocolate and Danish pastries which had been fashioned to look like small flying saucers. A waitress was serving up dessert and coffee to a couple of exhausted police officers who were still talking about the remarkable events that occurred over the summer. Their conversation was interrupted when the old folk singer picked up his guitar and came on for his last set. He started off by announcing that he'd written something new that he wanted to play for everyone.

"This is sort of a science fiction song; about all the craziness we've seen around here in the last couple of weeks. I hope you like it. It's a song I call 'Flying Over Stonebridge.'"

The lyrics went like this:

> *I was travelin' down to Stonebridge*
> *When saucers came out of the sky*
> *Cruisin' over cars along the turnpike.*
> *Hoverin' over Boston*
> *Shimmering with the city lights below.*

When the chorus started, the people in the cafe sang along. Scott and Christina joined in. Christina flashed a little smile as if to acknowledge all the secrets they shared from that crazy summer.

As they headed home, walking down Main Street, Scott and Christina noticed Abigail was out prowling on the rooftops as usual, gazing up at the sky, perhaps waiting patiently for another visitation from above.

Back up in the gentle rolling hills above Stonebridge, in that small cluster of unassuming houses, the skies above the Harrison house—after a very eventful summer—were finally calm and quiet again.

There were no plans for flights over Miller's Pond, or air car rides above the streets of Forestville, or dreamy moments where the *Mercury One* seemed to be headed off on a journey to the moon. Instead, the ship was hidden in the old work shed, lying under a grey tarp and sitting dormant. *For now.*

The End

About The Author

 James Schwartz is the author of *The Mind-Body Fertility Connection* (Llewellyn), *One Voice, Sacred Wisdom* (Career Press/Weiser), and a mystery series called *An Invitation to Murder*. He is a teacher and speaker who has been on numerous radio talk shows and has taught both in the U.S. and internationally. James is a graduate of California State University at Dominguez Hills and San Diego State University.

www.ingramcontent.com/pod-product-compliance
Lightning Source LLC
Chambersburg PA
CBHW032013310726

48972CB00002B/385